EVA CHASE

Eva C (signature)

CRUEL
MAGIC

ROYALS OF VILLAIN ACADEMY

Cruel Magic

Book 1 in the Royals of Villain Academy series

First Digital Edition, 2019

Copyright © 2019 Eva Chase

Cover design: Christian Bentulan, Covers by Christian

Ebook ISBN: 978-1-989096-38-3

Paperback ISBN: 978-1-989096-39-0

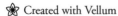 Created with Vellum

CHAPTER ONE

Rory

I f I'd known my parents would be dead in an hour, I'd have done a few things differently that Sunday morning. Made sure to fit in a hug or two. Offered at least one "I love you." And not dredged up the same old argument we'd been having for the last half a year, which didn't end up mattering anyway.

But I didn't know, so I took what appeared to be my moment. The three of us were sitting around the square white table in the breakfast nook just off the kitchen, warm California sunlight streaming through the broad windows. Dad was finishing up his French toast and eggs equally drenched in syrup, a contented smile curling his lips. Mom poured herself another cup of coffee and inhaled the steam with a pleased sigh.

I dabbed my last corner of toast in the runny yolk left

on my plate and washed it down with a gulp of my own bitter coffee. "I was looking at the listings online," I said. "There are a few apartments not too far from here that I can afford."

Mom let out a very different sort of sigh and gave me a look full of fond exasperation. "We've talked about this, Lorelei. You should be saving that money for your future."

She only pulled out my full name when she intended to end the conversation. I barreled onward. "I've really appreciated having the basement. You know that. But I just turned nineteen. Isn't my future supposed to be starting *now*?"

The first time I'd brought up the idea of moving out, they'd offered me the small basement apartment they'd been using for storage as a compromise. But the whole point had been to get a little independence, and it was hard to feel like an adult with my parents literally over my head. After being homeschooled most of my life, now that I was attending a few classes at the local college—and seeing how my classmates lived—it was becoming more and more obvious that I had to make a real break if I was going to figure out my future for myself.

Unfortunately, while I was making more than enough to cover rent and the rest, an artist with no credit history didn't look like the safest bet to potential landlords. To get a lease, I was going to need Mom or Dad to sign on as a guarantor. Which meant, somehow or other, I had to convince them it was a good idea.

Dad leaned his elbows onto the table. "You know the

drill," he said with a teasing glint in his eyes. "Pros and cons. Go."

We'd been playing that game whenever I'd proposed something my parents weren't sold on since I was seven years old. I'd like to think I was pretty good at it by now.

"Pros," I said, ticking off fingers as I went. "It'd be an important transitional step to becoming a completely independent adult. I'd be forced to learn how to look after myself. I could get a place that's closer to the college so it'd be easier for me to participate in the extracurricular stuff there and save maybe an hour in transit. I'd be building my credit score and a rental history. I'd have more space and more freedom to… to figure out who I am without you looking over my shoulder."

I hadn't let myself say that part before because I'd known it'd make Dad wince the way it had just now. Mom set down her coffee, knitting her brow. "You should feel like the apartment is completely yours, hon. We don't want to stifle you."

"I know." My hands fell to my lap, and I twisted one of the glass beads on the charm bracelet they'd given me for my tenth birthday and that I'd added to every year since. Each charm was a symbol of a love or a dream I'd shared with them. Why couldn't they understand this longing? "All you have to do is look out the window to see who's coming and going. Sound travels up. Even if you're not *trying* to monitor what I'm doing, I can't forget that you're right here."

"All right," Dad said. "That's fair enough. Maybe we

should have taken that more into consideration. And then cons?"

I held back a grimace. He wasn't going to let me fudge this list. "I'll be spending money I could otherwise be saving. If I have a few bad months in selling my figurines, I'll have to dip into the savings I already have. I won't be able to just pop up here and grab something to eat if I'm feeling hungry and lazy, but maybe that's a good thing?"

"It won't be as safe," Mom said. "You'd be living around strangers."

"I'm going to have to sometime, aren't I?"

"It'll be extra stress when you have your studies to focus on," she went on. "And you'll have a lot more pressure to keep going with your current job because you need that money, even if you decide you want to try something new that's more of a risk. In some ways, you'll have less freedom."

"It's not that we're trying to keep you here forever, Rory," Dad said. "We just want to make sure you get the best start we can give you. Why not wait another couple years until you can really launch a career for yourself, and in the meantime we can try to find ways to help you feel more independent here?"

It was hard to argue with that. There were tons of cons. I didn't know how to express how important the one main pro was to me in a way they'd accept without hurting them a whole lot more than I wanted to.

As I bit my lip in thought, Mom smiled, her voice falling into the softer lilting tone it often did when she was about to work her magic. "I know you've been getting a little stir-crazy, wanting to do some traveling too, so I thought we could finally take that trip to New York City this summer—see the Met and MoMA."

Her words did exactly what she'd intended. A spark of delight lit in my chest at the idea of jetting across the country to some of the most respected art galleries in the country. We'd done a bit of traveling as a family before, but only within the state.

With that joy came a knot of guilt as well. I was already planning my own solo trip—a week in Florence, Italy to see all the amazing galleries and architecture there —and I didn't need parental sign-off to do that. I hadn't decided yet whether I was going to wait to tell them until I was heading out the door or not until I was actually on the plane. Telling them now, months in advance, would only mean more arguing.

Mom couldn't feel the guilt, though. As a mage, she drew on joyful feelings to perform her magic, so she was finely attuned to only that aspect of my emotions. With a soft murmur and a flick of her hand, she set my cooled coffee steaming again. A bit of comfort to ease the sting of their disagreement.

"Thanks," I said. "And that trip sounds fantastic."

"I'm looking forward to it too," Dad said with a grin. "I'll see if the Conclave has any special projects I can take on. I expect we'll have plenty of energy to work with."

He was a mage too. The two of them could turn any joy they stirred up in each other or me—or anyone else we ran into—into power. Dad's specialty was healing. Around his ordinary accounting job, he volunteered at a nearby hospital, nudging people's recovery along. *Always be open to happiness*, he'd told me when I was little, half playful and half serious. *Every time I make you smile, it could save someone's life.*

Letting them turn my happiness into magic was as close to any kind of supernatural power as *I* got. From what I'd gathered from the little bits and pieces they'd revealed over the years, being a mage was hereditary. As an adoptee, I hadn't gotten the genetic benefit, and there was no way for them to teach me when I didn't have the power already inside me.

Maybe that was another reason I wanted to take at least a few more steps away from the house I'd grown up in. No matter what I did, I was never going to be as special as they were. Most of the time, I was okay with the fact that I was just a Nary, which was what Mom and Dad called regular people—short for ordinary, or as Mom had said when we'd had The Talk about their talents, *Nary a bit of magic.* Sometimes, though, the yearning prickled so deep it made me queasy.

I *was* ordinary, and eventually I was going to have to build a life with no magic in it at all. Might as well get it over with.

"We'll come back to this conversation when I can convert some of those cons into pros," I told my parents, getting up. Maybe they hadn't been able to teach me magic, but they'd definitely taught me stubbornness.

I brought my coffee downstairs and through the laundry room. On the threshold of the basement apartment, I paused for a moment, taking a sip and contemplating the space.

I really did appreciate having it, and I wished it'd done the trick. Even though the apartment was cramped and dim with storage boxes stacked against one wall, it wasn't *awful*. I just couldn't shake the growing sense that the longer I stayed this tied to my parents, the harder it was going to be to stand on my own when I really needed to. Until I'd started the college classes this fall, Mom and Dad had been the only people I'd regularly spent time with. I had a lot of catching up to do.

My pet mouse, Squeak—not the most original name, but it was her first owner who picked it, not me—was scurrying around her cage, nuzzling at the bars. The sunlight coming in through the little window over her perch made her fur shine: pure white other than a splotch of black on her left flank. I popped open the door and let her scramble up my arm to my shoulder while I considered how I wanted to spend the rest of my morning.

I *could* finish the last bit of the History of Modern Design essay that was due on Thursday… or I could get to work on that phoenix figurine idea that had come to me last night.

I wavered for approximately two seconds before grabbing my bin of polymer clay and my sketchpad off my desk. Squeak's whiskers tickled the back of my neck as she wriggled under the dark waves of my hair. Sometimes she liked to hang out back there like it was a nest or something, which, given how much trouble I often had getting those waves to behave, was kind of fitting. I started up one of my favorite playlists on my phone and sat down at the little kitchen table.

The first stage for any figurine was working out the design with pen and paper. I had to see what I was going to sculpt before I could start working on the actual pieces. My fingers flew over the sketchpad, bringing to life a fiery bird soaring up from a burst of flame. A giddy shiver ran through me as I filled in the details. Perfect.

It was going to be hard to part with this one, but now that I'd spent a few years building a name for myself online, I could make twice as much money selling just one of my little creature sculptures than I did with my three shifts a week at the art supply store downtown. I needed to pay for that Florence trip—and maybe to put down enough advance rent that some landlord would be willing to skip the whole guarantor thing.

When I was satisfied with the sketch, I started warming up the orange clay that would form the base of the phoenix's body. Its tangy waxy smell filled my nose. The feel of the clay softening under my fingers always took me into a sort of trance that felt almost magical. My art was the closest thing I had to a special power.

I was shaping the lump of clay, humming faintly with the song that had just come on, when the ceiling shook.

Bang. Bang. Two sharp thuds echoed from upstairs in quick succession, so violent my skin jumped. The clay slipped from my fingers.

Voices barked loud enough for the hostility to travel through the ceiling, but the words were indistinct. I jabbed the music off, my heart thumping. What the hell was going on?

One of the voices upstairs yelled again. Something made of glass or china smashed. I swallowed hard and grabbed my phone. As I slipped out of my apartment to the stairs at the other end of the laundry room, I dialed 9-1-1.

"What is your emergency?" said a woman on the other end, who managed to sound both pert and deadly serious.

"I don't know," I said, fighting and failing to keep my voice steady. "It sounds like someone broke into my parents' house. I'm in the basement—I can hear a commotion upstairs. It doesn't sound good."

"What is your address?"

I rattled it off.

"All right," she said. "We'll have the police there as soon as we can. You hang tight. Stay on the phone with me—and stay out of whatever's going on."

That was easy for her to say. It wasn't *her* parents going through God knew what up there. I kept the phone clutched by my ear, but I also slunk halfway up the stairs, placing my feet carefully so the steps wouldn't creak.

The voices got clearer. They must be in the kitchen— Mom and Dad often lingered there for a while reading or chatting after breakfast.

"…is she?" a man was demanding. "Out with it, or this can get much worse."

There was no sound of impact, but Mom let out a pained gasp as if she'd been hit. Was this some kind of home invasion? Couldn't she and Dad use their magic to turn the tables on these assholes?

I guessed there wasn't much joy in the room for them to draw on.

I couldn't help myself. Maybe some other girl would have stood by while thugs smacked around her parents, but not this one. I eased up another step so I could peek through the mudroom into the kitchen.

Mom and Dad were hunched on the floor at opposite ends of the room, Dad farther away with his back against the fridge, Mom closer to me, braced against the oven. Five figures stood over them, three men and two women, all dressed in posh black shirts and slacks like they should have been out at some exclusive dinner party and not here threatening random innocent people.

Except, what were they threatening them *with*? I didn't see weapons in anyone's hands. What the fuck was going on?

Footsteps thumped down the stairs at the other end of the house. "Second floor is clear," a guy hollered.

Clear of what? What had they thought might be up there?

"Check the basement," said the man who'd been warning Mom earlier.

Mom's back stiffened. A strange look came over her face, frantic but fierce.

"You don't have to," she said with a rasp. "I'll tell you where she is."

Two suspicions clicked into place in my head: The assholes were looking for *me*. And Mom was only pretending to give in to get the satisfied smile that crossed the man's face in that moment. A brief jolt of happiness was all she'd need to break out her powers.

Heaving herself to her feet, she thrust her arms out with a swift murmur. The man and the woman next to him stumbled backward. My heart leapt with hope in the instant before the man caught himself. He slashed his hand and spat out a word that wasn't from any language I recognized.

Mom's flesh tore open from the base of her chin all the way down her throat. Blood gushed out, streaming down the front of her pink cotton tunic. Her legs gave way beneath her as the color drained from her face. She sagged over in front of the oven.

My mind went blank with horror. *No, no, no.* I dropped the phone and threw myself toward my mother.

The man had already been swiveling toward Dad. "You deserve far worse for the crimes you've—"

He cut himself off as I hurtled into the room. I managed to catch Mom's head before it hit the tiled floor. Her blood washed hot over my forearms and flowed across the tiles. Her head lolled in my hands, her eyes glazed and lifeless.

My stomach flipped. I pressed my palm against the raw gaping wound on her throat instinctively, as if any part of me really believed I could still save her. "Mom," I choked out.

"Rory, get out of here! Run to—"

The woman closest to Dad said a word and twitched

her fingers, and his mouth snapped shut. Several hands grasped my arms to haul me away from Mom's body.

I tried to wrench away, to hit the people around me, to stop them somehow, but my feet tripped under me. One of the figures spun me around to face him. His fingers clamped on my shoulder, his bright hazel eyes catching my gaze from where he'd tipped his head close to mine.

"It's okay," he said in a low, gentle tone that penetrated the roar of anguish inside me. "We've got you now. You won't be trapped here anymore. We're going to take you home."

The words sounded as if they should have been comforting, and he said them like he meant them. With a weird rush of warmth, my body stopped shaking. I blinked, registering that he looked younger than the others, not much older than me. And he was one of the most striking guys I'd ever seen. Even if I hadn't been in the middle of the most horrifying scene in my life, with one glimpse that smooth face with its slicked-back black hair and those brilliant eyes would have burned it into my memory.

The most horrifying— Wait, had he cast magic on me to calm me down? My mind recoiled.

I didn't want these people to "get" me, and this was my home right here. That was my mother—

"I feel we need to send a message," said the man who'd murdered Mom from where he was walking toward Dad.

My heart lurched with a fresh jolt of panic. I yanked myself away from the gentle guy just as the man sliced both hands through the air in an X.

A matching X gouged through Dad's plaid shirt right into his chest. A spasm jerked his body, and a cry seared up my throat. I lunged at his attacker.

More hands caught me. The murderer muttered something under his breath that sounded like a curse.

"Knock her out," he said. "We've got to get going."

A few harsh syllables reached my ear with the swipe of a palm across my forehead, and my mind fell away into blackness.

CHAPTER TWO

Rory

I came to with a sway of the surface beneath me. My body was lying on firm padding, a smooth material against my cheek. My next breath brought the smell of leather into my nose. The thrum of an engine and another swaying sensation told me I was in some kind of vehicle.

My eyelids felt too heavy to lift. My thoughts were muddled. What had they done to me? The people in the kitchen—the man who'd ripped Mom and Dad open like animals in a slaughter house—

Nausea surged through my gut at the memory. I stiffened against the seat. Those monsters had killed my parents and dragged me off... somewhere. I didn't have any idea why or what they wanted, but every particle of my being clanged with fear.

The haze in my head gradually retreated. I eased my eyes open just a crack to take in my surroundings.

Some of my hair had fallen across my face, hiding my gaze from anyone watching. Between the dark brown strands, I made out thin sunlight seeping through the windows onto an empty burgundy leather seat that faced my own. I was in the back of a limo.

My only company was two figures up in the front, the backs of their heads just visible above the tops of the seats. The sunlight glanced off a glass privacy divider between me and them.

As I took that in, the woman in the front passenger seat turned to glance back at me. My breath stopped in my throat as I held myself perfectly still, watching her through my eyelashes. After a second, she looked away again.

The divider must have been a thick one. I didn't hear her speak, but a hint of a laugh carried through as if in response to a comment.

My captors wanted to keep an eye on me, but I guessed they didn't want me to hear whatever they might say about me or where we were going. Okay. A faint ache was spreading through my shoulder from lying prone, but I'd just have to pretend I was still unconscious until I decided what the hell to do next.

None of this made any sense. Mom and Dad had never given me any reason to think they had enemies, let alone the kind of enemies who'd want them *dead*. They'd spent their lives working with joy, for fuck's sake.

This morning—if it was still the same day—I hadn't seen any sign that they were worried about an impending attack. Everything had seemed so normal.

A lump rose in my throat. I shut my eyes against the burn of tears. That breakfast was the last time we'd really talked, and I'd spent most of it badgering them about letting me move out. If I could have erased the last day and stopped any of this from happening, I'd have happily stayed in the damned basement for the rest of my life.

I was pretty sure I was still wearing the same clothes, but no blood clung to my hands or arms. Someone had washed Mom's blood off me. Somehow that felt like a betrayal in itself.

A small shape shifted against the back of my head. I had to tense up to restrain a flinch. Then tiny claws prickled against my scalp in a familiar sensation.

Squeak—had she been holding onto my hair the whole time? I'd been so caught up in the attack that I hadn't thought about where she might have ended up.

A wry wisp of a voice tickled into my head. *Good, you're awake. We need to talk, sweetheart.*

I almost choked in surprise, and my mouse's claws pinched deeper into my scalp. *Quiet. Don't let them know you've come to. If you stay still and whisper to answer me, we should be able to have a decent conversation without them realizing.*

"Squeak?" I murmured, my thoughts spinning. My mouse could talk—or telepathically communicate, at least? Since when? She'd never acted like anything other than a regular rodent back home.

The name's actually Deborah, but when we're around anyone else, you're better off sticking with the mousey one. Sorry to spring this on you so suddenly. I'm just glad I managed to hang on to you while these bastards were hauling you off.

What…? Who…? I didn't know where to start.

Maybe Squeak—Deborah?—picked up on my confusion, because she nestled into her favorite spot at the nape of my neck and went on.

Here's the quick version: I used to be a joymancer like your parents. The Conclave worked some magic so that my mind could take up new residence in this mouse body. It's not such a bad trade, you have to understand, because I was just about dead from cancer when they offered. All I had to do to get a bunch more years was play pet and do my bit as your familiar if anything went wrong. I just wasn't expecting anything to go quite this wrong.

I couldn't wrap my head around most of that. Dad had brought Squeak home from one of his stints at the hospital, saying she'd belonged to a kid there he'd failed to save whose parents hadn't known what to do with the pet. He'd asked if I'd mind looking after her for a bit while he found a permanent home, and I'd ended up enjoying the little animal's company so much I'd told him I'd keep her.

"My parents knew?" I said quietly.

The deal was that I'd watch out for you and signal them if you needed help.

"You called yourself a 'joymancer.'" I hadn't heard that term before.

That's what we all call ourselves—the mages who take our magic from joy. I take it your parents never told you about the other kind. The ones that grabbed you are fearmancers. The same way we draw on happiness to power our spells, they draw on terror. As you've already seen, that leaves them with a pretty warped sense of morality.

Fearmancers. A cold shiver ran down my back. Mom and Dad had never said anything about other kinds of mages. I'd never even met any of their colleagues under the Conclave.

I forced myself to keep my voice low. "Why would these fearmancer people want *me*?"

I'm not sure, Squeak/Deborah said. *But I do know where they're taking you. They were talking about it while you were out on the plane. You've been down for the count for hours. They brought us on a private jet to an airfield in what I've gathered is northern New York. This is just the last step of the journey.*

"A journey to where?"

The fearmancers have a school where they teach all their awful practices. The Conclave has known about it for a long time, but they keep it well-hidden enough that we've never been able to shut it down. They've got some fancy name for the place, but most of the time we just call it Villain Academy. A lot more accurate, in my humble opinion.

Villain Academy. Another chill trickled through me. "I still don't get it. Why are they bringing me anywhere at all? I'm not even a mage. I'm just a Nary."

Deborah made a sound like a sigh. *Oh, Lorelei. Your parents really should have told you that part. The thing is—*

The limo jerked to a stop. Deborah froze and then scurried down under the collar of my T-shirt to hide beneath the fabric on my back.

My pulse raced as my captors stepped out of the

vehicle. Someone opened the door by my head with a rush of cool damp air. No, this definitely wasn't a California April anymore.

I narrowed my eyes to slits. A shadow fell over me. "We can't bring her in like this. Ashgrave, wake her up."

There was a pause, and then a low measured voice I recognized said, "She's already awake." Feet shifted against the ground outside as the familiar speaker crouched next to my seat.

"Hey," he said in the same gentle tone he'd used in my parents' kitchen. "I know you're probably really confused, but we're here. You just need to come inside, and we'll get everything sorted out."

Sorted out? Were they going to sort out the way they'd murdered my parents? The fact that they'd kidnapped me and dragged me from one end of the country to the other?

But the young guy with the gentle voice and the striking face hadn't carried out the killings. Okay, he'd tried to dull my panic with his magic, but then and now, he'd talked as if he wanted to help me. Was it possible not everyone here was a total villain?

Whatever the case, he could clearly tell I was faking.

I eased myself upright as if I'd only just woken up. The guy's black hair was a little rumpled from the trip, but his face was still as stunning and his eyes as brightly alert as before. He offered me a little smile with perfect cupid's bow lips. "Let's go. The headmistress is waiting for you— she'll explain everything."

I wouldn't mind a few explanations, but I wasn't in any

hurry to go anywhere with a bunch of villainous mages. I didn't feel all that safe in the limo, though.

The guy backed up as I scooted forward. I stepped out onto the smooth asphalt of a parking lot. Immediately, the cool air raised goosebumps on my bare arms. I wasn't dressed for northern weather, especially now that the sun was sinking low.

A couple spots away from the limo, a posh gunmetal gray sedan was parked. The other figures around me must have arrived in that. All six of the creeps—the fearmancers —who'd stormed in on my parents stood around me, watching.

Directly beyond the sedan lay a field framed by a dense forest that wrapped around to my left. The road my captors must have driven up veered away between the trees there. That was my chance at escaping.

To my right, a massive stone building loomed, looking like the illegitimate offspring of a medieval castle and a Victorian manor house. Turrets jutted here and there, their windows shuttered. A gargoyle hunched over the arched front doorway. Um, yeah, I'd rather not set foot in there, if I had a choice in the matter.

The trouble was, I didn't think I had any choice at all.

"Why am I here?" I said. "What do you want with me?"

The fearmancer who'd killed my parents stirred impatiently on his feet. "As he said, Ms. Grimsworth will do the explaining. That's how she wanted it."

I guessed what I wanted didn't figure into his plans. I

glanced toward the road again, and his underlings tensed around him.

I'd be kidding myself if I tried to pretend I wasn't generating plenty of fear to fuel their magic with every thud of my heart. I'd seen how easily the one man had slaughtered Mom and Dad. If I made a run for it, what were the chances I'd even make it across the parking lot before they caught me?

I squared my shoulders. They'd brought me here for a reason. I'd be able to come up with a better strategy for getting out of here if I knew what that was. *Know thy enemies.* Dad used to say that, jokingly, when talking about working around the hospital administration.

A punch of grief hit me in the gut. I clenched my jaw, holding myself steady against it.

I didn't have a clue what was going on, but I did know one thing for sure: no way in hell were these assholes getting away with what they'd done to my family.

"Okay," I said, hugging myself against a chilly lick of breeze. "Let's go."

My parents' murderer, who appeared to be in charge of this little squad, made a dismissive gesture with his hand, and three of his followers got back in the sedan. He, the young guy, and one of the women escorted me up the stone steps to the building. As I got closer, I could make out a crest carved into the peak of the stone arch just beneath the gargoyle. The crest was framed by prickly leaves, and at its center was a dragon's head. Not ominous at all.

Our shoes rapped loudly against the polished

hardwood floor inside. The huge front hall smelled like mahogany with a whiff of smoke, the former from the broad curving staircases on either side and the latter from the flames dancing in sconces along the stone walls. Their glow gave a wavery quality to the daylight that streamed from the high windows.

The man led us past the staircases and down a narrower, dimmer hall beyond them. It opened to a second entrance room with gold-gilded wallpaper and a single mahogany staircase directly in front of us.

Voices filtered from a side room, but we weren't headed there. The man strode up the stairs. I climbed after him, fidgeting with the glass charms on my bracelet as I went.

"That's right," a smoothly amused voice rang out from above us. "Let's see how you move with a real fire under your feet."

My head jerked around. Down by the right-hand end of the second floor landing, four guys were standing in a cluster. Or rather, as I reached the top of the stairs and could get a better look, three guys were standing in a semi-circle around a fourth.

My legs stalled as I stared. If my hazel-eyed "friend" was striking, the three young men looming over their target were heart-wrenchingly gorgeous. The kind of stunning I'd have assumed had been tinkered to perfection in Photoshop if they hadn't been standing before my eyes just ten feet away.

One appeared to have been built entirely out of muscle, with a chestnut-brown crew cut that emphasized the chiseled planes of his square-jawed face. Another held his lean body with a languid grace, his dark copper hair shadowing boyishly angular features that were made mature by lavishly full lips currently curved into a smirk.

Between them, directly in front of the scrawnier kid they'd caught, was the guy who'd spoken. I could tell it'd been him from the haughty tilt of his handsome face, which managed to look divinely innocent and yet devilishly hot at the same time, a mix of soft and hard lines so perfect that my fingers itched to try to capture them in clay. His golden-brown hair was just long enough to show a hint of curl, and his dark eyes, fixed on the kid, glittered with satisfaction.

The kid, who I'd have placed at sixteen or so, backed up a step, and the divine devil moved his hand. A spurt of fire shot up beneath the boy's shoes. He yelped, scrambled backward, and lurched forward again as the flames seared higher and hotter at his heels. His eyes had gone wide with terror. His tormentors laughed.

Fearmancers. What a fitting demonstration of their talent. Horror twisted tight in my chest. My three escorts had started across the landing in the opposite direction, but the last shaky thread of composure I'd been holding onto snapped.

This morning I'd been totally useless while one asshole had flayed my family. I didn't have to watch another one flambé this kid. I could at least create a distraction that'd give the boy time to flee.

"Leave him alone!" I said, marching toward them. "You're hurting him."

Three startled gazes leapt to me, the flames flickering down. The divine devil grinned.

"I'm teaching him a necessary lesson. Are you aiming to get schooled too?" His eyes skimmed down over my body, and I was abruptly aware of my wrinkled tee and loose jeans in comparison with the pressed dress shirts and slacks everyone around me was sporting. "You look like you could use it."

My eyes narrowed. "You're welcome to try."

Before I'd even finished speaking, his lips moved and his fingers twitched, and a streak of flame darted across the floor toward me.

If he'd thought he was going to shock me, he had no idea what I'd already been through today. I stomped my foot down on the fire, restraining a wince at the flare of magical heat, and glared. "Is that the best you've got?"

The copper-haired guy let out a laugh. The divine devil's mouth curled into a sneer, his expression as cocky as before, but a quivering sensation flitted through the air between us. It wriggled through my ribs and up to the base of my throat, sharp and heady, as if I'd bitten my tongue.

The guy whipped another lick of flame at me and the kid, and one defiant word crackled over my tongue. "*Freeze.*"

The quivering jolted out of me—and a sheen of frost raced across the floor, swallowing the flames and fixing the guy's loafers to the floor with a glint of ice. The kid dashed away.

My pulse stuttered. What the fuck? How did that—Had *I* done that?

Where had that power come from?

The jitter of uncertainty that hit me was my undoing. The guy recovered in a flash. He stomped his heel, the ice crinkling away under it, and the entire surface beneath me turned slick and hazy. I moved to take a step, and my feet shot out from under me. I landed on my ass with a sting of pain up my spine. The frigid layer of ice bit into my palms.

"Do you really want to keep going?" the divine devil said, managing to sound both teasing and menacing.

I scrambled up, and the woman from my escort grabbed my arm to steady me.

"This isn't the time," the man said, and motioned to the hazel-eyed guy. "Maybe you'd better fill them in. And you." He jabbed his finger at me. "*This* way, please."

"I look forward to seeing you later," the divine devil called after me as my two remaining escorts ushered me across the landing and around a corner.

As fascinating as he'd been to look at, I couldn't say I returned the sentiment.

I inhaled and exhaled slowly, trying to settle my nerves. I *couldn't* have conjured up that frost, right? I'd never shown the slightest hint of magic before. There had to be some other explanation.

We strode down a gloomy hall with varnished wooden doors lining both sides. The killer stopped at the door at the very end of the hall and rapped his knuckles against it.

"Come in," a woman said in a cool voice, as if she'd been expecting us.

The man opened the door and motioned me in ahead of him. I stepped onto a thick crimson-and-ocher rug in a room as big as my entire basement apartment. Built-in mahogany shelves lined the walls, stuffed with aged books, jars of indeterminate powders and oils, and assorted trinkets.

In the middle of it all, a prim woman of about fifty sat at a matching desk carved with a vine around the edge. Her eyes had a beady quality, her nose pert and her lips thin. Her long graying blond hair was wrapped into a thick coil at the nape of her neck, resting against the collar of a fitted indigo dress-suit.

She stood up as we came in with a bob of her head to my escorts. "Well," she said, fixing her beady gaze on me. "Here you are." She sounded satisfied but somehow not quite pleased, as if she was happy with the situation but not that she had to be a part of it.

"Go on, then," she said in the same cool tone, waving the other two off. They vanished, shutting the door behind them. The woman extended her hand toward one of the two velvet wingchairs that faced her desk. "Please, have a seat. As I'm sure you were told, I'm Headmistress Grimsworth. I'd imagine you have a lot of questions."

I allowed myself to drop into the chair, careful of the mouse clinging to my shirt between my shoulder blades. It seemed like I should probably pretend Deborah hadn't told me anything, or they'd wonder how I knew, but acting clueless didn't feel all that difficult. All the trauma and the confusion of the day washed over me in one huge wave. It took a moment before I could speak.

"Where is this, and why the hell am I here?"

Ms. Grimsworth's mouth curled into a narrow smile. "You're here because this is where you're meant to be. This is the Bloodstone University for Magical Edification, and you are Persephone Bloodstone."

CHAPTER THREE

Malcolm

"Who the fuck was that?" I said, my gaze following the new girl as she slipped out of sight. "And where the hell did she grow up that she comes here dressed like a feeb and jumping into other people's business?"

The junior we'd been playing with had scampered off. If he started spreading the word about how some random chick had saved him from Malcolm Nightwood, he'd find a whole lot more than his feet on fire.

Jude swiped a hand through his dark red hair, his lips curved with his typical smirk. "She looked pretty nice landing on the ground ass-first when you were done with her, I'll give her that."

Connar's grim expression broke with a soft snicker. His brawny arms flexed as he crossed them over his chest. "You know, she did. She should have realized she was outmatched the second she saw you."

I'd admit the new girl had a nice ass in general, even in her baggy jeans. I'd gotten a good look at it while she was leaving. Maybe she'd be fun to have around if she removed the stick she apparently had shoved up there.

We could certainly help her with that.

Declan fixed me with what I'd come to think of as his professor look. He'd always had a bit of a know-it-all vibe that must have come with being the oldest of us and the only one close to full baron. It had intensified since he'd gotten the teacher's aide gig this fall. I gave him a pass on it because he generally put that knowledge to use greasing whatever wheels we needed greased.

"*That*," he said in an authoritative tone, "was the long-lost heir of Bloodstone. So whatever you're imagining doing to her right now, you might want to revise those plans."

I blinked, momentarily losing my grasp on my composure. *Only* momentarily, of course. "The Bloodstone scion? They found her? Holy shit."

Jude cocked his head, his dark green eyes lighting up with curiosity. "Was she living with feebs, hence the clothes?"

"With joymancers," Declan said. "Which as far as I can tell amounts to almost the same thing. Their house could have fit in the front hall three times over. They do like to show off their modesty."

"Wait," I said, prodding him in the chest. "Did you get yourself invited along on the rescue party? Why the hell didn't you tell us anything?"

Declan's chin came up. "They asked me at the last

minute. Said it'd be good for her to have one of the other scions there—someone who'd have an idea what she might have gone through. We weren't supposed to tell anyone until we'd pulled it off."

Declan's mother had been killed in the same confrontation-turned-massacre where joymancers had claimed the lives of both the Bloodstones of our parents' generation. Sometimes I forgot that little piece of his past, because I'd only been three when it'd happened, so I didn't really remember it in the first place.

No one talked about the skirmish much anyway. It was kind of a sore spot among the older mages.

"You could have introduced her and saved her a little trouble." I peered toward the hall the girl had disappeared down, a tickle of exhilaration rising through my chest. So, that was the Bloodstone scion. She hadn't had any more idea who we were than we had about her. Totally fitting that she'd have started asserting dominance the second she'd walked into Blood U.

She'd be embarrassed when she found out who she'd actually been messing with. I had to smile, imagining her reaction.

Despite the shabby clothes, she'd been awfully easy on the eyes. And that brash spirit... Oh, yes, spring term had just gotten ten times more exciting.

"No one knows how much *she* knows about who she is or what happened to her," Declan said. "From the way she was acting, I don't think she had any idea. Grimsworth wanted to talk with her first."

"We'll give her a little time to settle in," I said

magnanimously, rubbing my hands together. "Find out what dorm they stick her in. We can stop by after dinner and give her a chance at re-doing first impressions."

Having a Bloodstone at the school… I wasn't going to let that tip the balance very much. The four of us who ruled Blood U and would someday rule the whole fearmancer shebang together—we'd had each other's backs for years. She'd have to prove herself ready to respect and return that kind of allegiance before we'd fully welcome her into our circle, the final point on the pentacle.

We'd make it clear who ran things around here and go from there. Once she got the picture, I had the feeling it'd be a productive friendship.

My thoughts slid back to the fierceness in her dark blue eyes when she'd tried to stare me down, the flush of color in her pale cheeks. Maybe more than friendship if I got my way. And, let's be honest, I usually did.

CHAPTER FOUR

Rory

I stared at the headmistress of Bloodstone University for the space of a few heartbeats before I regained control over my vocal chords.

"I think there's been a mistake," I said. "I would definitely remember if my name was something as weird as Persephone Bloodstone. I'm Lorelei Franco. Usually I go by Rory. Nice to meet you." I raised my hand in an awkward little wave.

Maybe I should have said "horrible to meet you," but from Ms. Grimsworth's pinched expression, I had the feeling that wouldn't have gone over well. I still didn't have a lot of options here.

The headmistress looked down at a few papers spread in front of her on her desk. A sharp ashy smell drifted past my nose from a cone of incense set on a burner on a nearby shelf. It made my stomach turn.

"You've been living with Lisa and Rafael Franco, yes?" she said. "For how long?"

"For—for as long as I can remember. They adopted me when I was two years old."

Ms. Grimsworth hummed to herself. "They or their colleagues kidnapped you, Miss Bloodstone. Did you know that they were mages—that they could wield magic?"

I nodded slowly. "Yes. They didn't keep that a secret from me. But why—"

"There are two types of magic-workers in this world," Ms. Grimsworth said. "The people who raised you were joymancers, working with feelings of elation. You've now met the first fearmancers I'd imagine you've had a chance to associate with in your memory."

"Fearmancers. Mages who use fear?" I said, as if Deborah hadn't already explained that much. Otherwise she might wonder why I wasn't more surprised.

"Exactly. Our communities have often been at odds. Seventeen years ago, a group of joymancers interrupted several fearmancers in the middle of conducting their business. Your birth parents were there, along with you. They were killed in the attack, and the joymancers took you with them when they fled the scene. We've spent significant resources over those years trying to track you down. They hid you well, but not well enough to foil us completely."

Her beady eyes glinted with satisfaction, as if the brutal murders of my *real* parents, the ones who'd raised me, were something to celebrate. My stomach churned.

Even if everything she'd just said was true, why the hell *wouldn't* mages like Mom and Dad have wanted to get a little kid away from a "community" like this? They'd been trying to give me a better life.

"You've been affected by your time with them, naturally," the headmistress said. "But as you realize how much they were denying you, how much they stole from you, I expect you'll adapt quickly. There's a reason this university is named after your family, Miss Bloodstone. The Bloodstones are one of the five ruling families among the fearmancers. You'll have great magical gifts that I doubt your kidnappers ever allowed you to use."

"I don't have any—" I started, and stopped, shutting my mouth so sharply my teeth clicked. On the landing, with those gorgeous asshole guys, I'd conjured ice. Not a lot of it, but... I hadn't known what I was doing.

The sensation of power that had come over me hadn't been joy—that was for sure. No, for one fleeting instant, the divine devil had been *afraid*.

And I'd drunk in that emotion and transformed it into power, as easily as breathing.

Fuck.

"I'm a fearmancer," I said quietly as the understanding sank in. "But I never—when I was living with my parents—"

"They would have had ways of suppressing your natural talents," Ms. Grimsworth said. "Mages of both kinds normally see their magical ability emerge sometime between their fifteenth and sixteenth birthday. For most of your childhood, they wouldn't have needed to even worry about it."

Between my fifteenth and sixteenth birthday. Icy fingers wrapped around my gut. The mouse currently nestled against my back, clinging to my shirt—Dad had brought her home just a couple of weeks after my fifteenth birthday.

Deborah had said her job had been to protect me, to let them know if I needed help. Had that really been just a nice way of saying she'd been my guard, watching to make sure my fearmancer magic didn't emerge despite whatever they were doing to hold it in?

Oh, God. No wonder they hadn't wanted me to move out or to travel anywhere without them. They must have needed me to stay close so they could work their spells on me.

I closed my eyes against the horror welling up inside me. No. My parents *had* been protecting me—protecting me from these people who they must have known were searching for me. From the dark magic they practiced. Any horror I felt shouldn't be because of them but the blood the fearmancers had spilled in my house this morning.

Somehow I didn't think I could simply say, *Well, that's all lovely, but I'd like to head back to spend the rest of my life with the non-psychopathic mages now*, and the fearmancers would fly me back on their private jet in a jiffy.

I looked down at my hands clasped together on my lap. The light from the ornate fixture on the ceiling glinted off the charms along my wrist that Mom and Dad had bought for me over the last nine years. Another wallop of grief hit me without warning.

How long would it take for someone to find them where the fearmancers had left them ravaged? Or had the mages who'd taken me magicked my parents' bodies away so the murders would never be discovered, and they'd simply vanish from existence?

All the pieces of my life with them, from my childhood through to this morning, were hundreds of miles away. All I had of *myself*, of my history as their daughter, was that bracelet and the old T-shirt and jeans I'd thrown on for a lazy Sunday morning.

And a telepathic mouse that was part guardian, part guard. Deborah's furry back shifted against my skin as she adjusted her position. I couldn't forget her.

Ms. Grimsworth had been waiting in silence as I'd wrestled with her revelations. I sucked in a breath and raised my head. "All right. What happens now? What do you expect me to do?"

She gave me a tight smile that might have been slightly sympathetic. It was hard to tell, her face was so rigid. "It seemed best for you to come here and remain until your education is complete. As the heir to the Bloodstone legacy, you'll have certain responsibilities. You're greatly behind in the training you'll need to complete to fulfill those responsibilities. The Bloodstone properties will be yours when you're ready to take your full place in society. They're currently inhabited only by maintenance staff paid for by your fortune."

I had properties. I had a *fortune*. This morning I'd

been worried about making a couple hundred bucks on a figurine. A hysterical giggle bubbled in my throat.

"Aren't there any other Bloodstones around who can handle this stuff?" I had to ask.

The headmistress pursed her lips. "Your grandfather served as temporary baron, despite being aged out, until his death seven years ago. He had a brother who took up residence in Portugal decades ago and who hasn't been heard from in almost as long. Your mother's younger sister passed away before you were born—a boating accident. By that series of unfortunate circumstances, you are the only definite living Bloodstone in existence."

Wonderful. Exactly how pissed off would she be if I chose this moment to vomit all over her expensive rug?

I dragged in a breath. Maybe the best option was also the easiest. I could play along for now, right? It wouldn't be such a bad thing to learn the basics of the magical talent I'd only just discovered. I'd wait for my moment, and then I'd run for the hills—or rather, for California. My parents had friends in the Enclave. Someone had to know what the hell to do.

"I guess it's up to me, then, huh?" I said with a weak laugh, and stood up. "How do I get started?"

Ms. Grimsworth said something under her breath and made a small gesture with her hand. "I've summoned the professor who'll serve as your mentor to show you to your dorm room. He'll explain more of the workings of the school along the way. Tomorrow morning, we'll conduct your assessment to determine your areas of greatest strength, and then he and I will draw up a course plan for you to follow. You'll find we aren't rigorously focused on classroom work here at the university. We find students learn best with a mix of assignments and more self-directed practice."

Like setting younger students on fire? I bit my tongue rather than mention that.

The headmistress got up and motioned at me from head to toe. "It also seems worth mentioning that the team that liberated you cast a locating spell on you to ensure we don't lose you again. You'll be able to roam the entire campus grounds and visit the town down the hill, but if you should find yourself whisked farther away, we'll be alerted and arrive as quickly as possible."

As she spoke, a shiver ran over my skin that might have been an echo of that magic. I thought I read a subtle threat in her gaze. If I tried to make a break for it of my own accord, I wouldn't get very far, no matter how stealthy I was. Shit.

There had to be a way to undo a locating spell. I'd just have to learn it.

A knock sounded on the door. Ms. Grimsworth swung it open.

In the hall stood a man I'd have put in his mid-forties. Tufts of light red hair—really it was orange—stuck up in various directions over his round head and along his equally rounded jaw. Like every other fearmancer I'd encountered so far, he was dressed to impress: a blue linen shirt that downplayed his barrel chest and gray dress pants.

"Miss Bloodstone," the headmistress said, "I'm pleased to introduce you to Professor Banefield, one of our specialists in Insight. He'll be acting as your mentor for your first year at the university, and perhaps longer if you get along well."

I didn't want to think about being stuck here for a whole year, let alone more than that.

Professor Banefield gave me a smile that had more warmth than I'd gotten from all of the other fearmancers I'd met combined and stuck out his hand. The warmth startled me so much it took me a second to realize he was waiting for me to complete a handshake.

"It's a pleasure to meet you, Miss Bloodstone," he said with a brisk pump. "Or if I might call you Persephone—"

"Rory," I said quickly. "My name is Rory." Maybe I couldn't argue the Bloodstone part, but I'd be damned if they were going to take away the first name my parents had given me too.

Banefield's gaze twitched to the headmistress and back to me. "All right then. Rory. I'm so glad to have you returned to us. You must be overwhelmed. Why don't you let me show you to your room here on campus, and then you can take some time to absorb everything you've learned?"

"That sounds good," I said, because it really did. If there was a place here I could be alone with my thoughts, let me at it.

"I hope you'll consider this school a home for as long as you're with us," Ms. Grimsworth said as I stepped out of her office. "If you should have any concerns, you can always come to me."

Professor Banefield set off down the hall with a

rhythmic stride. After walking alongside him for a minute, I realized he was a bit bowlegged.

"This building houses the staff offices and residences as well as the junior dorms—for students aged fifteen to seventeen," he said, and pointed at a door with a gleaming bronze name plaque. "If you need me, you'll be able to find me here. You'll be living in the adjacent Ashgrave Hall, which contains the senior dorms—for our students aged eighteen to twenty-one—and our extensive library."

That name rang a bell. When I'd gotten here with my parents' attackers, the head guy had called one of them "Ashgrave," hadn't he?

"Why Ashgrave?" I asked.

Banefield gave me a quizzical look but answered easily enough. "Each of the ruling families had a hand in creating this university. Yours had the distinction of giving their name to the entire school, but the others each adopted a building."

Someone who'd been part of the attack was a member of another ruling family. I wasn't sure what to do with that information.

"Bloodstone, Ashgrave... What are the other ruling families?" That seemed important to know.

"Nightwood, Killbrook, and Stormhurst. This is Killbrook Hall we're in right now. The classrooms are in Nightwood Tower, which forms a triangle with the two halls. And closer to the lake you'll find the Stormhurst Building for Physical Fitness."

Banefield rambled on as he led me down the stairs. "The university seeks to provide all students with both privacy and a communal experience. The senior dorms are set up with ten individual bedrooms around a common living and kitchen area, with a bathroom shared just by the ten or fewer in that dorm. Because of your status, you'll naturally receive one of the few corner rooms with a little more space and a view of the lake."

"Naturally," I muttered, and snapped my mouth shut when he shot me another of those puzzled glances. "So, what happens in this 'assessment' thing tomorrow?"

"Nothing for you to worry about. All you need to do is be present, and the assessors will take care of the rest. From what I recall, it feels like a brief, mild tingling."

If he was telling the truth, I could probably handle that much.

We stepped out through a side door into the cool spring air. The sun had dropped below the trees, and the shadows sprawled long across the ground. A paved pathway swerved through the neatly trimmed grass to another medieval-ish stone building that rose five stories to a gable roof.

Another path rambled across the way to a narrower cylindrical structure nearly twice as tall that easily earned the label Tower. Banefield pointed between Ashgrave Hall and Nightwood Tower toward a squat building topped by a dome farther across the green.

"Assessments take place in the main gymnasium," he said. "I'll come by your dorm to escort you there at nine o'clock tomorrow. We all understand it'll take you some time to get your bearings."

And yet they seemed perfectly happy to throw me into

this life with hardly an acknowledgement of the one they'd ripped me out of. Did fearmancers have so little conscience that it didn't occur to them that I might still be bothered by my parents' deaths even now that I knew Mom and Dad had supposedly kidnapped me? Was that fact supposed to erase an entire childhood of love?

The first two floors of Ashgrave Hall held the library. A few students were ambling between the shelves, glancing our way and then going back to their business. We hiked up three more flights to the top floor. No elevators to speak of, apparently. I was going to have killer legs if I stayed here very long.

"It's important to note," Banefield said as we climbed, "that we welcome a number of Nary students to the university to assist with certain aspects of our programming. They wear a gold pin shaped like a leaf that they believe simply marks their scholarship status. You must be careful to avoid discussing any magical subjects while they're within hearing and to ensure they don't pick up on any spells you cast on or around them. Discipline is rather strict in that regard."

I blinked at him. "You let Naries into your university of magical studies?"

He shrugged. "We prepare you for every aspect of the world you'll be venturing into. None of us can exist without some dealings with the Nary population."

The fifth floor landing offered four doors. Banefield swiped a keycard over a panel for the one marked C1, and the lock clicked over. He handed the card to me and pushed the door open.

The square room on the other side was four times the size of my living room back home, with a similar aesthetic to the headmistress's office, just fewer books and more seating. A thick rug covered most of the floor under the clusters of sofas, armchairs, and coffee tables. A ten-seater mahogany dining table stood between the living area and a kitchen with two stainless steel fridges along the far wall. Five wooden doors stood along the walls on either side of me, and another door next to the kitchen must have led to the bathroom.

A couple of girls around my age were sitting at one end of the table finishing off their steak dinners. The rich smell of sirloin laced the air. A few others were sprawled on the sofas. All of them had been looking toward the open bedroom door in the far left corner when we came in. Their gazes jerked to me and then back to the bedroom.

Another girl was poised just outside that door with her hands planted on her curvaceous hips. Perfectly neat waves of auburn hair spilled down to the middle of her back.

"I didn't agree to this," she was saying in an acidic voice.

"You can take it up with the headmistress then," a woman said from inside the room. She came out carrying a box, a stiletto heel protruding from inside. "Or them, I suppose," she added, lifting her chin toward Banefield and me. She walked along the line of doors to deposit the box in the bedroom closest to us.

The girl spun around. The beauty of her angelic face,

pale and smooth as porcelain, was ruined by the narrowing of her eyes and the disgusted curl of her lip.

"That was *my* room, Professor Banefield," she said, crossing her arms over her chest as she strode over. "It's been mine since I moved to senior last year. I don't see why I should have to give it to her." The disgusted curl deepened as she looked me over. I bristled automatically.

"Victory," Banefield said in an even voice, "this is Per — Ah, this is Rory Bloodstone. As a scion, she's owed the best room we can provide for her. If she'd been with us from the start, you wouldn't have gotten to enjoy the room for as long as you did." He turned to me. "This is Victory Blighthaven, one of our most talented students."

His compliment bounced right off Victory. From the glare she was shooting me, she wished the fearmancers hadn't found me at all.

That makes two of us, I wanted to tell her, but I couldn't figure out how to express my profound desire to be anywhere but here in a way that didn't offend her and every other mage around me even more.

The fact was, though, that I didn't really care about the room. If I had my way, I wouldn't be staying in it very long anyway. If having it would keep this witch out of my way, let her have it.

"I don't need a special room," I said to Banefield. "It's fine. I'll take whichever one was empty."

Victory brightened for the instant before Banefield shook his head. "We have standards for a reason. You've been denied your heritage too long, Rory. We aren't going to hold you back from it even here. I believe Victory's things have already been moved over?"

The woman who'd carted the box out reemerged. "Yep, we're good to go. I set up the wardrobe like Ms. Grimsworth wanted, too. Come on, Miss Bloodstone. Let me show you."

Victory's eyes burned a hole in my back as I followed the woman over.

With the two of us and Banefield in the bedroom, there wasn't much standing room left. A queen-sized bed filled about half of the space. Across from it, a small mahogany desk and chair sat beneath a huge picture window that showed the field between the hall and the athletic building as well as the sparkling water of a huge lake farther beyond that. A wardrobe that stretched almost to the ceiling stood against the wall next to the door.

The woman tugged open the wardrobe's doors. Silky blouses and dresses and several pairs of slacks hung in a row. Every piece was sleek and posh. A fearmancer's clothes.

"I bought undergarments and the like for you—new, of course," the woman said, motioning to the drawers at the bottom of the wardrobe. "They said you wouldn't be coming with much. If the sizing's off, just pass on the word to someone from maintenance. We had to go by the initial observations. There are a few pairs of shoes in there too—you can see if they fit. Harder to tell feet sizes. From the looks of you, they were right that her clothes should work."

"*Her* clothes?" I repeated.

"Your mother's. We picked out a selection from the estate that seemed appropriate for university life." The woman flashed me a grin. Then her expression turned more serious. "We wanted you to have something from your family as you get started here."

My mother. Something from my family. The Bloodstones, they meant. The birth mother I couldn't even remember. Not the one whose literal blood had drenched my hands less than a day ago.

A prickling rushed up behind my eyes before I could catch it. "Thank you," I said, as quickly as I could manage without being a total ass. "I, um, this is great. I think I just need to lie down for a few minutes."

"Yes, of course. I'll see you in the morning." Banefield ushered the woman out of the room and closed the door. The second it thudded shut, I sank onto the edge of the bed.

Deborah scurried down the back of my shirt and poked her little white head out from under the hem. *Lorelei, if you—*

"Not right now," I whispered hoarsely, and just like that, the tears I'd been holding in from the moment I'd woken up spilled out in a torrent. I bowed my head into my hands and let grief take over.

CHAPTER FIVE

Rory

T he first sound that penetrated my cloud of grief was Victory's caustic voice carrying through my bedroom door, pitched in a low but pointed way to give her plausible deniability while she fully intended to be overheard.

"I heard the Bloodstones have always been bitches. 'Oh, really, I'll take whatever room's available,' as if she didn't know they'd already kicked me out of the one she wanted. Looks like the line runs true."

At least a couple of someones twittered with laughter in response.

I rubbed my stinging eyes and pushed myself upright where I'd curled up on the bed. My head was muggy, and my stomach pinched with hunger. It had to be well past my usual dinner time now.

Mom had been planning a roast. I'd seen it thawing in

the fridge this morning, less than a day and what felt like hundreds of years ago.

I inhaled shakily and resisted the pull of another wave of tears. Crying wasn't going to help me. If I was going to get through this, I needed to pull myself together.

Tiny claws tickled the back of my hand. Deborah the mouse peered up at me from the bedspread. *I'm sorry I wasn't able to prepare you better. I didn't know about you being a scion. I was going to tell you the fearmancer part in the car, but there wasn't time. If I communicate with you like this around them, they might pick up on it.*

"It's okay," I said under my breath, with sharp awareness of how easily voices could travel through the door. "If you can talk to me like that, can you cast other kinds of spells too?"

Unfortunately, no. It's part of the familiar bond. A mage can tie their spirit to an animal, and there's a certain mental connection... Regular animals wouldn't be able to communicate in words like this, of course. I only can because my mind is human.

"My parents created the bond," I said. They must have, in some way I hadn't noticed at the time.

So I could watch out for you in ways you didn't realize you needed, Deborah said.

"Yeah." I wished they'd thought they could trust me with those revelations. "I guess we should find a home for you somewhere in here. I don't want to know what the assholes here would do if they found out I've brought a disguised joymancer along with me."

Yes, good thinking. I'd rather not discover the

consequences either. Her furry body shivered.

I poked around the room with Deborah perched on one of my palms, and we decided my sock drawer would make an ideal hiding spot. The notch in the front for pulling the drawer open was just big enough for her to squeeze in and out, and if a few mouse hairs got on my socks, I didn't think anyone would be looking closely enough to notice.

My stomach grumbled more insistently. Was there anywhere to get food on campus? Professor Banefield hadn't mentioned a cafeteria.

I went to venture into the common room, and my pulse jumped at how easily the doorknob turned. Banefield had given me a keycard for the dorm, but my bedroom door didn't appear to have any lock at all. No keyhole on the knob, no bolt I could slide over from the inside.

I'd assume respect for personal belongings operated on an honor system, except from what I'd seen honor wasn't a quality fearmancers valued highly.

When I came out, two different girls were at the dining table, perched at opposite ends. One fidgeted with her mousey-brown ponytail as she hunched over the bowl she was eating from. The other was cutting into a filet mignon, her tawny waves pulled back from her face with a silver clip in the shape of a raven. The girls who'd been eating steaks earlier had moved to a sofa at the other end of the room where they were paging through a fashion magazine together.

And Victory was lounging on the sofa closest to my

room, her bare calves sprawled over the lap of a girl with a shiny black bob. She'd thrown her head back in a laugh at some comment made by her other friend, whose ice-blond french braid was streaked through with purple and pink. At the click of my door, her gaze shot to me. I ignored her, but I could feel her narrowed eyes studying me as I tested my doorknob from the outside.

"No locks in here, your highness," she cooed. "But I'm sure someone as special as you can figure out other ways of keeping your door secure."

Oh. They must all use magic to prevent intruders. And if someone was better at magic than you, they'd be able to break in no matter what you did, if they wanted. Of course that was how security would work at Villain Academy.

At least I didn't have much in there I wanted to protect. The only things that actually belonged to me, I was wearing. Deborah could hide herself just fine.

I turned away from my room, fighting the urge to hug myself defensively, and considered which of my dormmates would be the safest to ask where I could find my own grub. I hadn't gotten any farther than eliminating Victory and her sidekicks when the dorm door whipped open, and four guys who definitely didn't belong to this room strolled in. Apparently even that lock opened to the right spell.

The guys moved through the common area with total confidence, as if they walked into girls' dorm rooms every day. Which for all I knew, they did.

At the head of the pack was the divine devil from

earlier, his wickedly flawless face split with an easy grin and a small cloth bag dangling from one hand. He was flanked by the redhead and the musclehead from before, which was no surprise, but ambling along behind them was the striking guy with the swept-back black hair and hazel eyes who'd tried to reassure me during my parents' murders.

"Mal!" Victory cried. She and her friends sprang up, and she sashayed over to give the divine devil a kiss on the cheek while the other two batted their eyes at the whole pack. Her hand lingered on his forearm.

"Hey, Vic," he said, his expression pleased if not exactly warm. The fact that he enjoyed this girl's attention only solidified my initial opinion of him.

The guy with the dark copper hair tugged on the end of Victory's friend's braid with a teasing smirk. "Does your hair just grow this way, Cressida? I never see you with it down."

The other girl arched her eyebrows, but an eager flush colored her cheeks at his touch. "Maybe someday you'll get to, if you prove yourself up to the challenge."

"What, you haven't been sufficiently impressed so far?"

The divine devil—Mal?—shot his friend a *knock it off* look, and the copper-haired guy let go of her braid with a breezy flick of his fingers. Victory gazed up at the ringleader coyly. "To what do we owe this visit? Got big plans you need company for?"

His gaze found me where I'd stiffened just outside my bedroom door. He aimed his smile my way with no hint of his earlier animosity. "I figured a little housewarming was in order for our newfound scion." He lifted the cloth bag higher. "We come bearing dinner, made by Jude's family chef. Best roast duckling you've ever tasted."

That wouldn't be hard, considering I'd never tasted roast duckling before, period. Why was this guy being so friendly now? Victory's smile had tightened, and she was as close to shooting daggers from her eyes as she could get without actually fileting me.

I'll admit that being homeschooled most of my life had its downsides, the main one being the isolation. The only people I'd socialized with on a regular basis were my parents. I liked to think that these days I didn't put my foot in my mouth anywhere near as much as I had in the first few months of college, but my capacity for complex social navigation was still pretty limited. And if the tricky situations I'd encountered at my old school had been algebra, this right here felt like advanced calculus.

"Um," I said brilliantly.

The divine devil's gaze darted across the room and settled for a moment on the mousy girl hunched at one end of the dining table. He murmured a few words with a clench of his hand. She slumped back in her chair, her eyes glazing.

My shoulders came up. I didn't need any practice to know how to respond to *that*. "What the hell did you do to her?"

He cocked his head as his gaze came back to me. "We can't talk freely when there's a feeb around. When I snap her out of it, she'll just think her thoughts wandered off for a minute."

For the first time, I noticed the gleaming leaf pin by the neckline of the girl's shirt. She was one of the Nary students Professor Banefield had mentioned.

And this jerk had talked about putting her into a stupor the same way you might mention leashing a dog.

He was already sauntering closer to me, leaving Victory to trail behind him. He tossed the cloth bag onto the dining table, and I caught a whiff of a meaty, citrusy smell that made my mouth water. My stomach probably would have gurgled again if it hadn't balled into a knot of repulsion.

"I think we got off on the wrong foot earlier. I'm Malcolm Nightwood, the Nightwood scion." He made a grand gesture toward himself and pointed to the copper-haired guy who'd come up beside him, who offered a cheeky wave. "This jackass is Jude Killbrook." Then to the beefy guy, who was watching me with a small smile that didn't really fit his otherwise stern expression. "Our resident blockhead, Connar Stormhurst." Then my former captor/rescuer. "And the stuffed shirt over there is Declan Ashgrave."

My eyes leapt to the guy with the bright hazel eyes, whose voice had been so gentle in the midst of the carnage this morning. "We met earlier," he said, in an even tone I couldn't read. "Welcome to the pentacle of scions."

So *he* was the Ashgrave I'd heard the head of the group talking to. He stood a little more rigidly than the others, but he didn't look any more bothered by Malcolm's casually insulting description of him than the other two did. Did he actually like this guy?

They were waiting—for me to return the introduction, obviously. "Rory Fra—I mean, Bloodstone," I said, stumbling. "Rory Bloodstone." For now. I motioned to the dinner he'd brought. "You really didn't have to."

Victory let out a sound like a muffled snort. The guys ignored her.

"You're one of us," Malcolm said. "We look after our own. You've made it to the right place, with the right friends—good-bye to the prissy joymancers."

That last remark took me from bristling to furious in an instant.

"What if I'm not interested in being friends?" I said.

Malcolm chuckled. "Who are you going to hang out with, then—the feebs and the wimps like you had before? We know where you belong."

My voice came out taut. "No. *I* know where I belong. And it's nowhere near jerks like you. So why don't you get the hell out of my dorm room and bestow your 'friendship' on someone who wants it?"

The room fell into total silence, all of my dormmates watching us. Connar's folded arms tensed. Jude let out a low whistle, but his smirk had hardened.

"You just got here, darling," he said. "It's a little early to start drawing battle lines."

A flush colored Malcolm's neck. His coffee-brown eyes flared with anger. "I think you need to remember who you're talking to."

"I know exactly who I'm talking to," I said. "A superficial, insecure asshole who cares more about family names than who someone is and has to resort to insulting and tormenting everyone he thinks is less than him just to feel good about himself. Why the fuck anyone would want that in their life, I haven't got a clue."

One of the girls gasped. If Malcolm could have incinerated me just with his gaze, I think he would have.

Despite his expression, his voice came out cuttingly cold. "If that's how you want to play this, be my guest. We'll see how quickly your feeb-dressed untrained ass comes begging us for a hand up when you see what the world is really like. And when you do, you'd better be on your knees and ready to open wide."

He spun on his heel and stalked out. The other three guys followed him, not even Declan glancing back. My chest twisted as he disappeared out the door.

It looked like he was just as much of an asshole as the rest of the scions. Why the hell had he tried to be kind to me this morning if he was going to stand by while his friend talked trash about everyone and everything that had mattered to me?

"You do know how to make an impression, don't you?" Victory said with a sharp little smile that looked a bit smug.

The adrenaline rush of my anger ebbed, leaving me empty. I gestured to the bag Malcolm had left behind. My stomach panged, but I knew if I ate one tidbit of the meal he'd brought, Victory would be running to him to crow about how I'd already accepted his charity.

"If anyone wants extra dinner, you're welcome to it," I said, and ducked back into my room where I could be alone with all the painful sensations inside me.

CHAPTER SIX

Jude

Saying Malcolm was pissed off was like suggesting the Atlantic Ocean was a tad damp. He kept his head high and his gait steady as we crossed the landing to his dorm room, but I'd known him my whole life, and I could read his anger in every tensed muscle and flick of his gaze. He strode into the common room, where a few of his dormmates were chatting around a coffee table, and swept his arm through the air.

"Everyone out. We need this space."

His smooth baritone penetrated the doors. It was nearly nine o'clock at night, but every guy in here knew better than to argue with Malcolm Nightwood.

The three in the living area scrambled up and hustled past us without a word or even eye contact. A couple of guys who'd been in their bedrooms slipped out and fled too.

Malcolm rolled a few syllables off his tongue that had meaning only to him, his fingers rippling like a piano player's as he scanned the room. He was confirming no one else was still in residence. When the spell had satisfied him, he spun around to face the rest of us.

"That brainless bitch," he snapped.

Everyone at Blood U knew better than to argue with Malcolm Nightwood... except our newfound Bloodstone scion.

I might have laughed at the memory of her trying to take Malcolm on, like a lamb bleating at a fucking lion, if Malcolm hadn't been so furious about it. If the conversation had happened in private, he might have brought her down a few pegs right there and left it at that. But she'd torn into him in front of the daughters of some of the most powerful families below the pentacle five, thrown his graciousness in his face, and he hadn't been prepared for a fight.

It was better that we'd left with one quick jab than stay and risk a larger fumble.

"She's brainless, all right," I said, flopping onto the arm of one of the sofas. "She's never worked a bit of magic before today, and she thinks it's a good idea to go up against the four strongest mages in the school? She'll regret that in no time flat."

"I should have flipped her on her ass right there," Connar muttered, cracking his knuckles.

Declan held up his hands, always the voice of reason. "But you didn't, because no matter what she said, she's still a scion." He turned to Malcolm. "She didn't really understand what she was getting into. She's only been here a few hours."

Malcolm scowled. "Somehow I don't get the impression she's going to turn all sunshine and roses as she settles in."

"So we teach her what her proper place is," I said. "And teach her quick, before she gets even farther into bad habits." I didn't care where she'd grown up or how ignorant she was, she couldn't walk in here and do whatever she wanted expecting everyone to accept her like that. We all had our parts to play, scions more than anyone.

If I'd pulled a stunt like she just had in front of that many witnesses… An uncomfortable prickle wrapped around my gut. The less I thought about that, the better.

Years of searching to finally pluck her from our enemies' grasp, the crown of scionhood dropped just like that onto her head where it should have been all along… You'd think she could show a little more gratitude.

"We'll teach her, all right." The eagerly brutal light that was my favorite look on him came over Malcolm's face. The corners of his lips curled upward. "Of course we will. We won't even have to work that hard. She's got a lot of catching up to do and an entire senior class looking for ways to earn for their leagues. A few well-placed blows, and she *will* come running to us begging us to have her back and help her learn the ropes. She might be a scion, but this place is ours. *We* decide what goes."

"Any blows you strike are going to need to be a lot more subtle than lighting a kid's feet on fire if you don't want Ms. Grimsworth cracking down," Declan said. "Having the Bloodstone scion back under her watch is a big deal to her. You can... *educate* her, but we don't want to come close to crossing any lines."

Malcolm scoffed. "Give me a little credit. She won't even know what hit her."

Connar looked from one to the other like a pit bull ready to spring. "What's the plan, then?"

I leaned back against the sofa. I knew what *my* role here was. If any of these guys would still give me the time of day if they had the full story—which was doubtful—it'd be for my ability to provide the entertainment. So I'd keep delivering.

"I don't think she should get to do much other learning until she's proven she can learn to give respect where it's due. She'll have a class schedule after her assessment. I can already think of a few fun ways we can make her wish she had us on her side."

"Do you have some new illusions up your sleeve, Jude?" Malcolm said.

I spread my hands. "Hey, might as well earn for my league at the same time."

He chuckled. "Whatever. As long as it's good, I'm down. What have you got?"

CHAPTER SEVEN

Rory

Professor Banefield had said he'd come get me for my assessment at nine in the morning. It hadn't occurred to me in the moment that I'd dropped my phone back in my parents' house and my dorm room didn't appear to have any clock. Maybe the other fearmancers had a magical way of telling time?

In any case, at least it gave me one reason to be thankful that I slept so restlessly that I was up with the rising sun.

When I ventured into the common room again, it was empty except for the Nary girl—the one Malcolm had called a "feeb"—who was eating a bowl of cereal in the same hunched defensive position I'd seen her in yesterday.

Now that I'd seen how the mages around her were inclined to treat her, I could understand why she might take that stance. She didn't appear to have suffered any ill effects from Malcolm's daze, which one of the girls must have finally snapped her out of after he'd left, but what the hell did I know about the effects of that kind of magic?

"Hey," I said tentatively, stopping by the edge of the table. She wasn't magical—she didn't even know magic existed—and weirdly that made her the only person I'd met so far that I could really trust. "I didn't expect anyone else to be up this early."

The girl gave me a wary look as she chewed the spoonful she'd just popped into her mouth. "I like to get out of here before anyone else wakes up," she said, in a tone that hinted at a whole lot of hassling she'd gotten when she didn't.

I glanced toward Victory's bedroom door with a grimace. "I can understand that. I'm Rory, by the way."

She bobbed her head, her ponytail swinging with the movement. "I heard. Ah, my name's Shelby. Sorry you ended up stuck with this bunch."

My mouth twitched into a smile, and her shoulders relaxed a little. Her gaze followed me as I puttered through the kitchen. The sink was stacked with dirty dishes, a sour smell rising off them.

"Doesn't anyone clean up around here?" I asked.

"The housekeeping staff come through in the middle of the day and take care of everything," Shelby said. "That's one thing I like about this place."

Because the posh fearmancers couldn't bear to pick up after themselves? Lovely.

I opened one of the fridges and noted the names

sharpied onto every container. "I guess there isn't any common food."

"No. There's, um, a cafeteria for the juniors in Killbrook Hall, and seniors are allowed to eat there too, but… no one does. It's basically social suicide."

I was pretty sure I'd already committed that at least twice since setting foot on campus. "Oh, well. Will you at least still talk to me when I'm shunned?" My smile shifted into a wry grin.

Shelby looked as if she was surprised to find herself grinning back. She rubbed her hand across her mouth and then blurted out, "If you want, you can have some of my cereal—and milk too, of course. It's nothing fancy."

A tiny spot of warmth formed amid the ache that was still squeezing my heart. "Thank you," I said. "That would be really nice. Fancy's not really my thing anyway."

By the time I'd poured myself a bowl, Shelby had already disappeared into her bedroom. How did the staff of Villain Academy convince Naries to come here? Or, maybe more pertinent, how did they convince them to stay here after the hell the regular student body must put them through?

Questions I guessed I'd have to save for another time.

I scooped an extra handful of cereal to carry in to Deborah and headed back to my room. She wriggled out when I opened the sock drawer. Her *Thank you* as I set down the cereal brought a pinch of guilt into my gut.

"What do you actually like to eat?" I asked, feeling a little ridiculous. She'd chowed down on the pet food and bits of cheese and fruit I'd brought her happily enough the four years I'd thought she was just a mouse, but maybe there was something she'd prefer now that she could tell me about it.

A hint of amusement crept into her dry voice in my head. *Oh, any kind of human food is wonderful, really. Although I have to admit I was particularly fond of cheese even before I became a mouse.*

"I'll see what I can do about getting you some then."

The woman who'd brought my birth mother's clothes had also thoughtfully left for me a basket of basic toiletries. In the bathroom, I stayed in the shower under water scalding enough to dull the inner burn of grief until I heard someone else come in. I wasn't sure I wanted to find out who. I waited until whoever it was had ducked into their own stall and then made a dash back to my bedroom.

The thought of wearing any of the clothes that had belonged to my fearmancer mother made my skin crawl, but my tee and jeans from yesterday kind of smelled, and maybe I'd get what I needed here faster if I looked more the part.

I pawed through the wardrobe until I came up with a silky blouse with a subtle print and navy slacks that matched. Neither showed a ton of skin or clung to my body too tightly, but my eyebrows went up when I looked at myself in the mirror mounted inside the wardrobe's door.

Holy shit. I was all sleek and professional-looking—I'd totally pass for a fearmancer now.

The sight made me want to tear the clothes right back

off. I reminded myself of my plan, confirmed that my birth mother's old shoes were too small, and slipped on my sneakers from home. The black suede didn't look *too* weird with the dressy outfit.

Good luck, Deborah said when I brushed my fingers over her soft fur, giving the black splotch on her flank an extra rub the way she'd always liked.

"Do you want me to get you, like, a book or something?" I whispered. Now that I knew my mouse had a human consciousness residing in her, leaving her to trundle around aimlessly for hours on end felt ridiculously cruel.

Don't worry about me, sweetheart. I just relax while the mouse instincts take over, and I don't really get bored.

I still hesitated before closing the wardrobe, but I did have to get going.

Rather than wait around while the other girls bustled around the common room, I headed downstairs so I could meet Professor Banefield by the entrance to the hall. I flipped through a design book in the library for about half an hour before I spotted his barrel-chested form pushing past the doorway. I hurried over to meet him.

"Rory," he said, no stumbling over my preferred name this time. "You're looking well."

I don't feel it, I thought, but I just gave him a smile.

"Are you settling in all right?" he asked as we set off along the path to the Stormhurst Building.

"I think so." Other than the fact that I'd managed to piss off the school royalty in less than twenty-four hours. A minor detail.

The athletic building smelled like floor wax and a lingering whiff of sweat that apparently not even magical cleaning practices could quite remove. We found Ms. Grimsworth and four other people who I took to be professors, two men and two women, waiting in a huge gymnasium. It looked bizarrely normal with the starkly colored lines crisscrossing the pale wooden floor and the basketball hoops perched partway up the walls. I'd gone to watch a couple of the volleyball games one of my classmates was competing in at my old college, and the gym there had been pretty similar.

"Good morning, Miss Bloodstone," the headmistress said, her voice echoing off the high ceiling. "Are you ready for your assessment?"

"I guess," I said. "What do I have to do?"

Her lips quirked into a wry smile. "Not a great deal. The process tests your innate proficiencies. The types of magic we do are divided into four major domains: Physicality, Illusion, Persuasion, and Insight. Knowing where your strengths lie will help us guide your studies. Most students here have one or two strengths. Your fellow scions each revealed three. I wouldn't be surprised if you show the same."

So Malcolm and his friends really were the most powerful mages around here. And I'd made enemies out of them in two seconds flat. Nice work, Rory!

"Okay," I said. "That sounds simple enough."

"Stand in the circle there," Ms. Grimsworth said, pointing to a blue shape marked halfway across the room. As I walked over to it, I realized the four professors formed a square around it, each an equal distance from me. I was right in the middle.

I came to a stop in the circle and let my arms hang at my sides, trying to stay relaxed.

"Just take it in and let your body react the way it will," the headmistress said.

I nodded, and the professors raised their hands.

Each of them spoke simultaneously, their voices blending together as they reached my ears. An erratic quivering of energy raced over my skin from all sides and delved into my flesh.

My body tensed instinctively. Something shuddered inside me, down in the place behind my ribs where I'd reacted to Malcolm's brief flash of fear yesterday. It whipped up like a whirlwind. For several seconds I couldn't breathe, the energy burst so forcefully against my lungs. Then it fell away as quickly as it had risen.

I'd closed my eyes without realizing it. When I opened them, the professors I could see were frowning. They walked over to consult with Ms. Grimsworth.

A faint draft raised goosebumps on my arms, and I rubbed them as I waited. Had they seen something about my magical capacity that bothered them? Maybe after having my abilities suppressed for years, I wasn't on the same level as the other scions. Oh, well. I'd work with what I had. I only needed enough to get the hell out of here.

The headmistress beckoned me over. "Miss Bloodstone," she said, "it appears we have a rather unusual result. The assessment revealed no effect at all."

I hadn't expected *that*. "No effect?" I repeated, wondering if the words meant something different than they should. I'd definitely felt plenty affected.

"It's the sort of response we'd expect to see from someone who has no magical ability at all," she said.

I blinked at her. "But—I could feel something reacting inside me."

"That might have been simply the magic of the test."

I didn't think it was, and besides— "I've already used my magic. Yesterday. I... had a disagreement with one of the other students about how he was treating a younger mage. I conjured ice on the floor, enough to freeze his feet to the ground for a few seconds."

Ms. Grimsworth raised her eyebrows. "Well, then. Do you happen to know which student this was? Perhaps we can get a testimonial."

Did I *want* a testimonial? It occurred to me, too late, that maybe I should want her to think I didn't have any magic. The fearmancers wouldn't have any use for me then, so I wouldn't have to stay here, right? But I'd already barreled on ahead. Too late to backtrack now.

"Ah, it was Malcolm Nightwood," I said, restraining a wince in anticipation of her reaction. "His friends—Jude and Connar—they were there too." I didn't know if Declan or my other escorts had been close enough to see what I'd done.

The headmistress only looked vaguely amused. "Ambitious, aren't we?" she murmured with a little shake of her head. "Well, you are a Bloodstone." She gestured to Professor Banefield. "Get Mr. Nightwood, Mr. Killbrook, and Mr. Stormhurst down here, will you? I don't imagine they should be too difficult to track down at this hour."

I sat on a bench by the wall while we waited for the guys to arrive, and Ms. Grimsworth fell back into conversation with the other professors.

How could I have shown *no* magic? It didn't make sense—not to me, and not to them either, obviously. Deborah was proof that even my parents had expected me to develop a power.

Finally, the divine devil and his cohorts swaggered into the gym. Even knowing what a callous, sadistic asshole Malcolm was, I couldn't stop the flutter that passed through my chest at the sight of his shockingly gorgeous face. Overnight I must have downgraded his looks in my memory to match his personality. With two more epitomes of hotness on either side of him, it was hard to look away.

Malcolm gave the headmistress a cherubic smile. "What can I help you with, Ms. Grimsworth?"

The headmistress motioned for me to rejoin the group. I walked over, watching the three guys uneasily. Their gazes skimmed over me as if they'd never seen me before. Somehow that unnerved me more than if they'd been glaring at me.

"Miss Bloodstone has informed us that she conjured ice in your presence yesterday," Ms. Grimsworth said. "I was hoping you could verify the incident."

"Ice?" Malcolm said, knitting his brow.

I gritted my teeth. "On the floor. Under your feet."

He shook his head. "I remember sending a little ice

under you to interrupt your tirade, but I don't recall you throwing any magic at me."

"I think Miss Bloodstone must have gotten confused, Headmistress," Jude said helpfully, flicking back his floppy copper hair. "Maybe she was trying to summon some ice at the same time Malcolm did. But I heard him cast the spell."

"Mr. Stormhurst?" Ms. Grimsworth said.

The brawny guy's chiseled face stayed blank. "As far as I saw, only Malcolm used any magic."

Oh, for fuck's sake. Malcolm shot me a triumphant flicker of a smile, and I forced myself to bite my tongue. What could I say? It was the three of their words against mine, and I was the newcomer here.

"All right, boys," the headmistress said. "I'm sorry to have interrupted your day."

"It was no trouble at all, Ms. Grimsworth," Malcolm said sweetly.

The three of them sauntered out. I turned to the headmistress. "I swear to you, I used magic yesterday."

She sighed. "Even if you did, if it isn't enough to register on the assessment, it might as well be none. This test has never failed us before."

"Could it be… My parents—the joymancers—were suppressing my magic before."

"Your rescuers examined you for lingering spells on your journey here," Ms. Grimsworth said. "By the time of your arrival, any magic used on you had already faded away. Spells of that sort are difficult to maintain without regular reinforcement."

No wonder my parents had kept me so close. Had they been casting magic on me every single night—or even more often than that—without me knowing?

"Then what do we do?" I asked. Despite the tightening of my throat at the thought of all those secret spells, my hopes stirred. Maybe I could get out of this hell right now after all.

"Well…" The headmistress rubbed her chin. "It's a highly unusual situation. In light of your heritage, I don't believe we should make any decisions hastily. We'll continue with a general spectrum of courses for the next month and see if we can't wake up your talent from whatever depths it descended to thanks to your captors' suppression."

A month. Okay. "And if I still don't show what you're looking for in this assessment after that?"

"I suppose we'll deal with that when we come to it. Most likely we'd have you take up residence in your family's properties with some private instruction on our society, and when you're ready to marry, we'll hope that your children fare better."

My *children*? Were they going to turn me into some kind of broodmare?

Ms. Grimsworth was studying me. "Were you hoping for something else?"

I opened my mouth and closed it again, thinking over my answer. These people hated the joymancers. I couldn't tell her I wanted to go back to my parents' people.

"I spent my whole life that I remember in California," I said. "If I'm not any use here, I'd kind of like to go back there." The fearmancers couldn't stop me from reaching out to the Conclave for help if I was in the same city.

The headmistress pursed her lips. "I don't think that would be at all advisable, Miss Bloodstone. The southwest is the epicenter of joymancer activity in this country. They've already ripped you away from your community and kept you prisoner once."

"But if I don't have any magic—"

"Do you think they'd believe that? You had no magic when you were two years old, but they knew you were a bargaining chip all the same. They're afraid of us, and people acting out of fear find it very easy to ignore rationality. You'll be safe as long as you're among your kind."

You're not my kind, I wanted to snap. But with her words, a sense of dread was sinking in. Not about Mom and Dad—I knew they'd cared about me. They might not have wanted me roaming too far out of their reach, but they hadn't treated me like a prisoner the way she was saying.

The other joymancers, though… If I was so important, why hadn't any of my parents' mage colleagues ever come by to talk to me? It was almost as if the rest of the joymancers had avoided meeting me. So I couldn't identify them if I defected back to my real "kind"? So they didn't have to worry about revealing any secrets?

Or so there was no chance I'd use my villainous fearmancer powers on them?

If they hadn't trusted me even while I had my parents there monitoring everything I did, what were the chances they'd trust me now? They might even think I'd *helped* those murderers kill Mom and Dad.

I swallowed hard. "Okay," I said. "I see your point."

Her expression softened just slightly, which maybe was as soft as that pinched face ever got. "We'll do our best to bring out whatever talent you have in you, I can assure you. It'll take us a few hours to work out your preliminary schedule. Why don't you take the rest of the morning to acquaint yourself with the campus at your leisure?"

"That sounds good."

I didn't set off exploring the campus, though. I headed straight back to my dorm, finding the common room thankfully empty for the moment, and shut the door to my bedroom as firmly as I could.

"Deborah?" I murmured.

Her little white head nudged the wardrobe open a few seconds later. I knelt down to scoop her up when she scampered to me and cradled her as I flopped on my back on the bed.

Trouble? she asked. *Other than the crapload of trouble we were already in, I mean.*

"I…" I inhaled slowly. "The joymancers were afraid of what I might do if I came into my powers even a little, weren't they? That was why my parents suppressed my magic—that was why they had you watching me."

She was silent for a moment. *They didn't want your magic to lead the fearmancers to you.*

"It couldn't have been just that, though. They never even told me. I'd have been so much more prepared if they had, but it mattered more to them that there wasn't a chance I'd turn against them. They didn't even tell *you* the whole story."

I'm sure they did what they thought was best for everyone involved, Deborah said, which wasn't exactly reassuring. She obviously didn't have anything to say that would prove the joymancer community would give me the benefit of the doubt now that I'd discovered who I was.

No way in hell was I staying here with these psychos any longer than I had to. But I was probably screwed if I ran back to California empty-handed too.

How could I show that no matter what my heritage was, I was on their side? That I was the girl—the woman —my parents had raised me to be?

How could I make sure the bastards who'd slaughtered my parents got what was coming to them?

The idea hit me so hard I tensed against the feather duvet.

"Deborah," I said slowly, "when you were telling me about this place, you said the joymancers had been trying to shut it down for ages, right?"

They just never got close enough to manage it, yes. Why?

"Well… you can't get much closer than this. What if *I* took down Villain Academy for them?"

Saying the words aloud sent a cool shiver through me. Dad's voice rose up in the back of my head. *Pros and cons, Rory.*

Pros: I'd destroy the institution that trained mages to become heartless killers. The information I could bring to the Conclave might help them interrupt all sorts of other fearmancer villainy. I'd avenge my real family. Oh, and as a side benefit, I'd get to see the cocky smile wiped right off Malcolm Nightwood's way-too-handsome face.

Cons: I might fail and face a fate that I couldn't imagine getting any worse than what I already had to deal with living with these creeps.

Yeah, when I laid it out like that, my decision couldn't have been clearer.

Are you sure about this, Lorelei? Deborah said, nuzzling my fingers. *If they catch you, fearmancers aren't exactly known for mercy.*

"That's a chance I'll just have to take," I said. "I'm the best shot my parents have at getting justice. The best shot the joymancers have at tackling this place." Just because I'd been born a fearmancer didn't mean I had to subscribe to their philosophies.

I sat up, resolve coiling inside me. I was going to topple this place, but that meant I had to stick around long enough to pull off what might be the most epic betrayal in mage history.

In one month's time, no matter what, I had to pass my second assessment.

CHAPTER EIGHT

Rory

You'd think a building like Nightwood Tower would be easy to navigate, considering it was pretty much straight up and down. Unfortunately, the perverse architect who'd designed it had decided to include two staircases, one on the north side and one on the south, each of which only gave access to two of the four classrooms on each floor.

I'd hiked up seven flights on the north side before I realized there was no way to reach my Seminar in Persuasion, room 704, from there. I had to hustle back down and up the other side.

Thankfully I'd set off for my first real class at Villain Academy with plenty of time to spare. My nerves had been twitching too much for me to sit still. I'd spent the last two days in one-on-one sessions with Professor Banefield between his regular classes while he tried to get me up to speed on the basics of fearmancy, but I still didn't feel particularly ready.

The trouble was it turned out I wasn't very good at being scary. Just as mages like my parents had to spark joy in someone around them to work their magic, I had to provoke fear. I'd done it with Malcolm the other day completely unintentionally. Approaching someone or something with the primary purpose of scaring them made my gut clench up. Especially when Banefield kept sticking things like adorable floppy-eared bunnies in front of me and expecting me to terrify them.

I managed to get a little reaction by stomping my foot or giving a shout, but the jab of guilt that shot through me afterward made it hard to concentrate on doing any casting or conjuring. After a while, Banefield had put a pause on applied magic and switched to theory and history to give me a break.

"You'll adjust to the process," he'd said with the confidence of a man who'd been taught his whole life that freaking out every conscious being around him was a totally admirable goal. "Another option would be to take on a familiar. Most of us end up taking one. The magical bond allows any fear your animal provokes to fuel your magic as well."

"Oh," I'd said. "Maybe later, if I can't get the hang of this on my own." I couldn't admit I already had a familiar who wasn't likely to terrify anyone. I got the impression the girls in my dorm weren't the type to scream at the sight of a mouse. They were the type to skewer it. I'd rather not risk her life to test that theory.

By the time I reached the seventh floor for the second time, my breath was coming short. I leaned against the cool plaster wall beside the classroom door to recover, and who should come strolling up the stairs but Malcolm Nightwood, looking as devilishly hot as ever and not the least bit winded. How was that fair?

He grinned when he saw me, but the curl of his lips had a hard edge. "If it isn't Glinda the good witch," he said wryly. "Finally came out of hiding?"

"I wasn't hiding," I said. "Strangely enough, I *do* have a little catching up to do."

"Hmm." He set his hand against the wall about a foot from my shoulder and looked me up and down. That close, I could practically feel his gaze traveling over my body with a flicker of heat I couldn't say I enjoyed. He might be the most gorgeous man I'd ever set eyes on, but he was also clearly dangerous.

"You cleaned up well," he said. I was wearing another of my birth mother's outfits: tapered pants and a V-neck blouse. It'd looked professional enough to me when I'd put it on this morning, but under Malcolm's gaze my chest felt abruptly exposed. He trailed a finger down my forearm to my charm bracelet, drawing a sharper line of heat to the surface. "Everything except for this. Did you buy it in some feeb dollar store?"

I jerked my arm away from him. "Just because something didn't cost thousands of dollars doesn't make it cheap. It was a gift from my parents."

He guffawed. "From your parents? As if the Bloodstones would ever—" His voice cut off, and his grin turned into a grimace. "You mean the joymancers. The ones that incarcerated you. Why the hell would you want to hold on to a memory of that? They weren't your parents; they were your jailors."

"You've got no idea what it was like," I retorted, and changed the subject before he could insult my parents any more than he already had. "Why did you lie to Ms. Grimsworth at my assessment? You *know* I conjured that ice."

Malcolm shrugged, his mouth shifting back into his previous cocky grin. There was more of an edge in his voice now. "Just living up to your expectations, Glinda, since you've already decided I'm an asshole. We play by our own rules at Villain Academy."

My body went rigid. How did he know—had he heard me talking with Deborah, or had someone else heard and told him?

Malcolm chuckled at my reaction. "Did you think we don't know what those sanctimonious pricks call us while they're looking down from their high horses? Let them think that."

Oh, okay, so the nickname was just common knowledge. "It doesn't bother you?" I couldn't help asking.

"Why should it?" He shrugged. "You know, if we were being really accurate, it wouldn't be about fear and joy. It'd be truthmancers and liemancers. We lean into what the world really is, how it really works. At least we're not pretending it's something it's not. If that makes us villains to them, who cares?"

"Says the guy who just lied about me in front of the headmistress."

Malcolm leaned a little closer with a glint in his dark brown eyes. He'd left the top two buttons on his perfectly fitted dress shirt undone, and the fabric gaped to reveal a triangle of toned chest. His voice came out smooth and silky.

"I was speaking a higher truth: thanks to the jailers you're still honoring, you don't have enough magic for us to bother acknowledging. If you want to change that, the other scions and I are ready to accept your pleas whenever you're ready to get down on your knees."

"I'd rather jump out that window," I said, jabbing my thumb toward the opening behind him.

"We'll see."

He pushed away from me and sauntered into the classroom with a completely carefree air. Fuck, he had the Persuasion seminar now too? I'd been hoping he'd just been passing by on his way to a different class.

The room I stepped into after him held three rows of three desks each—individual-sized, but the same posh mahogany as most of the furniture around Villain Academy. Three of them were already taken, the one in the middle by Victory's friend with the purple-and-pink-streaked french braid. Cressida, Jude had called her.

Malcolm dropped into the seat at the far back corner, so I took the one at the front closest to the door. Maximum distance seemed like a wise idea.

Professor Banefield had told me that most of the classes included students with a mix of experience levels so that those farther in their studies could develop a more thorough understanding of the subject by teaching the newer students. How many of these seminars was I going to end up sharing with Malcolm Nightwood—or the other scions, for that matter?

The teacher, whom my schedule told me was Professor Crowford, ambled in and stopped behind the larger desk at the front. He was obviously getting on in the years, only a few black streaks standing out against his silver hair and fine wrinkles creasing the corners of his eyes, but still attractive enough with his Roman nose and heavy-lidded eyes that you could tell he must have been a heartbreaker in his younger years.

His gaze came to rest on me, and he dipped his head in acknowledgment. "Miss Bloodstone, it's a pleasure to have you joining us. I'll do my best to make up for the delay in your studies."

"Thank you," I said, trying to shake the impression that an enormous spotlight had just been trained on me. Maybe I should have sat at the back after all.

A few more students filed in, only one of whom I recognized: the tawny-haired girl from my dorm. She had her shoulder-length waves pulled back with another silver clip today, this one a leaping fish.

Everyone gave me a curious look as they took their seats around me. I curled my fingers into my palms so I wouldn't fidget.

Word must have spread around campus by now. They'd be able to guess who the new girl was. Did they also know I'd flunked my first assessment?

Persuasion, I thought to steady myself, remembering what Professor Banefield had told me about this specialty. *Any magic that directly influences what another being thinks, says, or does.* Wonderful. I didn't think I wanted to do any of that unless it was to convince someone here to stick me on a jet back to California.

"For this morning's seminar, I'd like us to go back to basics," Professor Crowford said, and I felt several gazes turn my way again. "It's always useful to remind ourselves of the foundations of our magical practice. The core of persuasion is will—imposing our own will on another. Which is why…"

As he went on with his explanation, the surface beneath my butt started to prickle. A thin heat seeped through the fabric of my pants. What, was this place so fancy the chairs came with seat-warmers? I hadn't been particularly cold before. An off switch would be nice.

I shifted my weight, and the heat intensified. It crept up my back, sharp enough that a trickle of sweat rolled down my neck.

Crowford was gesturing to his temple. "…when choosing the angle of this sort of spell, it's important to consider the perspective of the target. How does the world look through their eyes? What's likely to be going on inside their mind? Naturally, insight can be a useful co-component, but even if you're weak in that area, you can still…"

My ass started to sting. I braced my feet against the floor as more sweat beaded on my forehead. This had to be a trick, a spell to unsettle me. Whoever was doing it—

Malcolm? Cressida? Some other enemy I didn't even know I'd made?—they wouldn't actually injure me in front of one of the professors, right? They were just trying to shake me up.

It was working. Professor Crowford was still talking, but I was only catching bits and pieces of his lecture. Too much of my attention was focused on tuning out the growing pain spreading along the bottoms of my thighs.

It couldn't get much worse than this. They'd have to stop soon. They couldn't—

The heat flared with a knife-like searing that cut me to the bone. I flinched and stumbled out of my chair with a choked yelp. Crowford's mouth snapped shut. Just like that, he and every student in the room was staring at me.

"The newbie seems like she doesn't really want to be here, Professor," Malcolm remarked. "She's very distractible."

Well, that answered the question of who. I swiped at the sweat on my forehead, restraining myself from glaring at him.

Crowford ignored Malcolm's comment. "Is something the matter, Miss Bloodstone?" he said.

No, I just liked to fling myself out of my seat at random moments for fun.

"My chair," I said, the ache still running through my backside. "It burned me."

The professor's mouth twisted in a way that could have been bemused or irritated—it was hard to tell. He stepped around his desk and walked up to mine, bending to touch the seat I'd vacated.

"It doesn't feel unusually warm at the moment," he said. "Are you sure?"

Of course I was sure that my ass had just about been scorched off my body. I opened my mouth to say so and hesitated.

The pain had faded away. When I adjusted my weight, letting my thighs brush together, the movement didn't provoke the slightest sting.

Oh, fuck, had that all been in my *head*?

I sat back down gingerly. No raw skin. No prickling blisters. No injury, like I'd assumed from the start.

A different sort of heat flooded my face. "I guess it wasn't real," I said. I wasn't going to pretend it hadn't happened.

Professor Crowford scanned the room. He definitely looked bemused now. "I suppose one of your classmates decided to fully initiate you into Bloodstone University, by an interesting choice of methods given the class. Credit to Illusion."

It took a second for his last words to sink in. "Credit?" I repeated.

His gaze slid back to me. "Did your mentor neglect to explain that aspect of school life? Every student is assigned to a league based on their primary magical strength after their assessment—or gets to choose one if they have multiple strong talents. Well-cast spells in that vein earn credits toward your league. At the end of each semester, the league with the most credits gets a feast prepared and served by the losers." The crinkles around his eyes deepened with a smile. "As you develop your abilities, you'll find such incidents are valuable opportunities to practice your defensive skills."

I sank lower in my seat as he returned to the front of the room. Of course this place didn't just look the other way but outright rewarded students for tormenting each other. Why would I have expected anything else?

Did they get *extra* credit for managing to mess with a scion? Until I could figure out how to get those defense skills into gear, I had the feeling I was going to be prime target number one.

CHAPTER NINE

Connar

One thing I could admit: from the moment I'd arrived at Blood U, it'd been easy for me to strike fear when I needed it. Also when I didn't need it. Pretty much all I had to do was walk into a room to set off a whole bunch of jitters of nervous energy.

No one talked about the reasons. No one dared to. But as I hurtled across the football field, I felt that energy expand inside my chest with the whites of the other guys' eyes and the tensed expressions as I wove between them.

Would Connar Stormhurst decide to blast right through them or fling them off their feet? Was there going to be blood spilled on the field today? Who knew?

I didn't think I'd used magic against anyone in the middle of a game in the entire time I'd been at the university, but that didn't matter. The possibility was there, lurking in everyone's minds.

The uncertainty could clear a path for me even without my really doing anything. I veered toward one of the juniors who'd joined in, baring my teeth, and he scrambled out of my way so quickly you'd have thought a hellhound had just snapped at his heels.

The goalpost loomed up ahead. I spun around, adrenaline from the run thumping through my veins, and raised my hands. "Open!"

Chandler Viceport hurled the ball toward me. No doubt he whispered a word or two to steady his aim. If he'd been off anyway, I'd have tossed out a little magic to swing the ball toward me, but it was flying straight into my arms. I yanked it to my chest and sprinted the last short distance to the goal.

"Touchdown!" one of my other teammates hollered for me.

As the teams gathered to regroup, I raised the undershirt I'd stripped down to and wiped the sweat from my face. The cool spring breeze was a relief after a workout.

I ambled over to join the other guys, and a few of them glanced up. I couldn't miss the way they braced themselves a little at the sight of me, even though we'd been playing on the same team for almost an hour. It twisted my gut and made me want to fake a lunge at them just to freak them out. Might as well meet their expectations and get that extra heaping of fear.

"Conn!" a voice hollered from across the field. The late afternoon sunlight glanced off Malcolm's bright brown hair. He waved to me, standing in his usual relaxed pose.

"I'll be right back," I said to my teammates, and jogged over to see what the heir of Nightwood wanted.

"Don't you ever get tired of dashing across the same field over and over?" Malcolm said, but his smile showed the teasing was good-natured.

"I never have to worry about losing my way," I tossed back.

He knuckled me on the shoulder. "You know I respect the hell out of you, but let's be honest, you probably would if they took the game someplace else. Will they survive a few plays without you?"

I shrugged. "If they don't, that's their problem. What's up?"

"I had another idea for our good witch. You're out here pretty often. If you see the Bloodstone scion heading into the woods on her own—even on the road into town —give me a shout right away?"

"Sure. What are you planning?"

"I'll share the story if it comes to be." His grin turned devious. "If I decide I need back-up, I'll let you know."

"And you know I'll be there," I said automatically.

I kind of wanted to ask what he planned on doing if none of his machinations brought her begging for forgiveness. Rory Bloodstone might have been new here, but she was a scion. I wasn't sure she was any more likely to back down than Malcolm was. She had been a bitch to him, and I'd be happy to see her brought down a peg for that, but the thought of their squabble turning into some kind of war within the pentacle didn't sit well with me.

What the hell did I know, though? Malcolm's teasing

was based on truth. Between the four of us, I was the last one anyone would call the brains. Even expressing a doubt felt like it'd be a breach of loyalty.

Sometimes I wasn't sure how much even Jude or Declan liked having me around. Jude's jokes strayed into caustic territory from time to time, and I'd seen that familiar wary look on Declan's face more than once.

Malcolm was the only person I knew who'd always treated me like he did, as he'd put it, respect the hell out of me, without concern or questions about what I or my family might have done. As if he simply assumed, because he knew me, that no matter how horrible the stories might be, there must have been good reason.

I wasn't a horrible person. And I knew that mostly because I'd have this guy's back or die at his side, no matter what came at us.

Despite his joking, Malcolm also gave me more credit for brains than even I generally did. He tipped his head to me. "If you notice a window of opportunity and think of a good ploy, feel free to jump right in there too. Gotta keep her on her toes until she gets the picture."

"I'll be watching," I said. It seemed unlikely, given that so far I hadn't crossed paths with Rory except briefly, but I'd do what I could for the cause.

"Excellent. A bunch of us are heading into town for drinks later. You in?"

"Absolutely."

He sauntered away, and I loped to rejoin the players on the field. The first rule everyone learned at Blood U was you didn't mess with Malcolm Nightwood. One way or another, Rory Bloodstone was going to figure that out too.

CHAPTER TEN

Rory

I knew something was wrong before I opened my bedroom door. A hint of scent burned my nose. I braced myself and shoved.

The door swung open into the dark room, and a wave of the smell, thick and choking now, gushed over me. It was the putrid sour stench of rotting food, like a restaurant garbage bin left out in the sun for a week.

Bile surged up my throat. I clamped my hand over my nose and mouth.

Deborah's voice reached my mind thinly across the distance between us. *Believe me, I have never wished more that I could still work my magic. Not that I can see there's much joy to be had here.*

Even with my stomach still roiling, the corners of my lips twitched upward at her disgruntled tone. Okay, it smelled awful. How did it look? I'd better find out what the full damage was.

I edged into the room, breathing through the sleeve of my blouse, which only filtered out a tiny bit of the stench. My pulse lurched when I flicked on the light, half expecting to see my bed drenched in butchered meat, but it looked... exactly the same as it had when I'd left it: the comforter rumpled, the curtain pulled back from a window that was now shadowy with dusk, and the wardrobe shut tight. I'd have sworn even the glass of water I'd left out for Deborah's use hadn't moved an inch.

I tugged open the wardrobe just in case, but my clothes hung untouched in their neat row. The only problem was the stench, then. Conjured, or maybe an illusion that only affected me. Would my familiar tap into any illusions that targeted my mind?

I heard them talking about the spell before they cast it, Deborah said, still hiding in the sock drawer—I couldn't really blame her. *The girl who was upset about you taking her room and a couple of her friends. If I could have stopped them...* A sound like a little growl carried into my head.

"It's not your fault," I said. So, it'd been Victory, presumably along with Cressida and the girl with the black bob whose name I'd determined was Sinclair. I couldn't say I was shocked.

The stink congealed deeper into my lungs, and nausea clutched my stomach. It didn't really matter that the room didn't contain any real source of the smell. I wasn't sure I could sleep in that space. I wasn't sure I could stand here five more minutes without vomiting. The hasty dinner I'd eaten before holing up in the library was churning around way too fast for my liking.

I closed my eyes for a second, fighting to get my bearings. My knees stung from falling on the paved path after someone's raccoon familiar had darted between my feet—on purpose or just a coincidence? The owner had smiled as they'd called the animal back.

At least a few times every day now, an eerie whispering would flit around my ears, murmuring words like "Pathetic" and "Keep on failing!" I couldn't count how many times I'd felt a finger prod my back or my ribs in class or walking across campus, but when I'd spin around I'd find there was no one close enough to have touched me —with their hands, anyway.

I couldn't defend myself. Six days after arriving here, I still hadn't managed to work any magic since my first encounter with Malcolm.

Had he sicced the entire student body on me, or had the others just observed him and followed his lead after the hot seat in our Persuasion seminar? Victory had her own separate beef with me, obviously. I wasn't sure it mattered with everyone else. This was what he'd wanted: for me to be badgered and berated into regretting that I'd snubbed his offer of "friendship."

I'd have asked Deborah if she had any idea how I could fix this, except I knew I didn't have the magic to combat this spell either. Should I risk sleeping in the common room on one of the couches? Should I go to Professor Banefield?

God, I didn't want to run off to the teachers like some

kind of kindergarten tattle-tale. That'd make me look even more pathetic. Anyway, from what I'd seen of things here so far, he was more likely to tell me to suck it up and give credit to the appropriate league than to come to my aid.

I had to fight my own battles. I just… didn't have any idea how.

Footsteps rasped across the floor outside my room. I tensed up.

As I turned around, the girl with the tawny hair and ever-changing silver clips—today's was a stag—peered into my bedroom from about a foot outside. She waved away the air in front of her nose. "Wow. They really outdid themselves, didn't they?"

Definitely not just an illusion then. Credit to Physicality for the conjuring.

"Yeah," I said. "I think I need to get out of here."

She backed up to make room for me to leave. Her mouth twisted with what looked like sympathy as she considered the putrid space. "I guess you still haven't got the hang of magically locking the door?"

"I haven't gotten the hang of magically anything at all," I admitted.

She twisted a lock of her hair around her finger. "I'd offer to lock it for you, but then *you* wouldn't be able to open the door. The smell feels like a pretty powerful spell, so I don't think I can just… turn it off, but I can encourage a breeze to wash it out the window if you want?"

That was the first help any other student had offered me since Shelby the Nary had shared her cereal with me my first morning. Relief punched me in the sternum, but at the same time, after the barrage of subtle tests I'd faced across the last few days, I found myself eyeing the other girl warily. "Are you sure you don't mind?"

She smiled, simply and genuinely. Her clothes were nice, but she didn't put on the same airs as the girls like Victory. Maybe she was okay.

"As long as you open the window for me," she said. "I don't want to set one foot in there."

"Fair enough."

Holding my breath, I dashed across the room to the window, yanked it up, and raced back out again. The other girl laughed at my haste and rolled a few syllables off her tongue.

I'd gathered from Professor Banefield that once a fearmancer had a handle on their abilities, they started coming up with their own private words for the spells they wanted to cast. *Eventually you'll be able to come up with the sounds and connect them to your meaning on the spot*, he'd said. *If no one can understand what you're saying, no one can predict how you're working the magic before it hits them.*

The air stirred. A light wind drifted past us into the room. The girl stepped back. "I don't know how long it'll take to clear that all out, but the smell will get better, anyway."

"Thank you so much," I said.

She ducked her head, a faint flush coloring her freckled cheeks, looking suddenly shy. "I'm Imogen, by the way. I, ah—I really hated how they messed around with you in Persuasion the other day. I'm sorry about that."

"It's not your fault." What could she have done even if she'd tried to step in? The professor had been fully aware that someone was harassing me, and he'd given them credit for it, for fuck's sake. "The whole week has been… Well, it's been. Let's leave it at that." I let out a short laugh. "Getting a little help makes for a definite improvement."

I expected her to slip away into her own bedroom, but she stayed with me as I walked to one of the sofas. "You really didn't know anything about this place before you got here, did you?" she said, sitting down at the opposite end. "I can't even imagine."

"I didn't know fearmancy even existed," I said. "I thought all mages worked with joy, like my—" My throat closed in hesitation after the response I'd gotten to calling Mom and Dad my parents before, but they *were*, and I wasn't going to let jerks like Malcolm browbeat me into denying it. "Like my parents."

"I guess it makes sense they wouldn't have wanted you to know where you were really supposed to be."

Here? I was never going to belong here. But saying that would have felt like throwing her kindness back in her face.

I wasn't going to be like so many of the mages here. They automatically sneered at the mention of joymancers, dismissing people because of the powers they were born with no matter what else they were like. I wouldn't do the same to fearmancers. Not every one of them was necessarily a villain. And I could use whatever friends I could get around here.

Not to mention, Imogen probably knew things that

could be useful for my whole taking down Villain Academy plan. I tugged at the hem of my blouse, deciding on the best way to ask some of the things I'd been wondering about.

Deborah had said the main reason the joymancers hadn't already shut down this place was that they hadn't been able to find it. The fearmancers must be using magic to hide it. If I could break those protections somehow or other once I had my own magic under control…

"From what people have said about my birth parents, it sounds like there's a lot of animosity between the two groups," I said. "Isn't anyone worried that joymancers will attack the school?"

Imogen snorted. "They couldn't even if they wanted to. My dad works here, you know—he's the head of the maintenance team. He says Blood U is the safest place any fearmancer can be in the whole country, there are so many wards around it."

That didn't sound like an easy job. "Does he help keep the wards up as part of maintenance?" I couldn't help asking.

"No, Ms. Grimsworth handles that in coordination with the blacksuits." Imogen paused. "They're basically the bodyguards and defenders for the whole fearmancer community, not just the university. The team that came to rescue you—they'd have been blacksuits."

Blacksuits. My mind flashed back to my supposed "rescue," to my parents' murderer in his posh shirt and slacks that had, yep, been black. My throat tightened. Add them to the list of people to take down.

"So, what is—" Imogen started to ask, and the dorm-room door clicked open. Shelby came in, her head ducked so the fall of her mousy-brown bangs hid her face. The rest of her hair was pulled back in her habitual ponytail. She saw me with Imogen and veered straight toward her bedroom.

Had Imogen hassled her before just because she was a Nary? Or did she simply assume I wouldn't want to talk to her if I already had company? There was one quick way to check whether Imogen was a fearmancer I'd actually want on my side.

"Hey, Shelby," I said, raising my hand to wave her over. "How's it going?"

She stopped but didn't move toward us, sucking her lower lip under her teeth for a fleeting nibble. "Um, okay. I saw you got your food situation figured out?"

I smiled. "Yeah. Thanks for saving me from starvation the other day." After my first mentoring session with Banefield that morning, he'd arranged for one of the chauffeurs the school had on staff to take me into the nearby town so I could do some grocery shopping. It'd felt a little weird getting driven around like some rich snob and even weirder when I looked at the balance on the Bloodstone bank account I'd gotten access to and realized I *was* rich.

Imogen looked from me to Shelby and back again, a faint furrow creasing her forehead as if she was puzzled by the fact that I'd even acknowledged Shelby's presence. She didn't say anything snarky, though.

"You should get the double-chocolate brownies at the

bakery counter the next time you're in the grocery store," Shelby said, her stance relaxing. "They're freaking amazing."

"With a recommendation like that, I think I'll have to."

"I've had those a couple times," Imogen said, slowly but warmly enough. "They are really good." She perked up, her focus narrowing in on me again. "Hey, why don't we go grab a drink in town? It's not like you'll be able to use your room for a while. You've got to get off campus now and then."

She obviously had only been including herself and me in that "we." Shelby started to turn away again. She didn't even look hurt, just resigned.

"Sure," I said. "Shelby, you want to come too?"

Imogen opened her mouth, surprise flickering through her expression, and seemed to catch her reaction. "Yeah," she said. "Why not? The more the merrier, right?"

Having Shelby along with us would mean we couldn't talk openly about anything magical, but the trade-off was worth it for the way the Nary girl lit up at the invitation. My heart wrenched at the thought of how many times she must have been shunned by our other dormmates in however many months she'd been living here.

"Yeah," she said. "For sure."

"Do we need to call for one of the school cars?" I asked.

Imogen waved that suggestion away. "No one bothers with those unless they're so wasted they're falling over. It's like a twenty minute walk. Come on."

Outside, night had fully settled in. Thin streaks of cloud blotted out most of the stars, but here and there a few tiny sparks twinkled down at us. The breeze that ruffled our hair had a cool edge to it that made me glad for the trim jacket I'd put on today, courtesy of my Bloodstone mom.

We skirted Killbrook Hall and meandered across the parking lot where I'd first arrived at the university to the narrow road that led through the woods into town.

"There's a walking path through the forest a little ways over too," Imogen said, gesturing. "But it's a little spooky for my tastes at night."

"I'm fine with the road," Shelby piped up.

We fell into awkward silence as we set off along the gravel-strewn shoulder toward town. Imogen seemed unsure how to talk with Shelby there.

From what I'd seen, the mage students avoided the Naries if they could rather than integrating them into their socializing. Even with my homeschooled background, I might have more conversational experience with non-magical types than any of my peers, just from days at the park and the past year of university classes.

"How long have you two been at the university?" I asked.

"I started right when I turned sixteen," Imogen said. A bit of a late-bloomer with her magic then, I guessed. "So, almost four years now."

"Wow," Shelby said. "I just started in the fall. It's pretty amazing, the set-up they have, even if people are kind of... intense."

Imogen glanced at her. "What's your concentration?"

"Music," Shelby said. "You guys have the best instruments I've ever played on here. I'm mostly cello. And theory, of course. The library has books I never could have gotten on loan back home."

Right. Professor Banefield had mentioned something about the Nary students coming under the pretense of individualized study around a few select areas. They shared a couple classes with the fearmancer students—in general areas like business and literature—and the rest of the time they kept to their own little pockets of focus. While we practiced our magic.

"Maybe we'll get to hear you play sometime," I said.

Shelby ducked her head, but with a smile. "Yeah. The five of us seniors in the music program, I think we're putting on a short concert at the end of term. What about you guys? What are you studying?"

Oh. Er.

"Biology," Imogen rolled off her tongue, answer at the ready. "Mostly human."

"Like, medical stuff?"

"I haven't been able to specialize that much yet, but yeah, heading that way."

A fearmancer healer? That was interesting. Shelby turned to me, and I grasped onto the one subject I knew I could talk about with university-level depth. "Environmental design. Which is basically like architecture, except you're focusing on how places are going to look on the inside. Or the design of outdoor areas like gardens or whatever."

That's what area I'd thought I was going to get into before all of this craziness had happened, anyway. The breeze picked up, and I hugged myself against the chill.

"That's cool," Shelby said.

We lapsed into silence again. A twig snapped under my foot, and a shiver of energy pierced my chest. I stopped with a jerk.

"What?" Imogen asked.

"I just…" I didn't know what I'd felt. I peered into the darkness between the trees. Some small creature rustled in the brush. Then everything was quiet again. "I guess I'm just jumping at shadows," I said sheepishly.

It wasn't that I'd been scared, though. The sensation had felt almost like… like that moment on the landing when Malcolm had realized I wasn't going to back down easily. The brief tremor of fear that had turned into power at the base of my throat.

Was it coming from the other girls, anxious about wandering along here in the night? But everything I'd learned said any power I gained had to be fear that *I'd* provoked directly.

I paid close attention to my internal reactions as we walked on. After a minute, a softer tremble reached me, one I might have missed if I hadn't been waiting for it. My toe hit a particularly large chunk of gravel, and as it rattled across the shoulder, a volley of tiny quivers pricked at my sternum. Something scurried away deeper into the forest.

The realization clicked into place with such a rush of relief I almost laughed out loud. I *was* provoking fear—in whatever forest animals were close enough to hear us passing by. It was a subtle effect. They weren't terrified of us, but we definitely made them nervous. Imogen must be feeling it too, or maybe she was so used to larger whiffs of fear that these little tidbits barely registered.

"Actually, hold on a second," I said. As the other girls paused, I left the road.

I only ventured a few steps between the trees, but that was enough to set off another round of fearful glints. I drank them in, my heart thumping a little faster with the faint buzz of energy collecting behind my collarbone.

I had power. Maybe not a lot, and maybe not enough to defend against everything this school wanted to throw at me, but more than I'd had before.

"Rory?" Imogen said.

"Just checking something," I said quickly, and hurried back. Before either of them could think too much of my weird behavior, I jumped into a new line of conversation. "So, what's the best place to get a drink in town anyway?"

"There are a few places that are pretty decent," Imogen started, and we spent the rest of the walk discussing the features of the various town eateries and our personal favorite drinks. I was abruptly grateful for the handful of parties I'd gone to with my former classmates to have some idea what my options were.

The trees thinned, and the town came into view up ahead, the streetlamps beaming brightly. We wandered past a couple of residential streets and then onto the main strip. Imogen glanced into a bar with a glossy black sign and made a face.

"Well, we're skipping that one tonight. The scions

always stake it out when they head down here. It's run by a Blood U alumnus."

In the amber light on the other side of the window, I made out a whole lot of familiar faces lounging in a few of the booths. That explained why our dorm's common room had been so empty tonight.

Malcolm had Victory perched next to him, stroking his forearm as he said something to Jude, who laughed and slung his arm around the shoulders of a girl who'd been in at least one of my classes. Cressida and a couple other girls from our dorm were squeezed in with Connar and another guy, throwing back shots.

My gaze caught on a sweep of black hair. Declan was tucked into the back of Malcolm's booth. He raised his lowball glass to his friends with a small smile.

A pang echoed through me as I jerked my eyes away. It might be stupid to have counted on anything from a guy who'd been part of the attack on my parents' house, but part of me felt abandoned by him.

"Where to, then?" I said, picking up my pace to leave Declan and the others behind.

Imogen pointed out a more modest-looking pub a few blocks down the street. We'd just reached the door when a jolt of panic hit me.

"I've never actually gone out to a bar before," I admitted. "Are they going to check my ID?"

"You don't have a fake one?" Shelby said, patting her wallet pocket.

"No problem." Imogen gave my arm a gentle squeeze.

"I'll take care of it if they ask. I'm *very* good at distracting bartenders." She winked at me.

She'd slip me by with magic, she meant—probably the same way she got herself by.

I laughed. "Then what are we waiting for?"

As the three of us pushed past the pub door, the good humor stayed with me, side-by-side with the hum of my newfound power. This was a different kind of power right here: people who'd lend me a hand when I needed it, people I could turn to.

If Malcolm wanted to break me, he was going to have to try a whole lot harder.

CHAPTER ELEVEN

Rory

My heart sank the second I stepped into my tenth floor Seminar on Insight and spotted Jude's dark coppery hair at the far end of the room. I'd been starting to think maybe I'd managed to avoid any classes with him.

Of all of the scions, I found him the hardest to figure out. Was he pissed off at me like Malcolm was? Did he find the whole situation entertaining in a sadistic sort of way?

Between the two of them, right now I trusted Jude even less.

Unfortunately, thanks to my door becoming mysteriously stuck this morning until Imogen had heard my banging on it and magicked it open, I'd gotten here at the last minute. The only remaining seat was right next to him, smack in the middle.

My heart sank all the way through the floor when I

noticed Victory at the desk behind it. She shot me a sharp little smile with a tilt of her angelic face. "For a girl with so much catching up to do, you cut it awfully close," she said with just a hint of venom in her coy voice.

Three guesses who had sealed my door, and the first two didn't count.

"I'll aim to be more punctual next time," I said, and dropped into the chair. My legs were a little wobbly from my sprint up the stairs. Holy crap, why didn't these magical assholes invest in elevators?

"If it isn't our ice queen," Jude said in an affected drawl, his lanky body sprawled out as if it didn't quite fit the desk. "No, wait, you didn't exactly rule over that ice. Maybe I'll just call you Slip'n'Slide."

"If that makes you happy," I said, not even bothering to look at him. If I looked at him, I'd have to notice how irritatingly stunning that angular face of his was. Under my desk, I twisted the charms on my bracelet, one tiny way to relieve my nerves.

A petite woman with coiffed blue-white hair and owlish eyes stepped into the room—Professor Sinleigh, I assumed. Like the teachers in a couple of my previous classes, she was joined by an older student who was acting as a teacher's assistant. Unlike the previous classes, today's assistant was Declan Ashgrave.

I tensed in my seat as he leaned his slim frame against the wall to the side of her desk, his bright hazel eyes sweeping over the room. I hadn't had any classes before this with two of the scions in attendance. But then, all Declan had done so far was *not* do anything while

Malcolm ripped into me. Maybe he'd feel a little more responsible for students' well-being while he was in this professional role.

A girl could hope, right?

"Miss Bloodstone," Professor Sinleigh said, peering at me as if through glasses even though she wasn't wearing any. "I understand you've had several private tutorials at this point to establish the essentials. Do you have any complaints if we jump right in?"

Would she really teach things differently if I said no? The faint buzz of magic I'd collected walking by the forest quivered at the base of my throat.

I hadn't known how to even start unraveling whatever spell Victory had cast on my door—Banefield had warned me that messing with other people's spells was a lot harder than casting your own—but Insight sounded like the simplest of the fearmancer skills. You figured out what people were thinking, what they wanted, and what they cared about, like normal people tried to all the time. We just had the benefit of magic to sharpen our perceptions.

And I was tired of looking like a clueless newbie around the people who were so eager to see me that way.

"No," I said. "That's fine."

"Good. If you find yourself confused, you can let me know—or Mr. Ashgrave, my aide, is available for extra assistance after class."

She clapped her hands. "As the rest of you know, we normally get started with a practice exercise. Middle row, turn to the student at your right. Left row, you two at the back work together. Pierce, Mr. Ashgrave will offer himself up for your use. Take turns reaching out to your partner's mind and mentioning one internal observation you're able to make."

It was clearly my lucky day. I glanced to my right and found Jude smirking. He swiveled in his seat to face me. "Looks like it's you and me, Bloodstone."

I turned like he had. I'd done a few exercises in "reaching out" with Professor Banefield, so I had the basic idea, but I'd never had enough magic in me to do more than get the briefest of glimpses. I couldn't say I was looking forward to what I might discover inside this guy's head if I managed to open it up.

Jude's dark green eyes fixed on mine for a second before traveling up to my forehead as if he was going to look right inside my head. He murmured his private casting word. I didn't know how to connect meaning to my made-up words yet, so I'd been using regular words that captured the right impression for me so far.

"Did you eat a Twinkie for breakfast?" he asked, his lips curling with disgust. "You might as well chow down on dog food. You're putting scions to shame here."

A couple of the other students glanced over at us, obviously having overheard him. A flush crept up my neck.

I *had* eaten a Twinkie, because they'd been one of Mom's guilty pleasures and a reminder of home, and the only food I'd had around that I could grab quickly to gulp down on my way to class. The sticky sweetness had gone a bit sour in my mouth, but the crinkle of plastic as I'd hustled up the stairs was still fresh in my memory. Was that how he'd picked up on that memory?

"I was in a hurry," I said flatly. "I suppose this is your specialty—your 'league'?"

He laughed. "Not at all. I'm an Illusion man myself."

Illusion. My mind leapt to the burning sensation that had seared my nether regions days ago. Jude hadn't been in that class, but maybe he'd helped Malcolm with the spell.

"Like Malcolm?" I suggested to see his reaction.

"Nah, Malcolm's strong there too, but he leans most to Persuasion. Of course, there's nowhere any of us are *really* weak."

Right. Ms. Grimsworth had said the other scions were strong enough across the board that each of them would have been picking between three of the four leagues.

Jude dragged in a breath as if to go again.

"Hey," I said. "It's my turn now, isn't it?"

He gave me a languidly amused look. "Go ahead and give it your best shot, then, Cold Feet."

I'd take that nickname over Slip'n'Slide. I gazed back at him, trying to see him as a collection of features—a straight nose, a jutting cheekbone, the sharp edge of a jaw—and not the dazzling picture those pieces created. A gold earring glinted in one of his earlobes, shaped like a tiny dagger.

I drew my eyes to his forehead, the skin pale where it peeked through the fall of his hair, like he had with me. "Look inside," I whispered, compelling a wisp of the energy inside me toward his mind.

For a second, I was worried nothing would happen,

despite the fizzing of power behind my collarbone. Then, with a little thrill, the sensation rushed over me of falling forward into a vast space—before my awareness slammed into a solid, blank surface.

My mind reeled backward, and I found myself staring at Jude. "You've got a wall up," I accused him.

His smirk came back. "Those who can, do. It's part of the exercise. But you're an all-powerful Bloodstone, right? You should be able to find a crack."

I glowered at him, and his smirk only grew. At the same time, I noticed the shadows beneath his eyes, the skin there just a little darker than looked totally normal. And the tilt of his head wasn't entirely relaxed, but kind of stiff, as if he were having to concentrate on keeping up.

Those weren't magical observations, just the kinds of things Mom or Dad would have pointed out to each other if they were coming up for a strategy for their joymancy together. To figure out how to stir up the deepest joy, you had to determine what a person was missing first.

"You're tired," I said, taking a gamble. "You didn't sleep very well last night."

Jude's mouth tightened. He looked annoyed, but I caught a fresh jolt of energy to join the dwindling supply in my chest. The fact that I'd hit the mark unnerved him.

Good.

I felt satisfied for the approximately second and a half it took before he started talking again.

"*You* cried yourself to sleep," he said, his wry voice taking on a razor's edge. "Finding the pressure of meeting expectations is getting to be a little too much, are you?"

I couldn't restrain a flinch. I'd been feeling more confident since my night out with Imogen and Shelby a couple days ago, but the grief and the general sense of being under attack still gnawed at me. He'd read right.

Before I could respond, someone snickered. Victory leaned her elbows onto her desk. "She hid her feeb clothes in the back of her wardrobe because she's scared someone will want to steal the hideous things."

"Wow," Jude said, launching right back in. "You nearly pissed yourself when that cat came at you yesterday. You're scared of an awful lot, huh?"

Victory picked up the thread with a note of triumph. "She thinks you're completely gorgeous even though she's *terrified* of you."

"Doesn't everyone?" Jude shifted back in his seat with a sly grin. "Poor girl, practically a virgin. Only one tumble between the sheets."

The idea of attractive guys must have jostled free memories I'd rather have kept buried. Jude's words brought them flying to the forefront, chased by a surge of panic that would only feed their magic more.

Victory shook her head. "And the guy ditched her right after. A Bloodstone gave it up for a feeb, and he wouldn't even look her in the eyes after in their stupid feeb school."

Every student in the room was watching the duo's little game now. I jerked my head around to seek out the professor, but she was watching us with an analytical eye, no sign she had the slightest intention of intervening. And Declan, across from her, was watching too, his expression so impassive it felt like a slap to the face.

Did you "rescue" me just so you could feed me to a bunch of fucking wolves?

My assailants weren't done. "And after all that, you've really thought about trying to run away from campus back to that awful place?" Jude tsked his tongue mockingly.

"She's all about the feebs, though. The one in our dorm is the only person here who makes her feel *safe*." Victory made the last word sound utterly pathetic.

My pulse skittered wildly. If they kept going, they might see something damning—they might find out about Deborah, or my plan to see the school shut down, or—

No. I couldn't let that happen.

Gritting my teeth, I shoved all the magic that had collected in my chest into a shield around my mind. I pictured it spreading out, solid and seamless, impenetrable as steel, to encase my entire brain. Every bit of strength and energy I had went into that wall.

Jude opened his mouth and hesitated. Victory fell silent too. For a minute, the three of us held there in a motionless, wordless battle of will. A prickling ran down my spine at the sense of fingers prying at my barrier.

It held firm. Victory backed off with a sniff and returned her attention to her partner. Jude gave me a slanted smile that had no warmth at all in it.

"So you can learn, Bloodstone. We'll just have to see if you can learn the right things."

He sank back in his chair. My shoulders slowly came

down, my heart still thudding. The space behind my collarbone felt unbearably empty.

I'd defended myself this once before the class had turned into a total catastrophe, but now every bit of the magic I'd been holding onto was gone.

CHAPTER TWELVE

Declan

I nodded to Jude when he got up at the end of the seminar. As I turned to ask Professor Sinleigh a question about our junior class tomorrow, I kept my gaze carefully away from any of the other students.

I'd hoped that once she'd answered it and headed out, everyone else would already have left. No such luck. One student had stuck around for my extra assistance.

Rory Bloodstone stood in front of the rows of desks, her slim arms folded over her cinched silk tunic. The indigo fabric brought out the blue of her eyes, so vibrantly dark they were almost the same hue. The loveliest part of her generally stunning face.

I tried not to let my mind stray to the pain I'd watched cross that face less than an hour ago, to the way she'd looked to me as if I could shield her from it. It had reminded me too much of the distraught girl I'd done my best to reassure in her captors' home.

I *had* wanted to shield her from the shock and brutality of that moment. Seventeen years ago, she'd lost so much more than even I had. But this, now—our situations were infinitely more complicated. Or at least, mine was.

"Did you have some questions about the material we went over today?" I asked in my most neutral voice, staying on the other side of the teacher's desk. That distance helped me maintain my own internal shields.

"Maybe just one." Her tone was direct and unassuming, but the slight huskiness to her voice touched me like a caress. Her gaze flicked to the door as if to confirm no one had lingered outside and then returned to me. "But not about the material. Why did you come with the mages who took me from my parents' house? You're not one of those blacksuits or whatever they're called."

Where was she going with this train of thought? "No, I'm not," I said. "The blacksuits thought, given the circumstances, it might help your transition to have someone along who had at least a little idea what you'd been through. The confrontation where your real parents were killed—the joymancers took down my mother too."

I'd only been four, just barely old enough to have kept a few blurry memories of her face, sometimes stern and sometimes grinning, and the rumple of her hand in my hair as she laughed at some childish thing I'd said. Rory mustn't remember her Bloodstone parents at all.

She let out a faint sound that might have been a restrained guffaw. "So, they made you come."

"No. They tossed around the suggestion. I said it sounded like a good idea and volunteered."

"Because you wanted to help me?"

Suddenly I felt as if I'd walked into a trap I hadn't seen until the barred walls closed around me. Rory's eyes held mine as she waited for my answer. It was probably too late to backtrack anyway. I'd rather not lie to her any more than I had to.

"Yes," I said. "Maybe I don't really have a clue what it's been like for you the last seventeen years, but I knew finding out the truth about your history was going to be hard for you, and if I could make it even a little easier, that seemed worth doing."

She leaned against the edge of the desk behind her. "I have another question, then. Why did you only care about helping me until I stepped through the front doors of the school? At what point did I stop being 'worthy'? When I wasn't going to put up with your friend's bullshit?"

An edge had come into her voice, but it sounded more hurt than angry. I swallowed hard.

"It isn't about Malcolm," I said. "Although you should probably figure out some way to make peace with him, because he's just going to make your life hell until you do. Insult a scion, and all bets are off. That's just how it works here. That's how it works out there." I gestured toward the window to indicate the wider world. "You have to learn how to defend yourself where there are more rules and boundaries, or you'll be eaten alive the second you leave campus."

I should know that better than just about anyone at Blood U.

"I see," Rory said. "You're staying out of it for my own good. Is that how you look at it?"

"Essentially, yes." We could leave all the other factors out of this conversation. "You're learning, aren't you? You managed to shut them out today."

"I guess it's too much to expect that I get a bit of buffer while I'm catching up."

"There *are* rules," I said. "And one of them is that as part of the teaching staff, I can't favor one student over another."

She raised her eyebrows at me. "Even a scion?"

"Believe me, if you ever manage to turn the tables on Jude and drag out a bunch of his uncomfortable memories for everyone to hear, I won't jump in on his behalf either." I couldn't stop the corner of my mouth from quirking upward at the thought. I'd defend him from any *real* threat—hell, I'd been protecting him and the other two from the moment I'd entered the realm of barons—but that didn't mean I always appreciated the guy's incisive approach to humor.

"All right then." Rory straightened up and headed for the door.

I should have stayed where I was and let her leave, but an impulse grabbed me. Before I could catch myself, I was striding over to open the door for her.

There wasn't a great deal of space by the door. Her

sleeve brushed my arm as she slipped past me. She glanced up to meet my eyes one more time, so close now I lost my breath for a second.

She wasn't just beautiful. I'd never seen the kind of determined ferocity with which she'd pushed back at Malcolm before. She had principles, and she was willing to fight for them, hard.

It made me want to fight for her. To hold her like I had so briefly in her parents' house. To find out what those lips tasted like when she wasn't using them in battle.

But I couldn't have that without destroying everything I'd spent my whole life working toward, so it was better I kept as much distance as I could.

She'd need to be a fighter to make it through her time at Blood U unscathed. At least there was that.

A question of my own tumbled out with the memory of Jude's comment about running away. "You aren't really thinking of leaving the school, are you?"

Rory stopped just outside the door and looked back at me. "Not until I've learned everything I need to," she said. "I'm not scared off that easily. Why? Would you miss me?"

She said the last question wryly, but the answer jabbed me in the chest. Maybe she'd only been here a week, but I'd seen enough of her to know that, yes, I would. She'd brought something different to this place.

"You belong here," I said instead.

Her mouth tightened, and she turned away without responding. I let the door swing closed as her footsteps tapped down the stone steps. I had a few minutes to gather myself, and then I needed to be off to my next class, as a student rather than teacher's aide.

I'd gotten about half a minute when my phone rang. I dug it out of my pocket and grimaced at the name on the display.

"Hello, Aunt Ambrosia," I said. "To what do I owe the pleasure?" *What the hell do you want now?*

"Declan," my aunt said with forced sweetness. "I just wanted to make sure you're fully prepared for the ritual next weekend. You did read up on all the proper procedures, didn't you? They're very particular."

Sure, they were. And she'd made *particularly* sure to include a few contradictory documents in the write-ups she'd sent my way in the hopes of tripping me up. As if she shouldn't know by now that I always did my own research straight from the source.

It was the sort of thing you learned to do when the aunt who'd been regent-baron in your place since you were four decided she was going to do whatever she could to hold on to that title. There were rules, yes, and I couldn't afford to break a single one.

"You don't have to worry at all," I said. "I'll be ready."

CHAPTER THIRTEEN

Rory

As I set my dinner plate in the dorm room sink, still a little uncomfortable with the thought of just leaving it there for someone else to wash up, Imogen sidled over and snagged my elbow.

"Hey," she murmured. "There's a senior party down at the lake tonight. First outdoor one of the year now that it won't be painfully cold after dark. Let's go."

I couldn't help tensing. "The scions will be there, won't they? And Victory with her crew?"

Imogen shrugged. Today's silver clip, a rearing horse, glinted against her tawny hair. "You're a scion too. Anyway, *every*one will be there. It's hardly exclusive. Well, other than…"

She glanced across the room, and I followed her gaze to where Shelby was just ducking into her bedroom. No

Naries at this party, then. When I glanced back at Imogen, she made an apologetic face.

"We need to cut loose every now and then without having to worry about what they'll see. It's fun. We make sure they don't even realize they're missing anything."

Part of me balked, but another part of me wondered how much talk there'd be if every mage in the senior class *other* than me showed up. Would Malcolm and Victory and the rest assume they'd cowed me into hiding?

Pros: I'd prove I wasn't scared off. I might learn more about how things worked around here while the students were more relaxed. I could even have some fun, maybe.

Cons: Various people might harass me some more. I was getting pretty used to that. Otherwise, none that I could think of.

Imogen would be there with me. If anyone got too obnoxious, I could always head back to the dorm.

"Okay," I said. "I'm in."

Imogen gave me a nudge toward my bedroom. "Go put on a dress—nothing too fancy—and I'll meet you downstairs."

As far as I was concerned, everything I'd inherited from my mother's wardrobe was fancy. I settled on a soft knee-length halter dress in pale lavender and grabbed a trim black jacket to pull over it, since I was pretty sure it was still going to be chilly down by the water.

The charms on my bracelet rustled as I pulled the sleeve over them. I hadn't taken it off except to shower since I'd gotten to the school, and I planned to keep wearing it all the way through, like a physical manifestation of the promise I'd made to my parents: I would get them the justice they deserved.

Deborah poked her head out of the sock drawer. *You look nice*, she said, her voice more distant in my head because she wasn't touching me. *Special fearmancer occasion?*

"Just a student party," I replied. "I've got to keep up certain appearances."

Maybe it'd scare them a little that I was still confident enough to show up at all, and I could collect some more magic just like that.

When I reached the front entrance to Ashgrave Hall, Imogen was waiting, her athletic figure hugged by a mint-green dress that flared out halfway down her thighs. Maybe I was underdressed. But she gave me a thumbs up and a grin, and motioned for me to follow her out the door.

As we left behind the main triangle and came up on the Stormhurst Building, the tang of wood smoke reached my nose. A bonfire flickered in the distance, its light stuttering with the silhouettes of dozens of bodies moving around it.

"How are the Naries not going to know they're missing out?" I said. The dressier flats I'd picked up at a little shop in town whispered over the grass when we veered off the main path onto a trampled dirt one. Strains of music carried across the field along with the smoke and the light.

"Oh, they can't see any of this," Imogen said in an offhand way. "You know that parts of the school are magically disguised so the Naries don't even know they're there, right?"

Professor Banefield had filled me in on that. "So they don't stumble in on us in the middle of turning each other into toads or something. But the whole *lake* isn't hidden."

Imogen laughed. "Of course not. Just for the party nights—we usually have one or two a month while the weather's warm enough—the teachers give us the go-ahead to put up a temporary illusion and repelling wards. Any Nary who looks this way will see the regular quiet lake, and they'll feel a distinct lack of desire to get any closer."

I appreciated the kindness Imogen had extended to me over the last few days, especially when she clearly didn't need to, but the flippant way she talked about the Naries still itched at me. At least she didn't call them "feebs" like most of the students here seemed to. When I'd finally asked Banefield about *that*, he'd admitted it was short for "feeble."

We don't encourage that sort of derogatory slang, but we don't believe in censoring the students' self-expression either, he'd said in a very responsibility-dodging sort of way.

It really did look like every senior on campus had come down to the lake for the party. Most of students drifted around the blazing bonfire, chattering and drinking. Several had wandered down the dock to the wide platform at the end, a few of them daring to dip their feet into the cool water. Others hung out on the rocky shoreline.

Someone had pulled a table out of the boathouse and laid it out with bottles of wine and platters of hors d'oeuvres that would have seemed more fitting at a dinner party than a college bash. A couple of ice-filled coolers with the necks of beer bottles poking from them gave a more down-to-earth touch.

I wasn't sure I wanted to risk getting tipsy, but I let Imogen grab me a beer. One shouldn't affect me too much. As she opened hers and then mine with a clink of the lid, a lightly sardonic voice piped up.

"Oh, look, even Frosty has come out. Watch you don't get too close to the fire! We wouldn't want you to melt."

My head jerked around to find Jude smirking at me from near the fire pit. The other scions stood around him, and Victory, Sinclair, and a few other girls from their crowd lingered nearby, all of them watching me. Jude took a swig from the bottle of wine he appeared to have confiscated for private consumption and handed it to Malcolm.

"It's the wicked witches who melt," Malcolm said, the firelight turning his hair an even brighter gold. "I'm not sure what'd happen to Glinda. Maybe she'd burn." He sounded as if he was considering finding out.

My gaze darted to Declan just a little behind him, even though I knew better than to expect anything from him now. His hazel eyes glinted with reflected flames under the sweep of his black hair, and then he looked away.

For a moment when we'd been alone in the classroom the other day, I could have sworn something had sparked between us. A hunger in his expression that had set off an answering flare in me, no matter how annoyed I'd been with him. But it had vanished as quickly as it'd come. Whether he cared more than he was willing to show or not, he was as walled off to me as Jude had been during the Insight exercise.

I returned my attention to Malcolm. "*You're* not melting," I pointed out.

He laughed and sauntered up to me. "If you expect me to deny that I'm wicked, I'll have to disappoint you." His smile sharpened as I stood my ground, my heart thumping. "It's good to see you without the feeb in tow. Now if only you'd left behind everything you should have." His hand leapt too fast for me to react, tugging at my charm bracelet.

I jerked my arm away and took a step back. "Thankfully I don't dress to earn your approval."

The girls started twittering. "Easy to make excuses for not going after what you're never going to get anyway," Victory remarked to the others with a sneer.

"You still haven't figured out where your allegiances ought to be," Malcolm said. "I guess we'll just have to keep working on you."

I'd actually be totally okay with you giving up, I wanted to say, but I could picture how much they'd laugh at that idea.

Malcolm turned on his heel and ambled back to his friends without waiting for my response. Imogen sipped nervously from her beer. I was searching for the right words to toss out before I found some other, very distant area of the party to visit, when a couple of guys having a tussle careened between me and the scions.

The one guy let out a drunkenly triumphant holler and pushed the other, but his sparring partner caught hold of his wrist at the last second. They spun around, and the first guy tripped on a beer bottle. Malcolm and Jude sprang to opposite sides, only just barely avoiding getting slammed into the bonfire.

"What the fuck are you doing?" a voice bellowed. I'd barely noticed Connar hanging back alongside the other scions, but all at once the guy was right there at the forefront, knocking the two interlopers back with a heave of his brawny arms. The line of his square jaw flexed as he clenched it. "Do you have eyes, or do you need me to remind you where they are?"

The guys cowered, backing away from the scions as quickly as their feet would take them. "Sorry. Really sorry. Total accident."

"Go have your fucking accidents somewhere else." Connar glowered at them like he was imagining exactly what shape he'd crush them into if they so much as brushed against his friends again. A shiver ran down my back. I hadn't had any direct run-ins with him, and I was abruptly very glad for that.

"You see," Malcolm's smooth voice said, so close behind me that I flinched. He'd circled around while I was staring at Connar. He set his hand on my waist, a spot of warmth my skin cringed away from. "We know how to look out for each other."

I whipped around, out of his hold, and crossed my arms over my chest. I didn't think it'd be wise to broadcast what I was about to say to the entire student body, so I pitched my voice low enough that only he would hear. "I'd take the joymancers over all of you any day."

Fury flashed across Malcolm's face. I dashed away to where Imogen had started backing toward the refreshment table, and to my relief, the divine devil didn't follow me.

"All in a night's fun?" Imogen said with a weak smile when I reached her.

"It's fine," I said. "They got to say their piece. Let's see the rest of this party."

We grabbed some food, and I drank a little of my beer as we wandered along the shore. I was starting to see what Imogen had meant about cutting loose without the Naries. Along with the college party antics I'd experienced back home, like that drunken playfight and the girls who were now egging a few of the guys into jumping off the dock into the lake, fearmancers found plenty of ways to up the ante.

Over here, a small crowd was whooping in encouragement while a guy gulped wine from a bottle that was floating magically several feet above his open mouth. Over there, someone had conjured a glowing illusion of a dragon that was doing battle with a lion made out of flames. Every time the creatures swerved to snap at some student's face, the casters would be drinking in jolts of fear along with their beverages of choice.

I realized after we'd made a rambling circuit of the party that everyone was giving the two of us a wide berth. The clusters of students shifted a little farther away from us as we passed by, though lots of them were happy to stare at me.

I raised my beer to my lips, and a taste so gaggingly bitter hit my tongue that I almost choked. I managed to spit it back into the bottle discretely. Someone had worked a malicious little transformation on my drink.

What was I even doing here? I hadn't decided to stay at Bloodstone University to party with the villains. I was screwing up any real fun Imogen might have been having while she stuck loyally by my side and accomplishing zip for myself and my plans.

"Hey," I said, touching Imogen's arm before we came back around to the bonfire. "I think I'm going to take a step back, maybe go for a little walk by the lake to clear my head."

"Do you want me to come with you?" she asked.

"No, I'll be fine. You enjoy yourself. And thanks for making me get out of the dorm."

She smiled with a hint of relief I had the feeling she was trying to conceal. "Text me if you need me."

Forestland stretched out along the edge of the lake on either side of the open area that held the fire pit, the dock, and the boathouse. A narrow dirt path led off through the trees on the east side. I set off along it, my shoulders coming down as soon as the sounds of the party faded behind me. The fresh night air washed my lungs clean. I felt safer here, alone in the dark, than I had in the middle of all those students back there in the firelight. Especially because with each muted thump of my feet, those tiny flickers of animal fear found their way to me.

I'd gone my whole life without magic, but now that I'd

had it, I couldn't imagine ever being at ease without at least a little at my beck and call.

The path had veered far enough from the lake that I couldn't make out the water anymore. I stopped and tipped back my head to peer at the intermittent stars between the leaves overhead. A twinkle here, a twinkle there. Too bad I didn't think wishing on one was going to get me anywhere.

Maybe some of the wards Imogen had talked about were out here around the boundaries of campus. Would I even recognize one if I passed it?

As I lowered my head to study the forest around me, footsteps crunched into the brush. I stiffened, but after a moment I could tell they weren't coming my way. A figure mostly hidden by the shadows and the tree trunks was pushing away from the path through the vegetation, heading toward the lake.

I paused for a few seconds and then slipped between the trees after them. My nerves jittered, but if someone was up to stealthy activities out here, it might be useful to know what. Then at least this night wouldn't have been a total waste.

The ground slanted upward. As I picked my way carefully through the underbrush, trying to make as little sound as possible, the figure ahead of me completely disappeared from view. I kept following the slope up, scanning the trees, until they fell away around a narrow clearing.

I stopped in the shelter of the forest. Less than ten feet away, the grassy rock-scattered ground fell away in a cliff over the lake. The music and voices from the party carried faintly over the water, but before me there was nothing but open water framed by arcs of trees and the sprawl of the night sky.

Near me, a log stretched across the clearing to the cliff edge. I looked past it and spotted the figure I'd been following sitting on the ground with his back against the trunk of a broad maple. In the dim moonlight, I could make out enough of his form to recognize him from the breadth of his muscular shoulders and the chiseled planes of his face.

I'd followed Connar Stormhurst.

My body tensed automatically. Why the hell had he left the party and his friends to come up here?

In the back of my mind, I saw the flash of his bared teeth as he'd run off the guys who'd nearly crashed into Malcolm and Jude. But the Connar in front of me didn't look rabid. He'd tipped his head back against the tree trunk, closing his eyes, and his hard features had somehow turned peaceful.

I had a little magic in me now, and he didn't have any of his friends to make for a completely unfair fight, if it came to that. Curiosity nipped at my heels and nudged me out into the open.

"What are you doing up here?"

Connar startled, his eyes popping open and his brawny body shoving off the tree in an instant. He caught himself at the sight of me, holding in a crouch. His brow knit.

"What are *you* doing up here?" he shot back.

"Strangely enough, I didn't feel incredibly welcome down at the party, so I figured I'd take a little hike. Somehow I don't think you had the same problem."

He hesitated and lowered himself back to the ground, not relaxing against the tree trunk like he'd been before, but not poised to attack either.

"I like this spot. It's completely away from… from everything else."

I wouldn't have thought Connar Stormhurst had an "everything else" he'd need to get away from, but he didn't look as if he wanted to delve any deeper into that answer. I shifted my weight and then asked, "Do you mind if I stay for a bit?"

He eyed me. I'd never been close enough to him to make out the color of his eyes, and now I found myself wishing I knew.

"You're not worried?" he said.

My pulse was thumping away, so he could probably taste how nervous I was, but I made myself smile. "Should I be? Are you in the habit of tossing people off cliffs for simply existing?"

The upward twitch of his lips felt like a victory. "No. Only if they really piss me off."

"Then I'll make sure to step well back if I'm going to do that."

To keep a safe distance from him, I hopped over the log and sat down there. The lake lapped at the jumbled rocks along the edge of the cliff about thirty feet below us. I couldn't make out the bonfire in the distance, only a hint of its reflected glow on the water and the dark line of the dock. The breeze licked over the bottom of my dress and my bare calves.

It was an incredibly peaceful spot with no one around and the murmur of the lake rising up from below. What made a guy like Connar seek it out still puzzled me. I glanced over at him and found him watching me. His expression was more curious than anything else, but my skin prickled anyway.

"What's your league?" I blurted out, just for something to say.

His eyebrows rose. "You can't guess?"

Oh. Er. "Physicality?" I ventured.

He grinned at me, and damn did his face transform when he really smiled. I hadn't seen it before. In his usual stoic mode, he looked gorgeously distant, look-but-don't-touch. That grin gave him a warmth that brought him to life. My heart skipped a beat despite myself.

There really should be laws against *anyone* being that good-looking, especially four of them in the same damn place.

"Did you each pick a different one, then?" If Connar was Physicality, Jude was Illusion, and Malcolm was Persuasion, then that meant Declan was Insight. Which made sense, given that he was TA-ing for that subject.

"A little friendly competition," Connar said. "And even though we're strong in other areas, you usually end up strongest in whatever type of magic you give the most focus. It seemed like a good idea to spread the talent around for when we're the ones in charge."

In charge. My skin prickled again with a different kind

of nerves. I was heir to one of the five ruling families. What that fact meant for life beyond this school hadn't really sunk in until just now.

Someday the four guys and I were supposed to reign over all fearmancer society.

I definitely didn't want to stick around for that. I wet my lips, wavering between finding some new line of conversation or calling it a night, and Connar shifted forward.

"What would you be doing if you weren't here?"

"I— You mean, like, here on this hill?"

"Like Blood U. If the blacksuits hadn't found you. What would you have been doing?"

He sounded as if he was genuinely interested in knowing. I hesitated, but I couldn't see any trap in answering. It was a straight-forward what-if.

"Working on assignments for the college classes I had back home," I said slowly. "I was studying design. Or making—I did these little sculptures of different fantasy creatures—people on the internet would buy them." My hands moved as if to form the shape of the half-started phoenix I'd left on my table, and nausea pooled in my stomach.

"Kind of like conjuring," Connar said. "Maybe you'll end up on the Physicality side too."

"Maybe." I hadn't thought about it that way. Physicality wasn't just about what you could do with your own body but creating solid things too. What kind of figurines could I create with magic as my clay? "I guess it must be easier to decide quickly if you've grown up knowing that you'll need to. And having an assessment that's not a flop probably helps too."

I shut my mouth before I babbled on any more, but Connar just kept watching me in that mildly curious way.

"It's hard for you, isn't it?" he said. "Dealing with everything here."

Possibly I shouldn't have been honest, but no one else had acknowledged that quite so frankly, and the words spilled out with a surge of relief. "Of course it's hard. I wasn't ready for any of this."

I looked away from him toward the lake, swiping my hand over my mouth. Connar leaned against his tree again.

"While you're here, you can leave all that behind too," he said after a moment.

We sat in silence for a few minutes after that, but it had a weirdly companionable quality to it, as if we were leaving each other to our own thoughts rather than simply unsure of what to say. Connar closed his eyes, his posture relaxing even more. I didn't know who he was down there with the other scions, but up here, away from everything, he didn't seem like a bad guy.

He was the only one of the four of them who'd acted as if my life before I'd gotten here might have been of the slightest bit of importance, for starters.

Imogen would probably be worried if I didn't turn up soon, though, and I did have a session with Banefield tomorrow morning. With unexpected reluctance, I stood up.

"I'd better get going. But—thank you for sharing this spot with me."

Connar blinked at me in apparent surprise. "Thank you for trusting me not to toss you off a cliff," he said after a couple beats.

It sounded like a joke, but as I headed back through the forest, I couldn't help thinking that his expression had been awfully solemn in that moment.

CHAPTER FOURTEEN

Rory

Professor Banefield answered his office door beaming with excitement.

"I think I've found just the thing for you," he said, ushering me into the book-lined space with its cluster of four armchairs at one end and desk at the other. He'd pushed the chairs and the coffee table that usually stood between them off to the walls. The click of clawed feet from the other side of the desk told me we were back to playing with animals.

My heart sank. "I don't know… I'm not sure terrifying furry creatures is ever going to be my forte." It was one thing to give them the unavoidable anxiety that came with any human presence in their natural habitat and another to purposefully scare an innocent being right in front of me.

Banefield didn't sound fazed. "But that's the trick of it." He ran his hand over his uneven orange hair. "You don't want to hurt them—you don't want them to be hurt. What if you were scaring one animal to protect another?"

He ducked behind his desk and dragged a large cage into view. This one held a plump house cat that was pacing restlessly behind the bars. Then he pulled out another cage from the other side of his desk: quite possibly the same adorable bunny I'd been unable to torment much before.

His meaning clicked in my head, and a smile crept across my face. "The cat tries to eat the rabbit, and I scare it away. Okay." I paused with a fresh twinge of guilt. "But it still doesn't seem fair to the bunny to put it in that position in the—"

"Which is why we're just going to dive right in," Banefield said, and snapped the cages open.

The cat sprang out in an instant, its gaze already fixed on the rabbit. The rabbit's nose trembled. It let out a squeaky sort of yelp and backpedaled to the corner of its cage as fast as it could go.

Banefield had known what he was doing—I'd give him that. My stomach flipped at the sight of the terrified animal, but this time I wasn't the one provoking the terror. I could be the one to save it.

"Shoo!" I hollered, stepping between the cat and the rabbit's cage. I flung my arms at it to motion it away. "Get away! Leave the bunny alone."

The cat hopped backward with a startled arch of its

back. As it hissed at me, a waft of fear, sharper and more potent than any I'd felt yet, rushed through my ribs to collect at the base of my throat.

The cat moved as if to try to dodge past me, and I stomped my foot. "Forget it! It's not your breakfast."

Another jolt of anxiety flowed into me with the smack of my shoe against the floor. The cat stalked away behind the desk. I straightened up, my pulse thumping giddily. Magic hummed from my throat all the way down my sternum. I didn't know how much it was compared to what fearmancers normally used, but it was a hell of a lot more than I'd had to work with before.

"Excellent!" Banefield said with a pleased clap. "There you go. The first hurdle crossed." He murmured something to the cat, and it allowed him to scoop it up and place it back in its own cage. "It may be more of a complicated process, but it'll serve our ends for now. We can arrange scenarios as you need to accumulate energy for your magic, and you should keep an eye out for parallel opportunities in your day-to-day life."

Like when I'd stood up to Malcolm to defend the kid he'd been harassing. Hmm. There were probably dozens of opportunities to scare off bullies from their targets every day here at Villain Academy, but I had the feeling taking up that banner was going to make me even more a target myself than I'd already become.

Not that I had any interest in becoming Miss Popularity—Victory was welcome to that title—but I really wasn't going to learn anything if my classmates turned every class I was in into a "let's beat up on Rory" session.

"Now what?" I asked.

"Now we can move past theory and get into the hands-on practice." Banefield sat down behind his desk. "Where would you like to start? What areas do you feel you could use the most additional work in before your next seminar?"

My mind leapt to that Insight seminar where Jude and Victory had picked apart some of my most vulnerable memories, but I'd managed to put up a wall they couldn't penetrate. All I needed was enough magic to sustain that. And my mentor's use of the term "hands-on" had brought up another memory—of talking with Connar last night.

"I have my first seminar in Physicality this afternoon," I said. "Can I try to, like, build something? How does that even work? Can I turn this energy into *anything*?" I tapped my collarbone.

Banefield chuckled. "I wish that conjuring were so easy. No, Physicality work mainly involves drawing on what you already have and, in essence, re-shaping it. You can make things appear out of thin air only if the materials are already on hand. So, for example, if you did conjure ice the other day, you'd have been pulling water molecules out of the air to create it."

Oh. "I didn't feel like I was doing anything that complicated." I hadn't really thought about it at all; it'd just happened.

"That's the beauty of being a mage," Banefield said. "To some extent, our powers naturally convert our will into the action we're seeking. We're simply honing them, learning how to use them more efficiently and effectively."

I nodded. "Got it. So… if I wanted to make a little sculpture of something with magic, I'd need to have the material I was going to use around. Or I guess I could make it out of ice and just pull that out of the air again?"

"Absolutely," Banefield said. "And don't get too tied to your literal ideas of what any given material can do. That's something you'll branch out into as you get into advanced Physicality, if you pursue that line. There have been great mages who can transform their own bodies into animals that appear twice their previous size or conjure a massive sword from the soil beneath a field. At their base level, many things contain the same essence as many other things, and what exists can always be stretched around our will."

I wasn't sure I could wrap my head around that idea just yet. "Let me just try…" I dragged in a breath. "Freeze," I murmured, letting some of the magic I'd absorbed vibrate up my throat.

Ice shimmered across the surface of Banefield's desk, which thankfully was mostly bare. But I didn't want some thin sheet just lying there.

I groped for the right word to capture my intention. "Together," I said, cupping my hands to model the motion.

The ice quivered and rolled up into a lump right in front of me. A laugh slipped out of me. I'd done that.

Let's see how far I could push this before my magic ran out. I focused on the phoenix I'd imagined all those days ago and made a stroking gesture on either side of the icy lump. "Shape," I said.

The lump erupted into a head and wings and tail. The outlines of feathers rippled over its surface. A beak protruded from the figurine's head and sculpted flames licked up at its base. Every detail I trained my attention on in my mind's eye burst into being, with another "Shape" whenever my momentum started to falter.

The energy inside me seeped away until my chest felt hollow. I stared at the ice sculpture I'd conjured. The phoenix was flinging itself up out of the fire just as I'd pictured it, even more perfect than if I'd tried to form it out of clay.

Banefield offered a round of applause. "Not bad at all for your first conscious attempt. I can see your artistic background coming into play."

"Is it going to start melting?" I asked, cocking my head at the icy figurine. Exhilaration shivered through me. I'd made something beautiful. Something beautiful out of fear.

"The magic you put into it will hold the chill for at least a little while," Banefield said. "Don't worry yourself —I'll disperse it before I end up with a puddle on my desk."

The thought of my creation being "dispersed" brought a little ache into my chest—but hey, if I could do that while conjuring ice out of thin air, imagine what I could do if I found myself a nice chunk of clay. Or maybe even some granite… So many possibilities.

A white shape loped past my chair. The bunny had

decided to brave the world outside its cage now that the cat was shut away. I watched it, the wheels in my head spinning. If I let the cat out now, I'd *really* have to scare it to stop it from getting its paws on the rabbit. The amount of energy—

My excitement dampened in an instant with the image of the bunny squealing in terror as the cat pinned it down. What was I thinking? I might not be fast enough. Even if I was, the rabbit would be scared out of its wits.

I'd been enjoying this magic so much that for an instant I'd been willing to risk that poor animal's life to get more of it.

My gut constricted around a lump of guilt. Banefield was studying me. "Is everything all right, Rory?"

"I just— Can we put the rabbit back in its cage before I face off against the cat again? Just to make sure I can protect it?"

"Of course." He didn't get up, though, just leaned over his desk with his hands steepled. "Maybe there's something else we should talk about first, in light of this experiment, and—I understand you've struck up something of a friendship with the Nary student in your dorm."

"Shelby," I said automatically. "Yeah. What about it?"

"I simply want you to be aware of how you're training your mind. With the kind of magic we work, the kind of mages we work around, identifying with those weaker than us is a weakness in itself."

I frowned at him. "Are you saying I shouldn't care about people?" Or fuzzy bunnies?

"No, of course not." Banefield sighed. "Living in secret as we do, our lives are already rather limited. As you've seen acted out here, fearmancers often prey on each other to develop their powers. The strong rise to the top, and the weak..." He made a falling motion. "When you care about someone or something that can't defend itself, you open yourself up to being hurt through that thing. Care about this rabbit, and any mage could draw fear from you by threatening it."

"So, what? We just let the weak get eaten?" Every piece of me balked at that idea.

"That's the way of the entire natural world, isn't it?" Banefield said, calmly enough. "We can work around your sensitivities for now. Just consider that you are the scion— and technically the baron, as soon as you've completed your schooling—of a ruling family. It's your *duty* to stand firm against any attempts to shake you. What might seem like kindness is an indulgence that fails both your community and yourself, and puts the object of your 'kindness' in more danger than if you hadn't intervened."

Because I'd make them a target too. Had the other girls been harassing Shelby more since I'd gotten friendly with her? I hadn't seen enough of how they'd treated her before to compare. Shit.

Some of what he was saying made sense, no matter how much I hated it.

Banefield stood up. "Shall we continue? You've got another half an hour with me."

I got up as well, squaring my shoulders. None of that political awfulness would matter if I saw my quest through and destroyed this place. The joymancers didn't work like that. I could prove to them I didn't either.

But for now, I had to work with what was in front of me.

I shooed the bunny back into its cage. "All right. Release the tabby."

CHAPTER FIFTEEN

Rory

D ad gurgled. Blood spilled over our kitchen floor in a flood that seemed to spread and spread, across every tile and past Mom's already limp body.

No. Please, no.

I lunged to reach him but couldn't seem to move, a scream bubbling in my throat—

And woke up, sweaty and shaking under my fluffy duvet in my Villain Academy dorm room.

Thin morning light seeped around the edges of the curtain to haze the ceiling. I stared up at it and sagged into the mattress as my pulse slowly settled down to normal speed and the images that were half memory, half nightmare faded from my mind.

Was that the fourth time or the fifth I'd revisited my parents' murders in my sleep? Enough times that I was losing track, anyway. The repetition hadn't dulled any of the pain or the panic, but at least I knew those would fade too, at least to the point that I could keep going.

When I sat up, the first thing my gaze landed on was a square of white paper fixed to the inside of my door. A paper that hadn't been there when I'd gone to bed last night. I leaned over to yank open the curtain and let the full sunlight in, and then peered at the note.

It's time, it said in bold black handwriting.

Well, wasn't that a charming sentiment and not at all foreboding.

"Deborah," I whispered, eyeing the floor in case whoever had left me that present had messed around with other things in my room. I'd made my best attempt at magically locking the door last night, but apparently it hadn't been good enough to keep vaguely threatening notes out. I wasn't sure whether the paper had been teleported through the door or placed there by hand by someone who'd opened it, or which of those possibilities was more disturbing.

Deborah poked her pale mouse face out of the wardrobe. She darted across the floor to scramble up a dangling fold of duvet and came to rest her front paws on my wrist. It was only a faint pressure, but her touch brought a little comfort all the same.

She was the only person here who had any idea what I was really going through, and she was hardly even a person.

What's the matter? she asked.

"Someone left a note inside my door overnight," I

said. "Did you hear anyone come in or feel any magic being worked?"

I was asleep a lot of that time myself. I expect I'd have woken up if someone had actually opened the door. But if they conjured it there by magic, I could have missed it. I'm sorry, sweetheart.

"It's okay. I just figured I should check." I exhaled, only a bit of the tension inside me dispelling with my breath.

What does it say?

"Just 'It's time,' whatever that means. I guess I'll find out." I swiped my hair back from my face, the dark brown waves so rumpled they were nearly curls. "Can you feel any other magic around the room?" I couldn't, but I didn't trust my own ability to sense it.

Deborah scurried away to traverse the foot of the bed, her whiskers quivering. She came back to my hand. *I think this room is safe enough. I could do some investigating, as well as I can, while you're going to your classes today. Perhaps I'll overhear something useful for you—who left the note, or what else the other students might be scheming about.*

The thought of her leaving the already precarious security of my bedroom to roam around the rest of the school made my chest tighten. "I don't think that's a good idea. Even if you could manage to stop any of the students from seeing you, a lot of them have familiars roaming around that would see you as a meal."

I'm pretty fast on my feet. Don't worry about me. My mission was supposed to be to look out for you, and I'd like to do a better job of that.

A lump rose in my throat. She'd had no idea she'd end up in this treacherous situation when she took on that mission, but she was willing to risk her life to keep protecting me however she could in her diminished form anyway. I couldn't help thinking back to the comments Professor Banefield had made yesterday about how caring about people could hurt both you and them.

Caring about me was putting Deborah in danger. I should be able to protect myself.

"You've done a great job," I said firmly. "I don't know if I'd have been able to hold it together without you here with me. You just focus on keeping out of sight around any of the assholes we can't trust. I'll look after me."

I tugged the note off the door, crumpled it, and tossed it into the garbage can under the desk. My charm bracelet clinked as I jerked open the wardrobe. Time to pick what to wear to face this day, whatever it was going to bring.

I set off for that morning's seminar in a collared ivory shirt and sleek slacks that made me feel like I was some kind of kickass lady CEO, ready to tackle the day with fierce professionalism. I'd put on the other pair of dressier shoes I'd bought: black Mary Janes with low clunky heels that hit the floor with a satisfyingly solid smack. The few remaining tremors of magic I'd held onto after my attempts at a locking spell swirled behind my breastbone.

The sun beamed brilliantly through the first-floor windows around the library. I stepped out into the warming air to cross the green to Nightwood Tower, and my strides slowed.

It was normal to see several students and maybe a few

teachers passing between the triangle of the campus's three main buildings at any given time. This morning, a whole crowd had gathered around the fringes of the green. There were dozens of students, most of them faces I recognized from my classes, and many of the teachers too. I even spotted Ms. Grimsworth lingering near a cluster by the back doors of Killbrook Hall.

I set off for the Tower anyway, trying not to let their presence unnerve me, but as I walked along the paved path, more and more gazes turned to follow me. My skin prickled.

I'd just reached the middle of the green when Malcolm came sauntering out of the crowd to meet me.

He had his hands slung in his pockets, the sleeves of his button-down rolled to his elbows, his entire stance radiating casual confidence: every bit the divine devil I'd pegged him as the first moment I'd seen him. His sly smile fit his aura perfectly.

My heartbeat thumped faster. I moved to dodge him on the path, and he sidestepped to block me, his smile widening.

"Hold on there just a minute, Bloodstone."

I halted, holding myself rigid so my nerves wouldn't show. He'd obviously called all these people here. I had to guess he was the one who'd left the note in my room. If I tried to make a dash for the Tower or even back to my dorm, how many steps would I make before he stopped me like we both knew he could?

Just enough to make me look as ridiculous as possible, no doubt.

So I stayed where I was and raised my chin. "'It's time'?" I said, quoting the note. "Time for what, Nightwood?"

"Time you finally recognize what you are and who you should owe your loyalty to," Malcolm said, his voice ringing clear across the green. "Time you stop carrying around an emblem of the self-righteous bastards who killed your family and would like to wipe us all out if they could. Time you got off that imaginary high horse." He raised his hand, and his voice shifted into a silky lilt. "Take off the bracelet the joymancers gave you."

Every bone in my body resisted, but his words wound through my body, loosening my muscles and jolting my nerves into motion. A startled gasp slipped from my lips as my hand moved of its own accord to undo the clasp on my charm bracelet.

Jude had said Malcolm's primary focus was Persuasion. Here was my first-hand demonstration. Professor Crowford had mentioned that the more your instructions went against the person's own will, the more power you had to bring to your magic for it to work. He must be expending an awful lot on me right now.

"Stop," I said. My protest held no power at all. I had to save the little bit of magic I had for when it could matter the most. My fingers curled around the dangling strand of charms. He couldn't take it. I couldn't *let* him.

But that wasn't what Malcolm wanted after all.

"Drop it," he said, as if I hadn't spoken.

My fingers twitched and released. The bracelet fell to the strip of smooth concrete with a rattle of the glass beads. I strained to snatch after it, but my body wouldn't respond.

"Smash them," Malcolm said in the same silky tone, but with a triumphant note now. "Smash every last one, like those fucking joymancers should be smashed."

Oh, God, no. I tensed every limb, calling on the threads of magic I'd been saving up, but my foot lifted against my will. I gritted my teeth and strained to pull it back.

The magic wisped through me to no effect. My heel slammed down on the bracelet. Glass crunched against the pavement. I flinched, tears springing to my eyes despite my best efforts. The words tumbled out. "Please, don't—"

"Keep going."

My foot rammed down again. Another crunch, another jab of pain right through my gut. Memories swam up of the trips to the jewelry shops, picking out each year's addition, Mom listening avidly as I explained what this or that one meant to me. Hope. Adventure. Creativity. Love.

Crunch, crunch, crunch, crunch.

I thought I heard Jude's mocking laugh somewhere to my left. The breeze cooled the damp streaks down my cheeks. My foot twisted, grinding the glass beneath my heel. Malcolm chuckled, low and satisfied, and all our spectators just stood and watched the show. Watched him reduce me to the pathetic weakling mage he saw me as.

My hands clenched at my sides. I wasn't weak. My parents had taught me that from the first days they'd revealed their magic to me, when I'd been just a little kid.

You don't need magic to be powerful, Rory. If your will is strong enough, you can do just about anything.

I had my will, and now I had magic too, if I just reached out and took it.

As I blinked the glaze of tears away, my gaze darted over the crowd. It caught on Declan standing back amid the spectators, his shoulders tensed, his mouth set in a grim line. He didn't look happy, but he wouldn't step in now any more than he had before. *You have to learn how to defend yourself.*

I could end this now. I could roll over like Malcolm wanted and prove him right, but every particle of my being screamed against that idea. He wanted this to be a fight. I'd give him a real one, by whatever means I could.

Fuck him and the assholes turning this torture into a spectacle. Fuck them all.

"Now let's give that one last—" Malcolm started, and I swiveled toward the nearest cluster in our audience.

"*You* want to try me?" I snapped at them, taking a menacing step forward. The breeze had dried the few tears that had trickled down my cheeks, and all my fury and frustration rippled through my voice. A few of the younger kids jerked back with a flash of fright that shot into my chest.

That was all I needed.

I spun back to face Malcolm, who was sucking in a breath to give another command, not looking at all fazed yet. Why should he be? Even with that whiff of power, I couldn't take him on head to head.

So I'd have to hit him hard and fast where it'd hurt the most, just like he had with me.

"Inside," I murmured, focusing on his forehead the way I had with Jude in the Insight seminar. What was he thinking about right now? What about this really mattered to him?

I caught an impression of an older man with the same golden-brown hair mixed with gray, a low measured voice saying, *Now that's a win befitting a Nightwood*, and a flicker of pride. His father?

Malcolm's expression shuttered. A wall hurtled up, jarring me out of his thoughts, but I had something to hold onto now.

"Hear his disappointment," I whispered, the first words that came to mind to fit my intention. I wasn't even sure if I was conjuring a real sound or the illusion of it for only him, or what it would say—I just threw all the magic I had into tearing through that sense of approval.

That low measured voice warbled across the space between us. "What the fuck were you thinking, Malcolm? How do you think you'll ever stand up among the—"

I wasn't sure if anyone could hear it other than him and me, but for an instant Malcolm's face stiffened in a mask of horror. A tremor ran through him before he could catch his composure. He snapped his stance into place again and spat out a syllable with a swipe of his hand. The voice fell away.

He jerked his hand again with another brief mutter, and a wallop of air shoved me backward. I fell on my ass on the pavement.

"I think I've made my point," the Nightwood scion said, all cool disdain again, but I didn't think I was the only one who'd have noticed his momentary lapse. He must have realized that too. His eyes blazed for the second they met mine, promising there'd be hell to pay. Then he stalked off across the green with a wave of his arm. "The show's over, folks! I hope you enjoyed it."

The show was over, but he hadn't totally won.

"Credit to Persuasion," Ms. Grimsworth said in a voice that carried. She sounded weary.

I eased myself back onto my feet as the crowd dispersed. The glinting shards of my charms scattered the pavement in front of me. Even the chain had snapped apart under my stomping foot.

A fresh wave of heat burned behind my eyes. I swallowed hard, fighting back the tears. As the last figures slipped away at the corners of my vision, I stayed crouched, staring.

Most of the charms were nothing but little shards. There was no fixing them by regular means. Maybe magic could have done it, but I had none left. Anyway, I wasn't sure I'd want to wear whatever my wavering talent could produce even if I summoned some more power. It'd remind me too much of this moment now.

But one shape wasn't quite as mangled as the others. I'd interrupted Malcolm soon enough to mostly save one. The little dragon bead I'd asked for on my fifteenth birthday lay amid the broken chunks, the coil of its tail snapped off but its head and body still intact.

My lips twisted as I looked at it. That was the only one Mom had balked over.

A dragon? she'd said. *That doesn't seem to fit you.*

It's courage, I'd said. *And strength. I want... I want to feel strong.*

She'd grasped my arms and squeezed them gently. *Of course you're strong, honey.*

Then I should have a dragon.

How could she have argued with that?

I fished it out of the broken bits. Had she been thinking that a dragon was too close to the predatory mage I'd been born to become? Was it a good sign or a bad one that this was my only surviving memento of their love?

I hadn't exactly fought fair just now. I'd threatened people who hadn't really been hurting me to scare them, and I'd hit Malcolm with the lowest blow I could. That wasn't who I wanted to be.

It was who I'd had to be to survive. To get the justice Mom and Dad needed, to make my way back home, the ends justified the means.

I stood up, and a movement caught the corner of my eye. My head jerked around. One member of our audience hadn't left after all.

Connar had lingered outside Ashgrave Hall, his hard face set in its usual impenetrable expression. My fingers tightened around the dragon charm. I didn't have any magic left, but I'd fight him with everything else in me if he tried to take this one last token from me.

For a moment, neither of us moved. Then his lips

curled just slightly upward in a hint of a smile, as if we were up on the cliff again in that secret spot away from the rest of the world. My heart skipped a beat.

Without a word, he headed into the hall.

I turned back to Nightwood Tower. I still had a class to get to. Clutching the dragon charm, I set off.

To get through the rest of my time here, I couldn't think of anything I was going to need more than a whole lot of strength and courage.

CHAPTER SIXTEEN

Malcolm

The first thing I heard when I answered my mother's call was my little sister crying in the background.

That sound was nothing new. Agnes was coming up on thirteen, and she still broke down way too easily. You'd have thought across all the years of our parents testing our limits and throwing our fears in our faces, she'd have developed more armor, like I had. That was why they did it in the first place: to harden us up before anyone else had a chance to take a jab at us.

Taking on the Nightwood name didn't come easy. She *needed* to toughen up, or someone outside the family might destroy her. If I'd been able to think of a way to prepare her that would have been more effective than my parents' tactics, I would have. Even at a distance, those sobs made my throat tighten.

She was old enough to be better at this, but she *was* also only thirteen.

"Hello, Malcolm," my mother said in her tersely blasé voice, without any hint that she was aware of and most likely responsible for the muffled weeping.

I leaned against the hard mahogany back of my desk chair, my legs stretched out in front of me, one of my dormmates' thrash metal songs filtering through our shared wall. He'd have turned it down the second I thumped on the wall, but I hadn't bothered because it fit my current mood.

"Hello, Mother."

I had the urge to ask her what had gotten to Agnes now, but showing concern wouldn't help me or my sister. It would simply be an opening for some new attack. My mother knew I could hear Agnes; she'd called me in the right proximity as a reminder that no matter what Agnes had been through in the last half hour, I could find myself in even deeper shit twice as fast.

The first thing I remembered learning from my parents was, *Never let your guard down.* Taught with the sting of a conjured electric zap up my four-year-old arm at random moments when my attention strayed too far from the adults in the room.

Another early lesson had been, *Hold your own counsel.* I wasn't going to ask her why she was calling either. She'd tell me when she was good and ready. Impatience looked like weakness.

"I trust your studies are going well," my mother said, a cursory formality.

"I haven't heard any complaints."

"I understand you've had some chance to acquaint yourself with the recovered Bloodstone scion."

There was the motivation behind this call. My gaze lingered on the view from my window across campus toward the lake. The rippling water reflected the pink haze of the sunset. On the other side of this floor in her own corner bedroom, Rory Bloodstone might be looking at nearly the exact same view right now.

Rory fucking Bloodstone, who kept throwing her preference for the pompous joymancers in the rest of our faces. Even this morning, she'd fought me. For what? For the pricks who'd slaughtered her real parents and Declan's mom, who'd left my grandfather with a twisted scar instead of an eye before I was born, who'd fucked up Dad's last big business venture, all of that no doubt with self-satisfied smiles plastered on their faces?

Cracking down on us every way they could, just as vicious as they accused us of being. At least we could own what we were. If Rory could have brought all her grit and fire to *our* side... But no, we obviously weren't quite there yet.

"I have," I agreed, slinging one foot over the other.

My mother had probably heard at least a few details of my clashes with Glinda the good witch. My family made sure to have at least a few staff members in their pocket at any important fearmancer institution, and if some of the witnesses had dished the dirt with their parents, as girls like Victory always did, word would have passed along through those channels too.

She cleared her throat meaningfully. "Are you sure this feud you've encouraged is the wisest approach? We need her ear—we need her to follow our lead once she's among the barons, or we'll never get anything done."

As if I hadn't heard her and Dad complaining about that enough times to know that. "You've managed for seventeen years without a proper Bloodstone baron on hand," I had to point out.

"We've been forced to delay policies we'd have liked to move forward with thanks to the uncertainty about her fate. We're tired of waiting. You'll have to deal with her even longer than we will."

I was the one already dealing with Rory's irritatingly stubborn ass and the power she managed to pull out of it at the most frustrating moments.

"I *started* with an offer of friendship," I said. "She threw it in my face. All that time with the joymancers screwed up her priorities. She'll come around. I've been breaking her down. It shouldn't be much longer now before she comes begging for mercy and forgiveness."

I wasn't going to talk about the defiance that had been etched on Rory's face when we'd stared each other down this morning or the tiny chink in my armor she'd managed to strike me through. She just hadn't learned yet that hitting back at me meant I was going to come down on her twice as hard next time.

"A cowed ally is certainly easier to mold than one on equal footing," my mother said. "See if you can't hurry the process up, though, won't you?"

"If you or Dad think you can do a better job of it,

you're welcome to drop by and take a shot at her yourselves," I said dryly.

My mother's tone turned acidic. "Surely we can rely on you to accomplish this one small task without assistance?"

"I said I'm on it, didn't I?" My fingers tightened around the phone.

I should have been able to answer this call with triumph after this morning's exhibition. I should have been able to report that I'd reduced the Bloodstone heir to a sobbing mess and then hooked her with a promise of redemption on my terms. But no. Even after I'd had Rory dancing to my orders, she still thought she was better than us. She still thought she could win.

"I hope to hear a more productive report soon, then," my mother said. "Your father would love to see you assert your leadership where it counts."

My stomach balled at the words. Didn't he see how much I was living out the principles he'd taught me? Maybe he'd be more satisfied with me if "where it counts" hadn't proven to be a constantly moving target that the two of them kept shifting out of reach.

There would be a day, before it was time for me to take over as baron, when he'd look at me and I'd be able to see in his eyes that he was finally totally convinced his heir could fill his footsteps.

When I'd hung up the phone, I tossed it on my desk. The sky outside had deepened to purple, the lake echoing it. The color of a bruise.

The joymancers must have broken something in Rory

for her to resist the natural instincts we all had so persistently. She thought she could prove the sanctimonious jackasses right if she beat us. We'd just have to break her all over again so we could put her back together right.

So she could be the marvel I'd caught glimpses of behind the front she put on, infuriating but so fucking tantalizing.

Everyone had points of weakness. It shouldn't be hard to figure out more of hers. She could talk back to me all she wanted, strike her blows where she could, but she didn't have the grounding of growing up with fearmancers, of knowing how to build her own armor.

I'd find the right vulnerable spot, and then I'd bring all her defenses crashing down.

CHAPTER SEVENTEEN

Rory

When I returned to the dorm after another morning seminar, it was a relief to find no one but Imogen in the common room. She looked up from the book she'd been reading and immediately waved me over. "How are you doing?"

I sat down when she insistently patted the sofa cushion next to her. "Oh, you know, getting by."

"Malcolm was horrible yesterday." She glanced around as if to double-check that no one else was in hearing distance. "I mean, he's always been kind of an asshole, but since you got here…"

"I bring out the worst in him?" I filled in. Lucky me.

"No one's ever stood up to him like you do." Imogen paused. "You know, if you ever feel like you just want it over with, and you did back down and at least pretend to grovel a bit, he'd lay off of you. The scions push people around plenty, but they don't keep kicking once they've knocked someone down."

Honor among fearmancers. I guessed the problem was I kept getting back up for more. I looked down at my hands. "I think I'd find groveling harder to stomach than anything he can throw at me."

Her lips curled with a slanted smile. "I was kind of hoping you'd say that."

I glanced over at her, studying her pretty freckled face. "Why are you so nice to me?" I asked abruptly.

Imogen blinked. She looked away for a second and then shrugged. "Maybe it'll sound kind of pathetic but— I've never been 'in' with the favored families. My dad might be head of the school maintenance team, but that isn't exactly the kind of position that draws a lot of respect. And then on top of that, my magical ability didn't kick in until later than most... I learned to keep my head down and my shields up, but I was hassled a lot when I was a junior."

I made a face. "I can only imagine."

"Anyway, I'm sick of watching people like Malcolm and Victory walk all over the rest of us, even though I'm too much of a coward to do anything about it. I really admire the way you push back." She scooted a little closer to bump her shoulder playfully against mine. "And I figure it can't hurt to have one scion on my side, right?"

I laughed and rubbed my hand over my face. "We'll see if that ever works out in your favor."

Shelby slipped into the room then, a book of sheet music tucked under her arm. She took in the two of us together, and her forehead furrowed with concern. "Is something wrong?"

By whatever means, Malcolm had arranged that no Naries would witness his spectacle yesterday. I sucked in a breath, trying to decide what to tell her, and Imogen jumped in.

"One of those assholes broke Rory's charm bracelet," she said. "Just shattered all the charms. It was awful."

Shelby's eyes widened with so much horror that I felt the need to reassure her. "I managed to rescue one," I said, pulling the dragon charm out of my pocket. I'd kept it on me since yesterday morning, afraid that if I let it out of my sight, someone would destroy it too. "I'll have to start a new bracelet or something when I have the chance."

"You know... Just a second." Shelby disappeared into her bedroom with a swish of her ponytail. When she re-emerged she was clutching a thin silver chain.

"It isn't anything fancy," she said, bringing it over to me, "but I don't like wearing necklaces when I'm playing so I haven't really been wearing it. You can borrow it as long as you want."

My heart squeezed. "Thank you," I said. "You don't have to."

"It's no big deal. Really."

The chain slid light and cool across my fingers as I took it from her. I strung the glass bead on it like a pendant and clasped the chain around my neck. The dragon settled against my sternum, as if guarding the magic inside me.

"I really appreciate it," I said firmly, holding Shelby's

gaze. Everyone else here was a jerk to the Naries, which only made it feel more important that she understood how honestly grateful I was.

She flushed as if embarrassed and bobbed her head. Imogen checked her phone. "Shit, I'd better get going, or I'll be late for class. Hang in there." She squeezed my shoulder with a quick smile and took off.

Shelby meandered over to the kitchen area to make lunch. She'd just reached the dining table when a shiver ran through her and her hand shot out to grip the top of the nearest chair.

I stood up. "Are you all right?"

"Yeah, yeah, I'm okay." She pushed herself straight again and swiped her hand across her forehead. Her earlier flush hadn't faded away, I realized. "Just a little under the weather. I think I've got a fever. Nothing huge."

Huge enough that I could see a bit of a wobble in her walk. "Isn't there a medical center on campus? Why don't you get them to check you out?"

Shelby shook her head vehemently. She ducked to grab a premade sandwich out of one of the fridges. "They'll either say I'm fine or tell me I need to stay in for treatment, and I can't risk missing any classes. It only takes a couple and they kick you right out of the program."

"Even if you're sick?"

"I don't know. They're pretty strict about dedication and all that. I don't want to take the chance."

She was running herself ragged to stay in a place where nearly everyone treated her like dirt. The pressure around my heart clenched tighter. "Is it really that important, if they're going to be assholes about it?"

"Yeah," Shelby said simply. "It is. There's no other school that offers the kind of specialized individual training they do here. Lots of people end up dropping out because it's tough, but the ones who make it through—I could get a spot in any orchestra I want, pretty much. I'm not losing that opportunity. I promise, it's nothing serious anyway." She sighed as she headed back to her room. "I just wish they'd fix that tree."

"Tree?" I repeated.

She waved toward the far wall. "There's a big oak by the west field. When the wind picks up, it's making this weird sound. That happened back home once, and it turned out the tree had gotten hollowed out by a parasite —it crashed all of a sudden when I was walking home and practically gave me a heart attack." Her eyes glazed in memory or maybe with the fever. "I told one of the maintenance staff, but I don't know if they cared. My skin keeps jumping every time I hear it."

She drifted into her bedroom with her sandwich and her music book. I debated marching her down to the medical center myself, but maybe it was just a cold, nothing serious. She'd know better than I would.

Of course Villain Academy would have to offer a huge reward to offset the torture the university put its Nary students through. I couldn't blame Shelby for wanting to hang on. But would she still think the torment was worth it if she knew just how much she was being used?

I wavered for a minute, torn between the impulse to

help her somehow and the worry that I'd ruin her dream if I intervened. In the end, I headed out of the dorm.

My own pickings in the kitchen were getting awfully slim. A walk into town to get away from this place and stock up on groceries—including plenty of cheese for Deborah—sounded appealing. I could take the path through the forest where I'd send plenty of wild creatures scurrying and stockpile some more magic.

Some seniors were playing a casual game of football on the field by the front of the school. It was warm enough that a bunch of the guys had pulled off their shirts. Most of them were pretty fit, but Connar's brawny form still stood out among them, the planes of his muscular shoulders and chest as much chiseled perfection as his face was. I watched him for a moment, wondering if I'd catch a hint of the connection that had seemed to be there yesterday, but his gaze slid right over me.

It'd be silly to expect more than that. I let all thought of him and the other scions go as I started along the winding woodland path.

It had rained overnight, but I only had to dodge a few puddles. As the rustling quiet of the forest closed in around me, something in my chest released. I drank in the fresh spring air and the tiny quivers of nervous wildlife.

I could keep doing this. I'd held firm this long. I was learning, getting stronger. Soon I'd be fully enrolled in the school, and as I expanded my powers, I'd be able to figure out how the teachers kept the campus protected. How to bring those protections down. How to remove whatever tracing spell the blacksuits had placed on me.

One step at a time, all the way home.

Browsing the grocery store alongside all the ordinary shoppers grounded me even more. By the time I set back off toward campus, two bulging bags slung over my shoulders, a little spring had come into my step.

The past was the past. I just had to let the garbage they threw at me roll off me and move forward.

Then a dark shape hurtled out of the woods with a growl and a flash of gleaming fangs.

A shriek escaped me with a lurch of my pulse. I stumbled backward, not fast enough to dodge.

The creature sprang at me, its massive paws shoving me back under its weight. I fell in a patch of mud by the side of the path with a smack of pain through my back and hot breath by my throat.

I lay there frozen as the creature glowered down at me, still growling. It was a wolf. A large one, with mottled gray-and-black fur and gleaming amber eyes. It snapped its teeth at me, and I flinched.

A whistle cut through the forest. The wolf's head shot up and around. A cool, smooth voice tinged with amusement reached my ears.

"I see you've met my familiar." Malcolm gave a shorter whistle and snapped his fingers by his side, and the wolf wheeled. It leapt off me and trotted over to join the Nightwood scion where he'd come to a stop on the path.

"Good boy," he said, scratching the fur behind its left ear. The smile he gave it was the softest expression I'd ever seen on his face. I couldn't expect him to aim anything like affection at me.

I shoved myself upright, abruptly aware of the damp stickiness coating the back of my shirt—and, ugh, my hair was full of mud too—now that I wasn't in imminent danger of having my throat torn out.

"Maybe you should keep it on a shorter leash," I snapped. I wanted to keep my composure, but my nerves were frayed. Fuck, he'd probably gotten ten times more power from my terror in the last minute than I had during the entire walk through the forest.

"That would defeat the purpose of bonding with an animal with such well-honed natural instincts," Malcolm said nonchalantly. "Wolves will be wolves."

And boys would be boys? I eyed him warily as I grabbed my bags from where they'd fallen. Cold droplets of moisture ran down the back of my neck, but the chill inside me ran much deeper.

We were completely alone. No witnesses, no one to comment if a rule or two were broken.

I didn't think Malcolm wanted me *dead*, but at this point that was about all I'd count on when it came to my well-being.

His gaze slid down my body, and a spark of panic lit inside me at the thought that he'd notice the dragon charm and force me to smash it too. But in my fall and recovery, it'd slipped under the collar of my shirt, out of sight—one small bit of good luck in an otherwise godawful situation.

"I'd rather have the wolf for company than you," I said.

Malcolm gave me a grin that was plenty wolfish itself.

"Eventually you're going to have to face the facts, Glinda. Some of us are predators and some are prey, and it's obvious which camp you fall into, no matter how big a front you try to put on. If you want to learn how to run with the wolves rather than getting chewed up, you've got to submit to the leader of the pack."

"Well, you can just keep waiting on that day," I said, hefting my bags over my shoulders. "Don't get your hopes up."

I walked past him, a prickle running down my spine as I left him behind. He could catch a whiff of how nervous I was, but I wasn't going to let it show any other way. My ears stayed perked for any sound of attack.

Malcolm didn't move to follow. "Careful when you're out in the woods again," he called after me. "Next time I might not be close enough to call him back. One of these days you could lose something you can't live without."

I didn't give him the satisfaction of a response.

The football game had dispersed by the time I reached the campus. A cluster of junior students had staked out the edge of the field with their lunches, and their stares followed my muddy back as I passed them. Cressida and a couple other girls from Victory's crowd noticed me crossing the green. She covered her mouth with a snicker.

"Love the new fashion statement," she said. "I didn't realize you could hit a bar even lower than feeb."

I ignored them and trudged into Ashgrave Hall. Halfway up the stairs, I ran into none other than the Ashgrave scion himself, on his way down.

Declan stopped at the sight of me, his eyebrows rising.

"Are you okay?" he asked, with just a touch of that gentle concern I'd heard in his voice that morning in my parents' house.

The last of my patience disintegrated. I looked at him, letting all the frustration running through me burn in my gaze. "If I'm not, are you actually going to do anything about it?"

He opened his mouth and hesitated, his hand twitching at his side. That was all the answer I had to see.

"All right then," I said, and marched on past him without a backward glance. An uncomfortable sensation sank deep into my gut—maybe not the lesson Malcolm had wanted me to learn, but one that was nearly as wrenching.

No matter what little kindnesses Imogen and Shelby extended to me, neither of them could offer any real protection. I was on my own.

CHAPTER EIGHTEEN

Rory

For the first time, my schedule directed me to the basement level of Nightwood Tower. I hadn't even realized there *was* a basement, but it turned out a little door stood around the side of the north stairs that opened to a second flight heading down. The air cooled as I descended, my footsteps sounding eerily loud in the tight space between the stone walls.

At the bottom of the stairs, I found a small room with wooden benches on either side and a large oak door at the opposite end. A girl I recognized from my Physicality class was sitting on one bench, so I guessed we weren't supposed to stroll right in. I sat down across from her. She didn't acknowledge me, but she didn't take any jabs at me either, so I'd take that as a win.

It didn't look as if this space, which had been marked on my schedule simply as Desensitization, was going to hold the usual eight or nine students that made up most of my seminars. More than four was going to be a tight fit.

Just as I thought that, our third classmate reached the bottom of the stairs with a flick of his dark copper hair away from his eyes. Jude looked at me, and his lips curled upward with his usual smirk. "Hey, Snow Cone. This should be interesting." He propped himself against the wall rather than sit on either of the benches.

I fought the urge to squirm on my seat. I had no idea what "Desensitization" entailed or why it might be interesting. Unfortunately, I hadn't had a chance to ask anyone who'd know since my updated schedule had arrived at the dorm this morning. Deborah hadn't had a clue. Somehow I didn't think I was going to get a helpful answer from the scion who'd enjoyed stringing up my embarrassing memories for everyone else's amusement.

One more student joined us: a gangly young man who eyed both Jude and me with apparent anxiety. He'd just sat down on the bench next to the other girl when the door swung open.

Four junior students filed out. One girl was hugging herself, her face wan. Another hurried for the stairs with a clenched jaw and red-rimmed eyes. One of the boys let out a laugh that sounded forced as the other flinched at the squeak of the hinges.

That didn't say "interesting" to me. That said, "Get me the fuck out of here."

A tall gaunt figure with a sheen of silver on his long jaw appeared in the doorway. He beckoned us in, his gaze lingering on me.

"Miss Bloodstone," he said. "This is your first session."

"Yeah," I said. "I'm… not totally sure what this is."

He chuckled under his breath, a weirdly warm sound in the chilly space, and motioned me after the others into a round domed room that I suspected filled the entire circumference of the tower. From the glossy tiled floor to the curving brick walls, every surface gleamed starkly black, making the space feel even larger in the pale light cast from the fixture at the peak of the dome.

"I'm Professor Razeden," the man said. "And the work you'll do here is a vital part to your education as a fearmancer. The rest of you have much more experience with this subject than Miss Bloodstone does. Who can explain for her why we go through desensitization sessions?"

The other girl raised her hand. "Learning how to prevent other mages from using our fears is just as important as learning how to provoke fear for our own use," she said confidently. "A mage who doesn't know how to control their emotions will find themselves controlled by others."

"Precisely," Professor Razeden said. "And why do we conduct these sessions in a small group rather than individually?"

"Because you need as much time off as you can get," Jude said sardonically, and the younger guy let out a nervous laugh.

Razeden cocked his head, but he didn't look bothered by the joke. "The real answer, please, Mr. Killbrook."

Jude took on a singsong voice as if reciting a quote.

"Because one of the greatest fears to master is the fear of having our vulnerabilities exposed."

"But nothing we see about each other in here gets talked about outside the chamber," the other guy jumped in, shifting on his feet. "What happens here stays private."

Razeden nodded, but I suspected if Jude caught a glimpse of anything juicy to do with me, he'd be passing it on to Malcolm within five minutes of us leaving the Tower. Not much I could do about that. And mastering my fears, making sure people like him and Malcolm *couldn't* turn me into a power source while they tormented me, sounded like a great idea.

I glanced around the otherwise empty room. "So, how exactly does that work?"

"You go one by one while the rest of us observe," Razeden said. "The magic in this room is a honed combination of insight and illusion spells. When I activate it, it will latch onto a point of fear in your mind and bring that impression to life, literally or more symbolically depending on the specificity of your emotions. Your fear will continue feeding the illusion until you can manage to control it. Then it will disappear, and your turn will be over. I will, of course, offer guidance as it appears you need it."

He gestured for us to step back to the wall and considered the four of us. "Since Miss Bloodstone is newly with us, I think we should let her do a little observing before throwing her into the lion's den. Mr. Killbrook, you seem quite energetic today. Why don't you start us off?"

Jude gave the professor a mock salute and strode into the middle of the room without hesitation.

What would he be afraid of? I had even less of a sense with him than I did with Malcolm.

"Begin," Professor Razeden said.

The light overhead blinked off, throwing us into total darkness. A hazy image swam into focus: Jude perched on the top of a crystalline spire.

He was swaying, bits of the glittering rock crumbling away beneath his feet. A chunk gave way beneath his heel. He stumbled and toppled off with a warble of wind I could hear even if it didn't touch me. He plummeted, falling and yet suspended before us at the same time.

Jude's hands flailed out with a flash of panic, and then his expression firmed. He stretched his arms out deliberately and spun his body around. His feet hit the ground with a loud but steady thump. He didn't even stumble.

The light came back on. Jude swept down in an exaggerated bow, his eyes glinting with triumph when he straightened up. He was afraid of heights? Of sudden falls? Whatever that imagery had represented, he obviously didn't need any help tackling it.

"Very nice, Mr. Killbrook," Professor Razeden said. "You continue to hone your reactions. Miss Scarlow, let's have you up next."

The fear the girl tackled must have been symbolic as well—I sure as hell hoped so, anyway. A bristling monster twice her height loomed over her and slashed at her with a razor-clawed hand.

As she dodged it, sweat broke out on her brow. She bobbed and ducked and dashed from side to side, but the beast kept after her. Her breath turned ragged. My legs tensed with the urge to run in there and defend her somehow.

"Remember, you must defeat it to overcome it," Razeden called out from the darkness. "How would you slay this creature?"

The girl fell on her side escaping the monster's grasp. She winced as its claws passed through her shoulder, even though the contact didn't appear to tear her clothes or flesh. It was an illusion, but I knew pain that was in your head could still hurt plenty.

She drew in a shaky breath and slid her palm across the floor. A narrow shining sword leapt into her hand from the same place the monster had emerged from. She sprang up and battered its claws away, weaving around the room for several more seconds. Her mouth pressed flat. She lunged forward and stabbed the thing straight through the chest.

Monster and sword disappeared. The light came on, and the girl walked back to the wall without any fanfare, wiping her damp forehead.

"Have you been practicing those exercises I gave you between sessions?" Razeden asked her.

She nodded. "It's just—it's harder when I'm right in the moment."

"More practice, and you'll get there. It's all a matter of training the mind." He turned to me. "Well, Miss Bloodstone, let's see how you fare your first time out."

Oh, God. I forced myself to move into the middle of the room, wondering what embarrassing scenario the room would conjure out of my head. What if it threw an illusion of Malcolm at me? Or even the scion currently in the room? Jude would have a field day with that.

"Begin," Razeden said.

The light went out, and suddenly I was surrounded by white. White tiles, white cabinets. And my mother, flung back against one of those cabinets as a dark shape just beyond my view slashed open her throat.

"No!" Not again.

I threw myself at her, pressing my hand against her neck. I had to be able to do something. I had magic—I was a fucking scion. I couldn't just watch her die all over again.

But where my fingers touched her skin, it flayed open even wider. The blood gushed faster. Mom's dulling eyes stared at me, horror twisting her expression.

I yanked my hand down with a gasp. It brushed her sternum, and her chest cracked open, ribs jutting up into the open air, more blood splattering my arms. I tasted a fleck of it in my mouth.

"No. No, no, no, no, no," I mumbled. My heart was thudding so hard and fast I couldn't make out anything else.

Professor Razeden's voice reached me as if from miles away. "Take deep breaths. Steady yourself. You can handle this. It isn't really happening. It isn't real."

"Yes, it fucking was," I shouted back in a voice gone raw.

The surge of anger that came with that retort gave me something other than terror to hang on to. Fury at the assholes who'd slaughtered my parents, who'd dragged me to their university to fend for myself among these villains, who put their students through horrors like this.

I would not let them beat me. I would *not*.

A thump sounded at the other end of the room. Dad slumped over, innards spilling from the gouge in his chest. My rush of anger fell away beneath a cold surge of fear like a tidal wave.

I shoved myself away from Mom and ran to him. My feet skidded on the blood-slick tiles. I tumbled down next to him, my fingers grazing the side of his head and just like that smashing open his skull.

His face crumpled. Bits of bone and gray matter mashed together beneath my hand. My stomach heaved. A sob caught in my throat.

I wasn't helping them—I was ravaging them even worse than the blacksuits had.

I crouched down, tucking my arms around my head to block out the sight. The sickly metallic scent of the blood filled my nose and mouth as I gulped for breath. Far away, someone was shouting at me, but the words all blurred together in the haze of my misery. A sound like a strangled whimper escaped my lips.

You killed them, a louder voice said, right inside my head. My voice. You *killed them.*

A hand touched my back, and I flinched. The next breath I drew in smelled only like damp basement air. The tiles beneath my feet were black again, and black walls loomed all around me. Not a speck of blood clung to my trembling arms.

Professor Razeden had bent down beside me. "The first few times, when you're not used to it, can be very intense," he said in a quiet, detached voice that offered neither sympathy nor judgment. "Now that I've seen what sort of scenario you may face, we can discuss strategies that should better prepare you to cope and rise above in the moment."

He must have ended the illusion. I certainly hadn't conquered my fear. I held there for a second longer, afraid to test my legs, and then straightened up shakily.

My throat stung when I swallowed. Had I been shouting—or screaming—more than I remembered?

When I blinked, I saw my parents' distorted faces, and the blood—so much blood...

I avoided meeting my classmates' eyes as I hurried back to the wall. Professor Razeden went to talk with the other guy before beginning his session. Jude sidled closer to me.

I tensed up, but the Killbrook scion's comment came out oddly tentative. "You really did love them."

He sounded... puzzled. My gaze jerked to him, but he wasn't even looking at me, his attention focused on the middle of the room where he'd have watched me go through that horror.

The fearmancers really didn't get it, did they? They had no concept of how the same people who in their minds had kidnapped and imprisoned me had also been the people I'd cared about most in the world.

Had *earned* that love with all the love they'd shown me.

At least, it'd seemed like love at the time. All my memories were jumbled in the aftermath of that almost-memory.

"If you only just figured that out, maybe you're not as smart as you like to think," I said, but without much rancor.

His eyes flicked to me then. He studied me for a moment, so intently my skin started to itch. I couldn't tell if he found what he was looking for. It was only that moment, and then another smirk slipped across his angular face.

"Had to get the teacher to bail you out of your own head," he said, with a tsk of his tongue. "Doesn't bode well for your academic success, now does it?"

"Shut up," I muttered, which was the cleverest retort I could come up with while my nerves were still scraped raw. Then, to my relief, the light switched off for the final session.

———

When I got back after Desensitization, I shut my bedroom door and braced the desk chair against it for good measure. Then I opened the wardrobe and sat down in front of it. As I tugged open the sock drawer, Deborah squirmed out from between the rolled pairs. She scrambled across them onto my waiting hand.

What did they do to you now, sweetheart? she asked without preamble, her dark mouse eyes peering up at me.

The tenderness in her tone made my throat constrict. It took me a second to speak.

"I just realized that I killed Mom and Dad."

Deborah made a sound like a snort in my head. *What are you talking about? I was there. You did everything you could to help them, putting your own self in more peril than I can really approve of, as admirable as it might have been.*

"I know. But I also— If they hadn't taken me in, the fearmancers never would have attacked them. If they'd never adopted me, they'd still be alive."

The last words came out ragged. I swallowed hard.

Deborah's tiny whiskers quivered against my palm. She nuzzled the heel of my hand. *That's hardly the same thing.*

"It's the same end result."

Do you think they didn't know the risks? It was their choice to make.

"Because they thought they had to protect the rest of the world from what I might do if they didn't suppress my powers."

No. I'd never heard Deborah sound so firm. *Listen, Lorelei... I can tell you something that'll show you what really mattered to your parents. I told you that I was brought on right after you turned fifteen, remember?*

"Yeah," I said. That was just further proof that they'd seen me as some kind of threat.

Well, after they did the whole consciousness transfer, I woke up in this body a little earlier than I think anyone had expected.

I heard them arguing with a couple mages from the Conclave who were overseeing the process. The Conclave wanted you to be moved to a more secure location, where several mages could keep an eye on you and your potential fearmancer powers.

A chill rippled down my back. If the other joymancers had felt that way about me back then, how much would it take for them to welcome me back now that my powers had awoken?

"They wanted to treat me like a literal prisoner," I said.

Deborah tickled my palm with her claws. *They were worried. They knew you'd be powerful. At the time, I didn't realize the heritage you came with. I didn't tell you about this before because I didn't want you thinking* they're *the enemy.*

"It's not exactly a stretch," I muttered.

My point is that Rafael and Lisa refused. They fought *to keep you with them, to keep raising you as their daughter, because that's how they saw you. Lisa said it just like that: "She's our daughter now." They couldn't imagine sending you off like some kind of delinquent for something you hadn't even done. For what your background was. Keeping you in their family for as long as they could mattered more to them than any danger that could come with that decision.*

"Oh." I ran my thumb over her back instinctively, as if she were still my pet mouse and not a person in mouse form. Deborah arched into the touch, so maybe she was mouse enough not to mind. I rubbed the black splotch on her flank. "They really said all of that?"

And a whole lot more. It was a long argument. But obviously they argued it well, because I went back with them to your house where you stayed for the next four years.

The ache inside me wasn't gone, but the story had eased it a little. I hadn't imagined the family I'd thought I had. They'd wanted me, risks and all.

I closed my eyes. "Thank you," I said, curling my fingers around Deborah and tucking her against me in the closest to a hug I could manage.

My fear had been a lie. But then, an awful lot of fears were, weren't they, no matter what Malcolm had said?

I couldn't let myself get so wrapped up in this place that I forgot who the real villains were.

CHAPTER NINETEEN

Rory

As Imogen and I came into the dorm room after a dinner in town, Victory and a few of the other girls brushed past us on their way out. Victory's lips curled into a sharp little smirk. Cressida let her purse smack my arm on her way past, and the girl at the back of the pack tossed over her shoulder, "Sleep well!"

The door shut between us with a mix of giggling and a hissed admonishment. I looked toward my bedroom door with a sinking sensation in my gut.

"Might as well see what the damage is," Imogen said.

"I thought I had a pretty good lock on the door this time," I said as we headed over. My abilities obviously weren't developed enough to stand up to Victory's yet. It'd probably take a while before they were. Professor Banefield *had* said she was one of the university's top students.

The door swung open easily. I braced myself for

another stink, but the air smelled clean enough, a hint of freshly mown grass traveling through the window I'd left an inch open. The dim light of the falling evening didn't catch on anything overtly concerning. I reached over and switched on the overhead light.

The fixture blinked on, and my entire bedspread started glittering. What the hell? I walked over.

Every inch of the duvet was scattered with tiny shards of glass, many of them burrowed right into the fabric. I'd slice open my fingers trying to dig them out. Somehow I had the feeling there were more underneath too.

A shudder ran through me. Victory had styled her conjuring to provoke emotional pain as well as physical. The mess on the bed echoed the smashed bits of my charm bracelet.

"For fuck's sake," Imogen muttered, coming up beside me. "I can give my dad a call. The maintenance staff can clean this up for you."

Resolve tightened around the hum of magic in my chest. "No," I said. "I don't want to have to go running for help. I think I can handle it."

I focused on the glinting slivers of glass, remembering how I'd pulled ice right out of the air the other day. This should be easier, right? I wasn't conjuring so much as simply moving.

"Come together," I murmured, drawing my hands toward one another at the same time. The shards quivered. Some of them rose off the bed, collecting in a clump near the foot. Others seemed to stick in the fabric.

I dragged in a breath and focused harder. "Come

together." Willing every bit of glass from within the duvet and beneath it, pulling them toward each other with the energy vibrating at the base of my throat. Prickles raced across my skin as I worked them all free.

"Come together," I whispered one last time, but I couldn't sense any more glass in the bed. I turned my attention to the floating ball I'd made of them.

What to do with them now? The hum in my chest stuttered. I didn't have much accumulated power left.

I could leave Victory a different sort of present. A smile tugged at my mouth, and I pressed my hands even closer together. "Mold and stick."

The shards melded together into a solid lump, all the sharp edges melting away. I released the shape, and it dropped onto my bed with a muffled thump.

Imogen picked up the thing and laughed. "It looks like a very posh version of a poop emoji."

I grinned back at her. "That's what I was going for. Might as well let Victory know exactly what I think of her attempt."

Imogen tossed it to me, and I brought the lumpy mass over to Victory's room. I didn't have a chance against her locking abilities, so I left it sitting just outside her door. She'd figure out what it meant.

"Let's see if we can really keep her out from here on," Imogen said when I rejoined her. "How did you seal the door last time?"

"I tried reshaping the latch so it wouldn't slide out when the doorknob turned." I twisted the knob to examine it. "I guess she smoothed it back out."

Imogen nodded. "You'd think a physical mechanism would be the best defense, but mental ones are actually harder for people to break. Next time, see if you can mix a combination of persuasion that they really don't want to come in and the illusion of feeling sick or scared or something like that. Scared is the best, of course, because then you get magic out of it too."

"Of course," I said, with a pinch of real queasiness. I wasn't sure I was ever going to get used to the casual way in which the students of Villain Academy fed off each other's distress.

My gaze slid to the wardrobe. So far I'd been lucky and none of my tormentors had messed with that. I couldn't count on staying that lucky. I owed it to Deborah to make sure I defended her as well as I could.

"I could use a little help figuring out another spell," I said, motioning Imogen into the room and closing the door. "If I wanted to make sure anyone who looked in my wardrobe didn't see one specific thing in there... That'd take an illusion, right? Are there any special tricks to doing that effectively?"

Imogen cocked her head. "What are you trying to cover up? It makes a difference."

I hesitated. But if I couldn't reveal this to Imogen after all the ways she'd been here for me so far, why was I even hanging out with her? I didn't have to tell her the whole story about technically having smuggled a joymancer into the school, only the part that would seem relatively normal for a mage.

"I have a familiar," I said. "But she's—well, she's a

mouse, and it seems like the vast majority of the other animals around here would happily have her for dinner, so I've been keeping her out of sight. I don't really want to know what Victory or the rest of them would do if they found her."

Deborah's voice reached my head distantly. *Are you sure about this? This girl is a fearmancer, isn't she?*

I couldn't answer her without raising questions I didn't want to answer. Imogen raised her eyebrows. "A mouse? Interesting choice."

"It's a long story." I knelt down by the sock drawer and eased it open. "I don't want anyone seeing anything other than socks in this drawer, even if they start digging around in there. How hard would that be?"

Deborah stayed hidden amid the rolls of fabric. She didn't risk saying anything else to me. Maybe Imogen thought I'd gone completely around the bend and was hallucinating this mouse, but she crouched down beside me, humoring me.

"If you want the illusion to hold even when things are moved around, the easiest way to make that stick is to take everything out of the drawer and start from there. Cast an illusion that people will see the bare base while you're looking right at it. Then add a few socks and layer another illusion on top. And so on in a bunch of stages until it's full again. Unless a person is paying really close attention, they aren't likely to notice they're being misled."

"Okay." That sounded like it was going to take a lot of energy. Maybe it was time for another walk in the woods.

Imogen straightened up. "Let me know if you run into

any problems, and I'll try to troubleshoot. I've got to get writing this essay for Modern Politics." She grimaced and headed off to her room, leaving me glad that I'd at least gotten a break in that area. Ms. Grimsworth had decided I was exempt from the general education courses until I got my magical abilities reasonably up to speed.

"I'll be back when I'm all charged up," I whispered to Deborah.

Outside, the clear sky had gone almost completely black, a half-moon gleaming amid the stars. I left behind the glow of the sconces around the university building doors and wandered toward the lake. Alone at night, I'd rather not meet Malcolm and his wolf in the wider woods on the other side of campus.

A few kids—juniors, from the sound of their voices— had gotten a rowboat out of the boathouse and were laughing and rocking it as they drifted across the water. Watching them, the realization crept over me that I could give them a good scare in a matter of seconds simply by flipping the boat over and dunking them. Just like that, I'd bet I'd have enough energy to fuel all the protections I wanted to put down in my room with more left over.

That was the strategy most of the other fearmancers would have taken. My stomach twisted, and I turned toward the strip of forest instead.

As unnerving as it could be walking around in the woods at night, there were also a lot more animals roaming around than there were by daylight. Wafts of fear fluttered into my chest with each step I made through the brush where I'd veered off the path so I'd make more noise to disturb them. Still, after everything I'd been through in the last week, Malcolm's voice echoed up from the back of my mind.

Some of us are predators and some are prey, and it's obvious which camp you fall into.

How was I ever really going to stand up for myself against him and the others if I only gathered power in dribs and drabs, meandering around like this or startling Banefield's cat now and then?

How was I ever going to gather as much power as they did without becoming just as much an asshole as the people I wanted to take down?

I passed the spot where the ground sloped up toward the cliff and paused. The memory rose up of the weird sense of peace that had come over me looking over the lake. Maybe if I left everything else behind, the right answers would come to me.

The underbrush was so thick that it took a little while to find the best route up the slope. No wonder Connar had found he could count on a certain amount of privacy up there. I guessed I hadn't made the quietest approach, because when I reached the edge of the little rocky clearing, I found him standing on the other side of the log, watching the forest for my arrival.

I halted, feeling abruptly awkward. "Oh. Hi. I didn't realize you were here. I just—it was nice up here last time, and I thought—"

He waved his hand to dismiss my fumbling explanation. "It's fine. There's room for two."

He moved farther along the log to leave plenty of

room where I'd sat before and hunkered back down himself. I hesitated. When he glanced back toward the lake, my lips moved instinctively, forming the word for one bit of magic I was coming to trust in the faintest whisper. "*Inside.*"

My attention focused in on Connar's head. The stretch of my awareness bumped up against a barrier—but it didn't feel as daunting as the one Jude had blocked me with. I narrowed my eyes with a tremor of the energy I'd just collected in my walk through the forest.

I didn't exactly push through, but I had the sense of the wall thinning to something more like a membrane. Impressions seeped into my head of calm and curiosity and something that tasted like… gratitude?

Was he *glad* I was here? I found that hard to believe, but I definitely didn't feel any hostile intentions in him. That reassured me enough to clamber over the log and sit down a few feet away from him.

A crisp but not unpleasantly cool breeze drifted off the lake. The rustling of the leaves behind us nearly covered the distant laughter of the juniors in their boat.

Connar glanced over at me, and his gaze settled on my new necklace for a second before lifting to meet my eyes. "You like dragons, huh?"

I touched the glass charm instinctively, my thumb catching on the rough edge where the tail had fractured. Strength and courage. "What's not to like?"

That slow, breathtaking grin he'd offered me the night of the party crossed his face. "I completely agree. Take a look."

With zero self-consciousness, he started unbuttoning his collared shirt. Heat rushed over my face. "Er," I began, but he stopped halfway and tugged one side down to reveal only his left shoulder.

I hadn't seen his whole back the other day when he'd been playing football. The moonlight caught on a dark shape etched on his skin. I leaned closer, and the shape came into focus as a dragon, wings unfurled across Connar's shoulder blade, not one but four narrow horned heads peering at me from their sinewy necks.

At least, I assumed it had to be a tattoo. The tiny green and bronze scales rippling across the dragon's body looked so vividly solid I couldn't stop myself from extending my hand to brush my fingers across them. For all they appeared to be real, all I touched was warm smooth skin.

The warmth quivered up my arm. I yanked my hand back. "That's amazing. Why the four heads?"

Connar tugged his shirt back up but left it unbuttoned. I couldn't say I minded the partial view I got of his sculpted chest. "It's to symbolize the barony," he said. "The four of us scions who'll rule together when it's time. My real family."

"Except there's five of us," I had to point out, even though I had less than zero interest in ruling over anybody.

He shrugged. "Sorry. When I got it, we had no idea when they'd ever find you or how that whole situation would play out. The guys—I grew up with them. Even before we started here, we'd see each other all the time."

"I suppose I'll forgive you," I said, and he smiled

again. I wanted to prod him about how his chosen family had responded to me—what did he think of Malcolm's and Jude's harassment?—but that was what he came up here to get away from, wasn't it? All of the conflict and the jockeying for power back on campus.

He'd grown up with that too. He probably saw it as normal. But even so, here he was being friendly with me rather than taking up Malcolm's mantle.

"So, Blood U must be pretty different from the schools you went to before," Connar said into my silence.

Understatement of the year. "I haven't gone to schools much, period," I admitted. "My parents mostly homeschooled me. I guess so they could keep a close eye on me." I hugged myself against that uneasy thought. "It was just recently that I started doing a few classes at the local community college. That place was… a lot more straight-forward." I could be diplomatic.

Connar chuckled as if he could guess how much I wasn't saying. "Maybe it's complicated," he said, "but it's got to feel right, too, finally getting in touch with your magical power. Realizing all the things you can do that you couldn't have known before. Doesn't it?"

"Yeah." I looked toward the lake, debating how much I wanted to tell him. Nothing that would hurt me if he happened to pass it on to Malcolm, but at this point, my skin was pretty thick. Why shouldn't I be honest, if he wanted to know? "My parents were open about their magic. With me, I mean. I thought I was Nary my whole life, and I wanted so badly to have the same kind of power they did. I just wish I could have found out differently."

Connar was quiet for a moment. "It's a pretty big deal even for us. We know we should come into our powers because they run in our families, but until you taste that first wisp of fear and direct it into a spell, you can't be completely sure you won't turn out to be some kind of dud. Fifteen years or more is a long time to wait to find out."

Maybe he could understand the awe of the discovery to some extent then, if not the pain of what I'd lost in the process.

"How old were you?" I asked.

"Just a month past my fifteenth birthday. For the families with the strongest bloodlines, it usually kicks in pretty quick. I've been here a little more than five years now. Can't say I'll be sorry to leave and get on with the rest of my life."

He set his hands on the log, leaning back a bit. It occurred to me that while he was being this open with me, I really ought to dig for the information that would help *me* get out of here.

"One of the girls told me there's wards all over campus to stop joymancers from finding the school," I said, which was technically true, because Imogen had told me that. Connar didn't need to know I'd prompted the information. "Why would we be worried about that? What would they even do if they found the place?"

What could *I* do that the fearmancers wouldn't want to happen?

Connar tipped his head to one side, his forehead furrowing. "It's never felt like a pressing threat while I've been here. But I suppose—joymancers can be brutal when they figure they're in the right. And they'd definitely disagree with a lot of the things we're taught here. They've killed fearmancers before—they've destroyed property... Basically the entire younger generation of fearmancers from across America is here most of the time, along with the best teachers in the magical arts. If they attacked the university, it could be devastating."

I didn't want to think about killing anyone. I doubted the Conclave would approve that kind of brutality anyway. The fearmancers assumed everyone operated the same way they did, just like they couldn't even conceive of the fact that I might object to anything they did. The joymancers might have ways of imprisoning the teachers and other major figures, though.

"But if the place was compromised and everyone got out, we could just set up school someplace else?"

"I don't think it'd be that easy. Not on the same level. My great-grandfather told me it took them fifty years for the staff to get the illusions and other barriers perfect so they could bring in Nary students without worrying about revealing ourselves. He was one of the first mages to attend with them. The desensitization chamber took a while to construct too. We couldn't just recreate everything like that." He snapped his fingers. "Better not to let them get at the place at all."

Well, that was certainly useful to know. A twinge of guilt ran through me for using him when he so clearly had no idea I had a hostile agenda, but I hadn't lied to him. I'd just asked, and he'd answered.

"Good thing for all the wards, then," I said.

"You're safe here," he said agreeably, which was such a ridiculous statement that it took all my self-control not to burst out in hysterical laughter. Maybe he caught a whiff of it anyway, because he added, "You don't seem to scare very easy anyway."

He could only say that because he'd never been the one scaring me. "Maybe I'm just good at hiding when I'm freaked out."

"It amounts to pretty much the same thing in the end. You've been getting the hang of things, from what I've seen."

"More or less."

"Hey," he said. "You're a Bloodstone, even if you didn't know it most of your life. You were born for this. And it shows."

The smile he gave me then was softer around the edges in a way that sent an odd flutter through my stomach. "You were born for it too," I said, just to break the moment.

A shadow flickered through his expression. He turned back to the lake. "Yeah. You could say that."

I had the impression I'd made a misstep, but I had no idea what it was. I shifted on the log. "If you'd rather have this spot to yourself again, I can—"

He held up his hand. "Wait. Watch. This is the best part."

The breeze had died down completely. The lake's ripples expanded. Then, with one last tremor, the surface of the water went still. The stars glinted down toward the glossy depths, and the lake reflected them back. Tiny glimmers speckled the dark water as if a whole galaxy lay down there as well as above us.

My breath caught in my throat. Right then, Villain Academy and all its horrors fell back even farther in the distance.

"You can see how amazing that is too, right?" Connar said quietly.

It took me a second to find the wherewithal to speak. "Of course. It's beautiful."

His gaze slid from the lake to me. He paused for a beat and then said, "So are you."

His low voice passed over me like a caress. My eyes jerked to him as the breeze rose again, shattering the underwater galaxy. "What?" I blurted out. "Why would you say that?"

He laughed and eased closer on the log, bringing his hand to my cheek. An eager shiver passed through me at his touch. "Because you are," he said. "Especially when you're refusing to take anyone's shit."

I was groping for an acceptable response to that when he leaned in and kissed me.

I'd only ever kissed two guys before: the boyfriend of two months who'd ditched me after the first time I'd slept with him, as Victory had gleaned from my memories, and some guy at a party a couple weeks later when I was trying to convince myself I didn't care. Connar blew them both away in an instant. His mouth pressed hot against mine, with a hunger that drew out an answering need in me.

My hand clutched the half-open front of his shirt in

the instinctive urge to pull him closer. He looped his arm around my waist as he kissed me again. His other hand lingered against my cheek, his thumb grazing over my cheekbone in a gesture that was almost as giddying as his kiss.

The taste of his mouth and the heat of his body dizzied me. What the hell was I doing? Why wasn't I doing more? After days on end of staying constantly on guard, the sensation of my body melting into his was nothing short of addictive.

It was just kissing. It couldn't hurt anything, could it? *He* hadn't hurt me, not really, not once. And his mouth on mine felt so fucking good.

He tipped his head, his tongue parting my lips at the new angle. I welcomed it to twine with mine. His fingers stroked a burning line over my jaw and down my neck. I adjusted my grip on his shirt, and my knuckles brushed his bare chest. He made an encouraging growl.

I dared to slip my hand right under the fabric to run right over those chiseled muscles, so hard under skin that was unexpectedly soft.

Connar kissed me harder, and his hand dipped lower. He teased his fingers along the curve of my breast through my shirt.

A pang of desire spread low through my belly. I pressed into his touch. His thumb swept over the peak, my breath stuttered, and a sense of alarm finally pealed out loud enough to wake me up.

This wasn't just kissing anymore. If I didn't get my head together fast, it was going to be a *hell* of a lot more than kissing. With a fearmancer. With a guy who called two of my most avid tormentors his family.

I pushed away from Connar with a sting at the loss of contact and scrambled to my feet. My whole body felt feverish, my lips raw, the air shockingly cool against them.

Connar stared up at me, his eyes dark with the same desire still echoing through me. His voice came out rough.

"Rory—"

"I think—I think I should go now," I said, and hurried down the slope before he could say anything that might make me forget myself all over again.

CHAPTER TWENTY

Jude

No one could ever mistake me for a cuddler. I rolled off Sinclair, she let out a satisfied sigh, and I motioned her toward her clothes where they'd fallen beside the bed.

She gave me a narrow look. "Can't a girl relax for a second?"

"If you wanted to relax, you should have picked a different time to come calling. My parents are due for the annual meeting in half an hour."

She sat up with a fluff of her black bob and reached for her panties. "You could have told me before."

"But then we might not have had this excellent quickie. It's not as if I didn't make sure you got yours." I grinned at her.

She made a face in response, but she couldn't stop her

gaze from sliding down to take another admiring look at my naked body.

Sinclair knew what she was getting into. We ended up in my bed together once every month or two, and other than that we barely spoke. She hooked up with other guys. I enjoyed various other girls as the mood struck me. We weren't even friends, just two people who found each other attractive enough to make our initial banging after one of last year's parties an occasional repeated occurrence.

No drama, no responsibilities. The perfect sort of intimacy.

She squeaked on her way to the door, and I caught a little spark of fear. "Your stupid familiar nipped my heel," Sinclair grumbled.

I laughed. "She's just helping you get going. Good work, Mischief."

My ferret chortled from where she'd darted under my desk. Sinclair glowered at me as she slipped out of my bedroom, and I got up to shower and pick out my clothes for the appointment. Better look snappy for the old man, or he'd have one more excuse not to look at me at all.

I swiped a bit of gel through my hair to keep it out of my eyes, tugged the sleeves of my gray button-down halfway up my forearms, and set off for the hall that bore my family's name.

It seemed a little ridiculous that we continued to have parent conferences once we were seniors. I was just a few months shy of twenty—men had waged actual wars at my age without having to check in with Ma and Pa first.

But that was the way things were done at Blood U,

since we weren't considered fully qualified mages until they sent us off into the wider world sometime during our twenty-first year. Every year before that, on the anniversary of our arrival at the university, every student's parents dropped in for a chat with Ms. Grimsworth about our progress.

I found mine waiting in the front foyer right on time. My mother's face lit up when she saw me, and she held out her arms for a hug. My father's gaze followed me as I ambled over to her with the sort of expression a person might direct at a cockroach they'd have stepped on if only they hadn't been in bare feet. Then it flicked away. I gave Mom a quick squeeze and Dad an even quicker smile as if I hadn't noticed.

Every time he saw me these days, he looked as though he were finding it increasingly hard to swallow. Not that he'd ever been a cuddler either. The closest thing to a hug I remembered getting from *him* was a fleeting moment when he'd patted my head after I'd pulled off some reckless childhood stunt to impress him—absently, his hand snapping away when he'd realized what he was doing.

Most of the time I got nothing from him at all. I might as well not even exist. It was fitting, in a way he didn't know I could understand.

"Shall we head up?" I said brightly. "Wouldn't want to keep the old bird waiting."

I caught a slight wince at the flippant way I'd referenced the headmistress, but otherwise Dad didn't react, let alone speak.

As we climbed the stairs to the teachers' residences and

offices, Mom peppered me with questions about my latest pursuits, and Dad remained stolidly silent. Over the years I'd come to the conclusion that she filled the space around me with twice as much chatter and energy to try to make up for his void.

Ms. Grimsworth's secretary was waiting by the door to see us in. The headmistress stood up behind her desk with a respectful bob of her head, presumably a little lower than she'd have offered a parent who wasn't a baron. My father smiled thinly at her.

"Well, Baron and Mrs. Killbrook," she said as we all sat down, "I'm sure you realize this is mainly a formality at this point. Jude continues to perform at expected levels in all his classes, in line with his excellent initial assessment. He has earned many credits throughout the year for his chosen league, and he commands deference among the student body with ease. The only small matter that was brought to my attention…"

She shuffled through the reports on her desk, and apprehension pinched my gut. I had a feeling I knew what she was going to say.

So what? Let it come out. Let's see what Dad made of it. How good a poker face could he keep? Would he dare to berate me for *this* supposed failing?

"Ah, here we are." Ms. Grimsworth peered at the paper. "Professor Viceport has noted that Jude is not progressing at the pace she'd expect in some of the more advanced areas of Physicality. Durability appears to be a particular concern." She looked up at me. "Do you have any thoughts on what might be holding you back in that area, Mr. Killbrook?"

I spread my hands with a shrug. "The knowledge that it would be unfair if I topped everyone at everything?"

Or, more accurately, the fact that durability was the one aspect of shifting and conjuring it was particularly hard to fake with an illusion. I could make something look and feel real in the moment, but anything meant to last after I left the room… If I stretched myself too far and the spell fell apart in a revealing way, Professor Viceport would realize I'd been faking all over the place.

Dad could probably guess that. I glanced over at him, debating how pointed to make my look. I wasn't really sure what I'd want him to do or say, but I couldn't get sicker of the way things were.

He was nodding at Ms. Grimsworth, his expression bland. "It builds character when not everything comes easy to you. I'm sure he'll find his way over that hurdle in time."

"Well, if you should decide you want to arrange for extra assistance, I'm sure you're aware of the summer training session in Maine…"

The headmistress went on for a little longer about my options for magical development, and Mom thanked her profusely on our way out. Dad barely waited until we'd crossed the hall before muttering, "Quite the drive out here just to hear a lot of nothing for fifteen minutes."

I'd thought about how useless these conferences were myself, but his vacantly dismissive tone lit a flare of rage in me on the pile of kindling he'd been building since he arrived. I bit my tongue, but in my mind's eye I imagined his head smashing in like Rory Bloodstone's joymancer father in her desensitization session, all with one swipe of her hand. Skull cracking, blood spurting...

My mouth stretched into a grim smile. What a lovely picture that would make.

The satisfaction I got from it dimmed at the memory of Rory's pretty face crumpled in anguish. What was it like to have a parent you cherished that much even after finding out they'd told you the most horrible lie?

I didn't have a clue, but the question lingered with me as I saw my parents to their car and waved them off. Dad didn't take his eyes off the road for a second. Mom waved back until she had to twist around in the passenger seat. I turned away from the parking lot and meandered around the side of Killbrook Hall, the memory of Rory trailing after me. Rory after the session, her voice taut as she said, *Maybe you're not as smart as you like to think.*

Her breakdown in the chamber should have been perfect fodder to spread around the school. I hadn't told anyone, though. Every time I remembered it, my stomach clenched with the impression that what I'd seen wasn't real weakness at all.

She was a strange one, the Bloodstone scion. Unconventional and unpredictable, and that made her interesting. I could set her off with a few well-placed words, but underneath that defiant temper she had an iron core. And no one could have denied she was particularly stunning to look at when she was pissed off.

I found myself smiling again and shook myself. Why

the hell was I giving her this much thought? As long as she refused to make amends with Malcolm, she was a thorn in all our sides, undermining our authority with every day that went by.

The way she'd slipped past my shield somehow that first day in the Insight seminar… I had no idea how she'd managed it, but if she'd dug very far, lord. The thought nauseated me.

She hadn't gotten any farther, though. I'd stabbed back hard—enough to both stop her and to make her terrified of trying again, I'd imagine. Until she was ready to surrender, we'd just keep tipping her off balance.

I snatched at the first idea that crossed through my mind and said a few words under my breath over my closed hand. When I opened it, an illusion of a wasp flitted off into the air to find its target. Only Rory and I would be able to see it, hear it—feel it. She was going to have some trouble concentrating for the next few hours.

Oh, yes, she'd be begging for a change in tune soon enough.

CHAPTER TWENTY-ONE

Rory

"You've been coming along well with the casting skills," Professor Banefield said as we strolled across one of the campus fields together. The spring day was so clear and bright that he'd suggested we take my mentoring session outside for a change of pace. "I suspect at this point it's just your blocks around generating the fuel you need that are holding you back."

My reluctance to terrify random people and creatures out of their wits, he meant. *I think that's called a conscience. Most of you here should look into that.*

I kept that snarky remark inside and searched for one that was more diplomatic. "Everyone here grew up practicing this stuff. It's a pretty big mental shift when you didn't."

"I realize that, and I've been thinking about the progress we have made. Clearly, you find it much easier when the fear serves a constructive purpose. Perhaps we can do more with that framing."

"What did you have in mind?"

He stopped and pointed to a boy who was sitting in the grass with a book about ten feet away from us. The kid looked like he might not be any older than fifteen, still a bit childishly chubby.

I might not have been raised by fearmancers, but I'd absorbed enough of their perspective in the last few weeks to be able to look at the boy and immediately recognize him as prey. In a cat-and-rabbit scenario, he was definitely the bunny.

Who was the cat, though? I glanced around, but there was no one else in view who appeared to have any interest in tormenting the kid.

"You know why your peers have been practicing provoking fear their entire lives," Banefield said. "It's what our community runs on. Those who are the most in control of others' fears—and their own—are the greatest masters of their own destiny. Don't go over and terrify that junior because you'll enjoy it. Terrify him because he needs to learn, in every possible way, how to deal with being terrified so that he can handle himself in the world beyond this campus."

Every muscle in my body balked. "I don't know."

Banefield cocked his head at me. "Look at it this way: Who would you rather see as that boy's teacher—you or Malcolm Nightwood? You don't have to be vicious about it. Just shake him up a little for his own good."

Okay, so my mentor knew me pretty well. Of course,

at some point Malcolm probably would terrify this kid in his callous way no matter what I did right now. But... was it possible that the kid would cope with *that* better if he'd already seen he could survive a more restrained offensive from me? That did make a certain kind of sense.

I didn't want anyone to be terrorized, period, but if they had to be, maybe it wasn't such a horrible thing for me to insert myself into the process. I just had to find the right way.

"I'll see what I can do," I said with a nervous jitter in my stomach.

I walked over to the boy. His head jerked up as my shadow fell over him, and just like that, a jolt of sharp fearful energy raced past my ribs.

Wow, human fear was so much more potent than animal. That one instinctive emotional reaction topped a half hour walking through the woods.

This didn't have to be hard. The kid was already scared without my saying anything. I didn't have to threaten him or hurt him. Just remind him that people could.

And ignore the fact that he'd be assuming I was talking about myself as well.

"Do you really think this is a good place to take a break?" I asked in the coolest tone I could summon, folding my arms over my chest. "Look at how easily I came right up on you. You've got nothing at your back. A lot of people around here would take that as an invitation."

The boy scrambled up. More of his fear flooded me with every shaky movement of his body. "Sorry. I'll get out of your way," he said, and hustled toward the nearest building.

I watched him go with shame tainting the exhilarating rush of power flowing through me. I'd hardly done anything. I'd made perfectly good points.

It wouldn't always be that easy, though. And I could taste how that sense of power could start to override even a solid conscience.

Professor Banefield came up beside me. "There you go. That was satisfying, wasn't it? Deal out a little tough love once or twice a day, and we can really get going with your magical work."

"Yeah," I said. It seemed wrong to feel this excited and this uncomfortable at the same time.

Banefield nodded to a couple of girls walking along one of the paths not far away. Gold pins glinted by the collars of their shirts. "You can always use a similar strategy with the Nary students. They may not need to be prepared for quite our level of competition once they leave here, but being toughened up a little can only benefit them in the long run."

Assuming they didn't leave here outright traumatized. Or dying. I remembered Shelby in the common room, swaying with her fever.

"Don't you think the university is a little hard on the Naries?" I said. "At least the regular students know what they're getting into. They shouldn't be killing themselves just to stay here so we can torture them."

Banefield's eyebrows jumped up. "What makes you put it that way?"

I gestured toward Ashgrave Hall with a jerk of my hand. "The Nary student who's in my dorm—she's pushing herself to go to classes even though she's sick. She won't even go to the medical office to get checked out because apparently the teachers are so hard on the Naries they threaten to kick them out if they miss a class or two to look after themselves."

"I'm sure under extreme circumstances, exceptions would be made," Banefield said. "We keep high standards because of the benefits an education here offers them in the end."

That was how Shelby had justified it too. It still didn't sit right with me. "We've got to cut them a little slack. They're not mages—they don't have the same talents to help them cope. They *can't* perform at the same level. It's cruel to expect them to and then punish them for not managing."

"I'm sure Ms. Grimsworth would be happy to entertain your thoughts on the matter if you want to take it up with her." Banefield's dry tone suggested that she'd entertain my thoughts for about five seconds before filing them away as nonsense.

I exhaled in a rush as we headed back toward Killbrook Hall. "She—the Nary student—said there's a problem with one of the trees on campus too. It's making some strange sound like it's going to fall over soon."

Banefield hummed to himself. "I can mention it to the maintenance staff, but I wouldn't be surprised if it's only some students playing pranks. If nothing else, we do teach every student here to be very cautious about taking anything they've believed for granted."

He stopped by the door to the hall and turned to me. "I think this has been a productive session. No need for you to come back to my office. Everything appears to be coming along well for your second assessment."

I paused with a skip of my pulse. "What?" I said. After the work I'd been doing in class, I'd started to put the idea of another assessment out of my mind. "All of my professors have seen me work magic by now. *You've* seen me work it. No one thinks I'm some kind of dud anymore, do they?"

The corners of Banefield's pale eyes crinkled with amusement. "I'm sure they don't. But the assessment process is a formality we can't simply skip. While you have demonstrated emerging magical talents, the faculty still needs to confirm you possess at least one area of ability strong enough to warrant using our resources to continue teaching you. From what I've seen, you have nothing to worry about. I expect you'll show at least two or even three like your fellow scions."

His confidence didn't settle my nerves. "And if I get the same weird result as last time?" I'd been able to cast magic before the last assessment too, and that hadn't helped me any.

"I highly doubt that," Banefield said. "But if you did, then it's nothing to be ashamed of. It wouldn't be your fault if your talents were stunted by your upbringing. You would return to your family home and could engage the services of a private tutor to continue encouraging what skills you have along."

Banished from the university named after my own family. Yeah, I was sure none of the fearmancers would see that as shameful at all. And how the hell could I work at exposing the place if I wasn't allowed to stay here?

Banefield patted my shoulder. "Focus on your studies, and don't worry about the rest," he said as if it were that simple, and headed inside.

I dragged in a breath and might have steadied myself if a well-built figure with a head of gleaming golden-brown hair hadn't sauntered around the edge of the building just then with a vicious grin.

"Well, well, well," Malcolm said in his smooth voice. "For all your 'goodness,' your position here at Blood U is awfully precarious, isn't it, Glinda?"

Of all the people who could have overheard that conversation, why had it been him? My shoulders tensed. "I plan on sticking around."

"I guess we'll have to see if you can handle the heat when push comes to shove." His dark eyes glittered with cold amusement. "You know what happens if you screw up and they send you off? The only way you can get back in here and take a spot with the real mages is with permission from the barons. That's my family, and Jude's, and Connar's, and Declan himself. So, you bow down now, or you do it later. Either works for me."

"Keep dreaming," I said, swiveling on my heel.

"I'll see you in our seminar," he called after me.

Oh, fuck, I had Persuasion with him in just a couple hours.

———

At the very least, my legs were getting stronger. I reached the seventh floor of Nightwood Tower without more than the slightest burn in my calves and only a little out of breath.

I'd shown up just before the start of class, preferring not to extend my time around Malcolm. All the seats were taken except one at the back, across the room from Imogen, but that was just fine. Malcolm had chosen one in the front row by the big window that overlooked the south field. It had been pushed fully open, letting a warm spring breeze saturate the room and ruffle the papers on Professor Crowford's desk where he was reading over a chart of some sort.

I started for the empty seat, and Malcolm's voice rang out. "Where do you think you're going?"

"Maybe if you give it a little thought, you'll—" I started to retort, and he flicked his hand.

"You're going to stop right there," he said with the lilt of a persuasion spell, and to my frustration my feet jarred to a halt under me, so abruptly I had to catch the desk next to me to keep my balance. The girl sitting there glared up at me.

Professor Crowford glanced up, his heavy-lidded eyes shifting from me to Malcolm. He didn't say anything, though. I guessed as far as he was concerned, this was just Malcolm putting his lessons to use.

"Is this really necessary?" I said, keeping my voice as steady as I could despite the hitch of my heart. "Haven't you got anything better to do?"

"Oh, I think this is pretty important," Malcolm said. "We all need to be aware of our limitations. You seem to figure you've gotten pretty strong, but the truth is, I'm more in control of what you do than you are. I could make you jump right out that window if I wanted to. *Walk*."

The thrum of magical energy in his voice conveyed his full meaning. My feet turned under me. One lifted and then the other, carrying me toward his desk and the window beyond it. The window with a seven-story drop on the other side.

The breeze didn't feel so warm anymore. I groped for control over my limbs, but my legs kept walking, one firm step at a time. The fear I'd absorbed this morning buzzed behind my sternum, but I didn't know how to use it to stop him. Was I supposed to be able to understand that instinctively? How the hell was I going to pass any assessment if I couldn't even summon enough power to keep myself *alive*?

No doubt that was exactly the point Malcolm intended to make.

I concentrated on the churning energy inside me and willed it into a steel shield around my mind like I had with Jude in the Insight seminar. My feet kept moving. Malcolm kept grinning. His spell had already wormed its way inside my mind. How could you dig something like that out?

I'd almost reached his desk. The window stood just a couple steps past that. My gaze darted to Imogen, rigid in her seat—she might not have had the power to stand up to Malcolm even if she'd dared too—and to Professor Crowford, who was watching the situation unfold with detached curiosity.

He wouldn't let me climb right out the window and jump. Right? Would Malcolm even try to push things that far? I had to think he only wanted to make the point. He'd bring me to the brink and benevolently let me off the hook while I teetered on the edge of the deathly fall. The fearmancers hadn't gone to all this work to rescue their stolen heir of Bloodstone just to see me break my neck less than three weeks later.

That was one tiny scrap of security in the middle of a heap of shit. I didn't want his fucking benevolence sparing me. I wanted to *stop* him.

"Good girl," Malcolm said as I reached his desk, in the same tone he'd used with his wolf. "Just keep on going."

"Out," I murmured as quietly as I could. Find the persuading spell inside my head and then tear it out of me.

My own magic prickled through my mind, but Malcolm's must have been woven in too deep, too tightly. I took another step. My blouse quivered with a waft of the breeze. I could see across the field all the way to the forest and the spire of the town church in the distance beyond it.

Sweat trickled down the back of my neck. If I couldn't break his spell, what else could I do to control myself?

It was hard to unravel someone else's magic-work. Easier to cast your own to oppose it. That was one of the first principles Professor Banefield had told me.

"Wall," I whispered with a rasp of magic over my tongue. The breeze snapped away, the air stilled, and my knee smacked into an invisible barrier not around me but in front of me, blocking my body from continuing across the last short span to the window.

Even so, my legs kept trying to walk. My foot and then my other knee banged against the wall I'd conjured.

I must have looked ridiculous, but I didn't care. All I cared about was the narrowing of Malcolm's eyes.

He muttered something, and the wall shuddered. I spat out the word again, focusing all my attention on holding the barrier in place.

Magic coursed up my throat. An ache spread through my chest at the speed with which I was throwing it forward, but I could feel the pieces of my security net crumbling as quickly as I was rebuilding them.

This was the best I could do. I could catch myself on the verge of catastrophe for however long I could sustain my magic. I couldn't snap out of Malcolm's hold. I couldn't walk away. And as soon as my limited reserves wore out, he'd have complete control again.

I might have helped him make his point even more thoroughly than if I'd just gone along with his stunt.

A sense of hopelessness quivered into my voice. Malcolm leaned forward, clenching his hand with a tight utterance, and my wall smashed. My foot swung forward. I gasped the word, heaving the barrier back into place, but the effort wrenched the remaining hum of energy up from my chest. This was my last defense. When he shattered that too—

"That's enough," Professor Crowford said evenly. He waved his hand, and just like that, both my wall and the compulsion to walk through it disintegrated. "A very fine demonstration of persuasive ability warping natural instincts, and a decent effort at creative countering. Credit to Persuasion and Physicality. Let's give the other students a chance to do some work now, shall we?"

I stumbled backward and then whipped around to find my seat. My legs were trembling.

Did Crowford know how close I'd been to losing the battle? If I'd somehow moved one of the professors of Villain Academy to pity, I was worse off than I'd been afraid of.

Malcolm shot a smirk my way as I sank into my chair, not looking all that disturbed by the interruption. He knew he'd landed his blow. And I knew it too.

Nausea crept through my stomach as I sat back to take in my next lesson, however much I'd get to use it.

CHAPTER TWENTY-TWO

Rory

Y ou'd think a library twice the size of the public one near my house back home would have *something* useful in it. I scowled at the pungent leather-bound volume I'd just flipped through and slid it back onto the shelf carefully so the cover didn't crumble any more than it already had.

This whole section of the library on the second floor was devoted to magical texts, bespelled to ward off the Nary students. Apparently most writings on magic had been compiled centuries ago, from the look—and smell— of the books around me. Some of them were written in languages I couldn't read or lettering I didn't even recognize. Maybe there was a spell to conjure a translation? Simply pointing at the table of contents and saying, "English!" hadn't gotten me anywhere so far.

The ones I could read prattled on about energy

transfers and conduction of intent with a complexity of terminology that left me feeling like a sixth grader trying to decipher a graduate-level engineering textbook. Fearmancers sure did like to talk a lot in very flowery language about how amazing their abilities were.

What I could really use was an introductory treatise or two—magic for kindergarteners. I'd sat through a lot of seminars in the last few weeks, but for the majority of my life I'd done most of my learning on my own with books or on the internet. Homeschooling might not have given me the greatest social skills, but the various assignments Dad had set up for me had left me an expert at independent study.

I just had to find a book that started with the basics.

I wandered farther, my gaze skimming the titles, and swift footsteps scraped against the hardwood floor. Declan ducked into my aisle, his black hair falling forward by his temples, his hazel eyes oddly frantic. He grabbed me by the elbow.

"Come on," he said under his breath. "We've got to get you out of sight."

"What?" I protested, but his urgency made me lower my voice too. I hurried with him down the aisle.

"I'll explain after—here, this'll have to do. They were right behind me."

He muttered something at a door in between two of the bookcases and shoved it open. At his tug, I darted after him into the tight space on the other side. He yanked the door closed, and the room went dark except for a thin line of light that seeped in along the doorframe.

The smell of old books was even stronger now. A shelving unit pressed into my back and the shape of another loomed behind Declan. Beside us, a table and chair took up the rest of the space. When I squinted, I made out a book sitting there with a gaping split down its spine. Maybe this was a repair room?

The space was so narrow that Declan and I had ended up just a few inches apart. When I shifted on my feet to get a better sense of balance, my chest almost brushed his. A warm cedary scent rose off his body, cutting through the dry leather tang. I had the unfortunate urge to lean into it.

"What the hell is going on?" I whispered instead.

His gaze stayed fixed on the door as if he could see through it. "I overheard Victory and a couple of her friends going by downstairs. They knew you were in here —they'd figured out some way to get you in trouble with the teaching staff. Something to do with the rare books, I think. I only heard a little."

"So you came racing over to find me first?" I couldn't keep skepticism from creeping into my voice. Declan didn't have the best track record when it came to rescuing me from trouble.

"Just because I'm not going to fight all your battles for you doesn't mean I want to see you expelled. You don't deserve that."

He really should have a chat with his good friend Malcolm about the subject, then. I'd be willing to bet the large sums of money I now possessed that none other than the Nightwood scion had suggested expulsion to my other harassers as an ideal cause to take up.

"Why didn't you drag *them* off into some dark room where they couldn't be assholes, then?" I said, and the answer came to me before the words even finished leaving my mouth. "Because we wouldn't want anyone to think you're showing me any 'favoritism.' Right."

Declan sucked a breath through his teeth as if he were going to argue with my conclusion—or maybe just with the tone I'd taken—but then he jerked a finger to my lips to silence anything else I might say. My mouth tingled at his touch.

Cressida's voice filtered through the door. "She's got to be around here somewhere. We'd have seen her if she headed out."

"Maybe Sinclair wasn't paying enough attention," Victory muttered. "I should have left you to keep an eye on the stairs instead."

"Well, if she's gone, it's not as if she'll never set foot in the library again. We'll just…"

Their voices faded away as they left our nook behind. I sighed in relief where I'd tensed against the shelves. Declan's hand dropped from my mouth. I resisted the impulse to lick my lips to sustain the impression of his touch.

"They might not have totally given up," he said. "We should give them a little while to leave, and then I'll go out first to make sure the coast is clear."

"And then I just never set foot in the library again? Wonderful solution."

"Once you've passed your assessment and been

officially enrolled, it'll take a lot more for anyone to call your place here into question."

"That would be great," I said, with an edge I didn't bother restraining, "if I wasn't in here specifically because I'm trying to make sure I pass that assessment."

He turned his head. It was too dark for me to make out more than the vaguest impression of his expression, but I could tell he was looking at me.

"Where do you feel you need extra help?"

The frustration of the last several days bubbled over in a flood. "Oh, I don't know, how about not having to spend every class fending off whatever new harassment technique your friends and their sycophants have thought up next instead of actually learning? That would be pretty nice, but it's not going to happen, is it? Because torture trumps everything else at Blood U. What do you even care?"

"I'm trying to help you the best way I can," Declan said, his own voice going terse.

"Yeah, right," I shot back. "You're trying to help me the *easiest* way you can. Out of sight, where no one might actually find out you disagree with what they're doing. But hey, you get to feel good about 'doing your best'."

Declan adjusted his weight, resting his hand on the shelf beside my shoulder. "I haven't had a single thing easy my entire life. Everything I have, I had to fight for, and I have to keep fighting, or I'm going to lose it all over again. You have no idea what the hell you're talking about."

"Of course I don't. How would I? You've barely said

anything to me since I got here. Go ahead, why don't you tell me about it?"

He was standing so close I felt his hesitation in the tensing of his body. I grimaced. "Of course not. Talking to me like an equal would be treading just a little too far outside the party line, wouldn't it? God forbid you act on your own conscience even when we're totally alone in the fucking dark without a single person watching."

I waved my hand at him, and my fingers swept across his chest. A surprisingly solid chest considering how slim he was. I was abruptly twice as aware of just how little space remained between our bodies.

Declan caught my wrist. His thumb swept over my palm with a flash of heat.

"You—" he said in a rasp, and then his voice cut off as his mouth collided with mine.

I was still angry with him, but I'd also wanted to kiss Declan Ashgrave from the first moment that striking face had appeared in front of me in the midst of the worst horror of my life, and both of those facts in combination were... confusing.

My lips parted in surprise, and he tipped his head to kiss me harder. My free hand shot up to push him away, but somehow instead my fingers just closed around the folds of his shirt, clutching onto him.

His mouth tasted like sugared coffee, perfectly bittersweet. He kissed as if he were searching for something in the claiming of my mouth. I wanted to give it to him, and I also wanted him never to find it if it meant he'd keep kissing me like this.

He pressed forward, his body aligned with mine from head to foot and scorching hot as he held me against the shelves. A little noise that was somewhere between a protest and a plea for more worked from my throat.

Maybe it was the sound that shook him out of whatever had come over him. All at once, he was shoving back from me as far as he could go, which wasn't far. His back smacked into the opposite shelves. A book fell to the floor with a thump.

"*Fuck*," he said, sounding so pissed off my body went rigid. "Stay right there. Don't move. Don't touch me."

My own anger flared back to the surface. "What the fuck are you talking about? *You* kissed *me*. It wasn't my idea."

"Do you think I don't know that?" he snapped.

"No, from the way you're talking, it isn't immediately obvious."

"Just—just stop." He inhaled raggedly. "It isn't going to happen again. It shouldn't have happened at all."

He paused, and a sensation rolled over me that snuffed out my anger in an instant. A waft of fear, thick and prickling, surging up through my chest from where he stood.

"Could you please not tell anyone about this?" he said quietly.

"It'd be your word against mine anyway," I muttered, but I couldn't put much force behind the remark.

Declan Ashgrave was *scared* of me. Scared of what I could do if I revealed this moment of indiscretion.

That was what a fearmancer would do, wasn't it? Make use of every weakness they could.

"And it won't be my word at all," I added before he had to say anything else. "I'm not interested in hurting you. I don't want to hurt *anyone*. That's not who I am."

A ragged laugh escaped him. "It's too bad you ended up here, then, isn't it?" He leaned close to the door. "I think it's been long enough. I'll go out. If I haven't come back in five minutes, assume you can get out of here without Victory coming at you." He turned back to me just for a second. "And after this, stay away from me."

He ducked out without another word, leaving me alone in the dark.

CHAPTER TWENTY-THREE

Rory

I t was a good thing I had to stop for a second to fish in
my purse for my dorm keycard, because that gave me
the chance to hear Victory gloating on the other side of
the door.

"And *then* when he was done begging, I told him I'd
consider going out with him again only if he can get us
into Fuchsia next time."

Her minions laughed approvingly. I backed up a step,
dropping my keycard back into my purse.

I'd had a few hours to simmer down from the close call
in the library—in all the assorted ways I needed to—but I
wasn't sure I could take another round of the Victory
treatment tonight without probably screaming and
possibly doing something that would get me in trouble
without any scheming necessary, like setting her hair on

fire or choking her with the lovely glass sculpture I'd made for her.

Better that I found something else to occupy myself with until she either headed out for a night on the town or went to bed.

I meandered back down the stairs uncertainly. The library was a no-go zone in case an ally of hers spotted me going in and alerted her. It was getting dark out, the sun having just dropped below the western treetops. I guessed I could discover how much the social suicide of having dinner in the junior cafeteria could lower my already rock-bottom status. I didn't feel all that hungry yet, though. My stomach was still twisted up from this afternoon.

Just beyond the main doors to Ashgrave Hall, a lean figure with dark red hair was standing at the edge of the green. As I halted, debating between retreating or making a show of not being fazed, Jude crouched down and clucked his tongue. A sleek brown ferret with a dark mask across its paler face came darting through the grass to meet him. It had a little gray-furred body clamped in its jaws, a dribble of blood coloring the tiny chest.

"That was a quick hunt," Jude said to the ferret. "You must have been hungry. Eat up."

He straightened up again as the animal tore into its meal. I jerked my gaze away from the raw flesh to his face. "Your familiar?"

He didn't startle before he looked at me, so he must have noticed me coming out even if he hadn't acknowledged me. "A handy companion," he said breezily. "What do you figure we should get for you, Ice Pop? I can think of all sorts of creatures that would make excellent meals for the existing university menagerie."

The question echoed my worries about Deborah too closely for comfort. "I think I'm fine without one for now," I said stiffly. "Don't let me interrupt your dinner."

I had even less interest in eating anything myself now. I set off toward the fitness building, thinking maybe I could work out a little of the tension coiled inside me on the machines.

"FYI, I'd steer clear of the lake if I were you," Jude remarked to my back. "Connar headed that way a few minutes ago looking pretty fierce, and I'm sure you've seen what he's like." He phrased it like a warning, but his eager tone suggested he hoped I'd take it as a dare and find myself in a tough spot with his fellow scion.

He didn't know that I *had* seen what Connar was like —and that the guy had a hell of a lot more to him than the "blockhead" Malcolm used as a bodyguard.

That meant Connar hadn't told the other scions anything about what we'd talked about or what had happened between us in that spot over the lake. Whether he'd guarded that secret for himself or for me, I didn't know, but suddenly I was sure that the lake was exactly where I wanted to go.

I didn't even bother walking down to the open area of shore. I veered straight into the forest, cutting across the path and making my way up the slope. My heart beat faster as I neared the peak with a potent combination of anticipation and apprehension. Was this really the best idea? I didn't know. I just—

I stepped out from between the trees, and my feet stalled.

I was alone on the clifftop. The clearing was vacant.

Wherever Jude had seen Connar heading, it hadn't been up here.

My spirits crashed as if they'd been pummeled by a wave way bigger than anything the lake could produce. I swallowed hard.

It shouldn't matter. It wasn't as if I could even really call Connar a friend. But I'd wanted an escape, and as peaceful as this spot was, it wasn't the place that had made me feel momentarily at home.

It'd been him.

I started back down the slope, disappointment condensing into a heavy lump in my chest. I'd made it about halfway down when a snapped twig farther below brought my head up.

Connar stopped several feet below me, catching sight of me at the same moment as I noticed him. For a second, I just stared at him, a little dazed.

His chestnut brown crew cut gleamed even darker than usual, the short strands lying damp along his forehead. His pale green dress shirt clung to his muscular chest in a few places as if it were damp too.

He must have gone swimming. The thought made me shiver. I'd dipped my feet in the lake from the dock a couple days ago and winced at the chill of the water.

"Hey," he said.

"Hey. I—I just thought you might be up there. Jude said something about you coming to the lake…"

"I'm heading up there now. I felt like I needed a quick swim first." His forehead furrowed. "Are you all right?"

After weeks of putting on my best brave face for everyone, even Imogen and Shelby, even Deborah, something in me cracked open with the honest answer.

"No."

He crossed the ground between us with a few quick strides, but he stopped with a couple feet of distance still between us. "Do you want to go up there now?"

"Yes." Apparently I only had the capacity for single-word answers at the moment.

Connar didn't seem to mind. He touched my wrist to nudge me to follow him, and rather than pulling back, he let his hand slide down to clasp mine. My pulse sped up again, but this time it was only eager.

With each step, the cracking sensation inside me expanded. By the time we reached the clearing, I could hardly breathe. I turned to Connar, and his jaw tightened at my expression. His arm came up around my back tentatively.

I let myself tip my head against his chest and then lean into his embrace. The smell of him filled my lungs, slightly watery from the lake but with a smoky edge that reminded me of one of the essential oils in my parents' collection. Vetiver, maybe.

The pressure in my chest didn't exactly release, but it did ease. Everything about Connar's reaction told me that I hadn't been crazy to come here. Maybe it was *only* here that we could be this close, but that was enough. He hadn't jerked me around. He cared not just about how I was now but who I'd been before. I could be real with him in ways I wasn't sure I could be real with anyone else in my life right now.

God, did I need that.

"Do you want to talk about it?" he asked after a bit.

I shook my head. "Leave everything behind, right?"

I heard his smile in his intake of breath. "That's the beauty of this place."

The word "beauty" tugged my mind back to the last time I'd spent here with him—the way he'd talked to me, the way we'd kissed. A giddy quiver ran down through my belly, but there was something I needed to know before I ended up repeating that moment.

I pulled back and looked up at him. For once, it was still light enough, with the sun only just about to set, that I could make out the color of his eyes. They were pale blue like the sky on a slightly hazy day. I wanted to drift in his gaze like a cloud.

"Last time," I made myself say, "why did you kiss me?"

Connar's eyebrows drew together. "Because... I wanted to?" he said, as if he had the feeling he'd stumbled into a test and that the only answer he had might not be satisfactory. But that was exactly what I needed to hear. No sign of ulterior motives or regrets. He'd wanted to, and I'd wanted to kiss him back, so that was that. Honest attraction.

"Excellent," I said. "A perfectly good reason."

He relaxed with a chuckle. "Is that an invitation to give it another shot?"

My innards were still too tangled up for me to jump right in. "Can we just sit for a bit and see how it goes?"

"Sitting is pretty much all I usually do here, so I don't see why not."

At the far end of the clearing stood a tree that looked as if it'd once been two that had grown too close together and merged into one trunk. We sank down with our backs to it, Connar keeping his arm looped around my waist. I carefully let my shoulder rest against his.

Despite his swim, his body was plenty warm. The heat of it flowed into me everywhere we touched.

"So, you're okay with what happened last time?" he said. "You left in a pretty big hurry."

"Yeah, I—" I struggled to decide on the right words. "I guess I'm a little… jumpy, with everything being the way it's been."

Connar could obviously translate that vagueness just fine. His mouth twisted. He hesitated for a moment. "You know, I think there might be a way to end this before it gets any worse. A way that'll leave both you and Malcolm happy. If you knew him better—and he knew you better — There's definitely some common ground. I'm still figuring things out, but—"

An ache squeezed around my heart. I touched his chest to stop him. Was he really offering to negotiate with Malcolm on my behalf?

"I don't care about making Malcolm happy," I said. "I'd be happiest if he just left me alone. Maybe you shouldn't worry about him so much either—he seems to look after himself pretty well."

"That's not— The way it is with the scions—"

"I know," I said, softer than I'd have thought I'd be able to talk when the subject involved Malcolm in any way. "Four heads of the same dragon."

An idea struck me with so much certainty that I sat up straighter. Connar watched me curiously as I leaned forward and spread my hands over the ground.

"Hold on," I said. "I want to give you something."

Energy whirled behind my collarbone. Closing my eyes, I reached it out into the earth beneath me, the acres of rocky terrain all around, and murmured, "Metal. Together."

Shivers raced up my arms as the shreds of material wriggled up through soil and stone. I gathered it in the air between my hands like I had the shards of glass on my bed, like the ice I'd conjured in Professor Banefield's office. The lump of metal grew until it felt the right size.

"Shape." A fresh wave of energy surged through me as I molded the lump with my mind and instinctive motions of my fingers into the form I was picturing.

When I opened my eyes, I held a little dragon figurine of mottled gray metal, half the length of my palm. Its wings curved around it and its single head peered forward on its arched neck, its stance defiant but its expression gentle.

I held it out to Connar. He accepted it from me, his eyes wide with awe, and turned it over in his hand gingerly as if he were afraid he might break it.

"I hope you don't forget that you're *you* too," I said quietly. "At least some of the time, that's got to come first."

He inhaled sharply. "If you knew *me* better, you might not say that."

"I know that you're more than your 'friends' give you credit for. I know you're the only one who's bothered to really listen to me—to acknowledge who I am and what I've been through—since I got here. Why do you think I came to you?"

He looked at me with so much emotion shining in his eyes that my breath caught. "If I can be that guy for you everywhere you need it—I'll try. I'll do what I can."

"You're here," I said. "That's a start. That matters."

Connar glanced down at his dragon again. He tucked it into the pocket of his slacks. Then, in one smooth motion, he stroked his fingers over my hair and drew me into a kiss.

The press of his mouth against mine brought just as much of a thrill as it had the other night. I gripped his neck, wanting closer, wanting more.

With a careful nudge, he eased me around and onto his lap without breaking the kiss. My ass settled onto his thighs, and the heat between our bodies turned searing. A tremor both nervous and needy tingled between my legs.

He kissed me harder, and I slid my hands up under his shirt to explore the muscular planes I'd only briefly gotten to know last time. He groaned against my mouth. My lips parted with his, and he took the opportunity to capture my mouth more fully, his tongue sweeping hot over mine, his teeth grazing my lower lip. A shaky groan of my own slipped from my throat.

He tugged my blouse free from my slacks and trailed

his fingers up over my ribs to the band of my bra. As I ran my thumb over one of his taut nipples, he traced the line of the band to the clasp at my back. His mouth left mine to nip my jaw and devour my neck. His fingers pulled, and my bra released.

My skin caught fire all along the path he charted with his lips. As he nibbled the crook of my shoulder, his hands slipped under my loosened bra to cup my bare breasts. My nipples pebbled against the shifting fabric as he stroked the undersides of those curves. The faint friction, the longing for more, and the flick of his tongue over my neck left me gasping.

A sharper heat was kindling low in my belly. Maybe I didn't have a whole lot of experience in this area, but I knew that sensation. I wanted him, simple as that, insane as it might seem.

Pros and cons, I thought automatically, and whimpered as his thumbs swiveled over the peaks of my breasts with a heady spark of sensation. *Pros...*

Fuck it. It *was* simple, simple and straight-forward. I wanted him, he wanted me, and I could already tell how good it would feel. No promises, no expectations like I'd had last time. Just whatever it was in the moment, without any strings attached.

Could I have asked for a scenario more perfect, really? Tomorrow if I crossed paths with this man he'd pretend nothing had happened between us, but I'd pretend it too. It'd be a secret we shared together. Completely the opposite of the jerk who'd discarded me without warning like a piece of trash.

I yanked at Connar's shirt, and he leaned back so I could peel it off him. The sight of his naked torso up close made my mouth water. I took it in, resting my hands against his ridged abdomen and drawing them up his body to his pecs. Then I flexed my hips to sink deeper into his lap. His chest hitched at the same time mine did when the bulge in his pants met my core. The pang of need that shot through me then was nothing short of ecstatic.

"Rory," Connar said roughly, and tugged my mouth back to his. We kissed, wild and hungry, and then he stripped off my shirt and bra in a couple of brisk motions. The cooling evening air teased over my breasts. He gazed down at them, flicking one of my nipples with a jolt of pleasure and smiling when it perked up even more.

"So fucking beautiful," he said. He cupped that breast and lowered his mouth to it.

I tried to suppress a moan as his attentions sent a surge of bliss through my chest. I didn't know if anyone else was down by the lake, but a loud enough sound could travel all the way to the dock.

Connar sucked my nipple harder into his mouth, and I decided I didn't care who heard. I dug my fingers into the short but soft strands of his hair and arched my back to meet him.

He lay me on the ground with a murmur that spread a cushiony feeling beneath me. The wonders of magic. It occurred to me to question where he'd learned that trick and who else he might have used it with, but I shoved those thoughts away.

He was with me right now. He was looking at me as if he'd never wanted anyone more.

Connar hooked his fingers into the waist of my pants. His voice came out thick with desire. "I want to worship you, Princess Bloodstone."

I nodded, only half understanding what he meant but happy to take anything he'd offer when he said it like that. He slid my pants and panties down together and bent over me, kissing my belly, the dip just below my navel, and finally the sensitive center of my core.

My hips jerked up with a gasp at the brilliant pulse of pleasure. Connar stroked my thigh and brought his mouth to me again.

The heat of his breath and the movements of his tongue sent flash after flash of ecstasy through me, building into a heady flame that simply burned on and on. It flickered hotter and sharper as his tongue dipped right inside me. He grazed his teeth over my clit and then sucked hard, and I burst with a cry I couldn't restrain, bucking against his mouth.

Bliss washed over me, but the release didn't delve quite deep enough. I grasped Connar's shoulder to urge him up my body. "Please."

The mumbled request lit a fire in his eyes. He kicked off his slacks and boxers in two seconds flat. But he took his time easing down over me, one arm braced next to me, the other hand caressing my cheek.

All the concerns that had been drilled into my head woke up. "Do we have to worry about—"

He shook his head with a grin and wiggled his fingers. "Magic. I'll look after you."

After the way he already had, I believed him. He kissed me hard on the mouth and on the corner of my jaw. His cock slid against my core, and I raised my hips to meet him. With a breathless murmur that sent a faint tingling through me, he gripped my thigh and dove into me.

"Fuck," I said at the blaze of pleasure that came with him. He filled me with a delicious burn.

He laughed raggedly and kissed me. "Fuck, yes, absolutely." Then he was pulling back and plunging into me again, and both of us lost even that limited vocabulary.

I rocked up to meet him, clutching his arm, stroking his dampening chest, lost in the feel of him inside me and over me. Connar groaned and thrust faster. My second climax swelled with a quivering like magic all through my nerves.

His lips crashed against mine, and his cock pushed deeper than ever before. I clenched around him. Ecstasy swept through me, curling my toes, sizzling through my mind.

For one instant, as he made a choked sound and followed me over, not even the cliff or the lake or the ground beneath me existed. Only Connar and me.

CHAPTER TWENTY-FOUR

Connar

Nestled against me, her head tucked under my chin, Rory's body felt so delicate it sent a weirdly thrilling pang through my chest. She *wasn't* fragile—I'd seen plenty of evidence of her incredible strength—and I wouldn't have wanted her to lose that toughness. But she'd let down her guard with me, out of everyone she could have turned to. She'd let me in both emotionally and in ways that made my groin stir at the memory.

It was a brand-new sensation, one that left me a little short of breath. Alongside the exhilaration, I couldn't help wondering how long this could possibly last.

There were so many things she didn't know. *I* could leave them behind when I came up here, but I doubted anyone else would do me the same favor.

For now, I might as well enjoy every bit of the grace I'd been granted. I kissed her forehead, inhaling the caramel-sweet scent that laced her skin and her silky hair. Rory scooted even closer to me and raised her head to catch my lips with hers. The kiss was soft and tender, but my cock did a whole lot more than just stir at that.

Dear God, I did hope we got to do this again after tonight.

"I should probably go," she said, with enough regret in her voice that I couldn't have taken it as any kind of rejection. "I've got an early class tomorrow, and I haven't even eaten dinner yet."

That should have been my cue to offer to go grab a bite with her. My stomach knotted.

She grabbed her clothes and carefully reassembled her outfit, her beautiful body disappearing piece by piece beneath layers of fabric. I sat up. The night air had cooled, and it raised goosebumps on my skin now that I'd lost her warmth.

"Sometime," I said, "after I've had a chance to smooth things over, I'll take you out to dinner in town."

Her gaze snapped to me, startled. Then a smile that could have wrenched my heart in two and stitched the pieces back together spread across her face.

"I'd like that."

I watched her go, slipping into the forest both wary and confident, comfortable in the dark. The image lingered in my mind after she'd disappeared from sight.

When she'd first stumbled on me up here, I hadn't expected us to end up like this. My first instinct had been to scare her off from the spot I'd come to think of as mine. But she'd stood there so uncertain and yet defiant, not half as nervous as most of the people back at the party were of me while she asked my permission to stay a while, and it'd hit me that I could play a different part for once.

Whenever the scions had a problem, I was the automatic bad cop: the intimidator, the implicit and sometimes explicit threat. With Rory Bloodstone, Malcolm and Jude already seemed to have that role covered between them. Which left an opening for me to be the good cop. Put her at ease. Get her talking about her thoughts and feelings. Figure out how to lead her into the fold where she belonged. End the war without any more bloodshed.

That'd been the plan, anyway. Maybe it was a stretch for me, but I'd figured it was worth a shot.

The problem was, the more we'd talked, the more I just wanted to keep talking with her for the sake of getting to know her. She wasn't like anyone I'd ever known.

And she didn't see me like anyone I'd known ever had.

I reached for my shirt and pulled it on, considering my best move with Malcolm. There had to be a way I could make him see he'd taken his campaign far enough. Wouldn't it be better to have a fierce woman like Rory Bloodstone on our side, unbroken, than to keep battering away at her strength?

He was pissed off because he thought she'd attacked him first in an attempt to challenge our authority here. To him, this was a battle for dominance. But everything I'd seen and heard from Rory told me it wasn't like that for her at all. She didn't give a shit who ruled Blood U. She was fighting tooth and nail just to survive.

I knew what that kind of desperation tasted like.

The others didn't. The three of them had been scion from the day they were born. I just had to figure out how to put it to Malcolm so he'd understand. I was still working on that part.

After I tugged on my pants, I touched the left pocket to make sure Rory's dragon hadn't fallen out. The feel of it under my fingers brought a smile to my face.

I texted Malcolm on my way down from the cliff, and he replied that he was in "the basement." I headed to Ashgrave Hall.

Before we'd even been moved over to seniors, Malcolm had found out about the half-empty storage rooms under the library and demandingly cajoled Ms. Grimsworth into letting him turn one of them into a private lounge area just for the scions. When I came in, he and Jude were standing around the pool table, Jude bent over to take a shot. The leather couches at the other end of the room around the widescreen TV and video game systems were unoccupied.

Sometimes we brought down other students we were feeling friendly toward, but it was nice to have a space that was only ours.

Jude's shot sunk two balls. He laughed at Malcolm's disgruntled curse and turned to face me. "Conn! Cooled off sufficiently? Our Ice Queen headed your way not too long ago—I hope you didn't take her head off."

"As far as I know, it's still attached to her neck," I said in as mild a tone as I could manage, and went to the bar cabinet that the maintenance staff kept stocked for us.

I had to find the right way to explain myself soon or this mess would just keep getting bigger. I poured myself a scotch and tossed back a gulp that burned all the way down to my stomach.

Malcolm sank a ball with a clatter. He leaned against the pool table as Jude considered his options.

"Darksend was making noises about shipping you off to that tourney again," Malcolm said. "The man doesn't know when to quit. I reminded the administration how *very* important it is to the rest of the scions that we continue our education together."

My stomach had dropped at the mention of the professor's name. Since I'd been in his class two years ago, Professor Darksend had been campaigning to have me join an international tourney in Physicality that basically amounted to a magical MMA competition. "It's only a couple of months away from your studies!" he'd go on. "An excellent opportunity to show off your skills and make a name for yourself."

It didn't seem to matter to him that I'd prefer not to build my name beyond where it already was by bashing around people I didn't even know and had nothing against. And unfortunately, my parents loved the idea. If it hadn't been for Malcolm's periodic interventions whenever the registration re-opened, I'd have already found myself in a deathmatch either in the ring or at home.

"Thanks," I said, that one word not enough to cover the rush of relief and gratitude that swept through me.

"Hey," Malcolm said with a grin. "I need you here, not off on a rampage for some stupid title."

He'd never made me explain why I wasn't interested. I'd just told him I wanted nothing to do with it, and that was all he'd needed to know.

Jude took his next shot with an extravagant flourish that bit him in the ass—he only nicked the ball he'd wanted to hit. He spun the pool cue in his hand as if he didn't particularly care, which knowing Jude he might not.

"What's the next step in our rampage against the Bloodstone?" he asked. "We've only got a week before she's up for re-assessment."

"I've got Victory gathering intel so we can make the next big hit really count," Malcolm said. "She was incredibly happy to pitch in to the effort. I'll hassle her if she doesn't report back soon. In the meantime, just keep on keeping the good witch on her toes."

"Not a problem." Jude smirked. "I've been enjoying the view along the way."

Malcolm smacked him in the leg with the end of his cue. "Don't get any ideas," he said in a tone that made my insides clench up.

"Who, me?"

"I know what you're like, Mr. Hit and Split."

"Oh, and you figure this girl's too good for that?"

Malcolm gave him a narrow smile. "She *is* a scion. There's a lot more to her than a pretty face and a nice ass. I'm looking forward to finding out what she can do with all that spirit once we smash the spite and show her what it's like to be a real part of the pentacle. On the off-chance that my charms have no effect, you're welcome to step in and see if she likes yours better. Until then, she's off limits."

Jude rolled his eyes, but with only casual annoyance. "I didn't realize you had a crush."

"Oh, please. As if you hadn't noticed she's the most interesting thing to walk through those doors since we started here." Malcolm's smile softened slightly around the edges, and my gut constricted into one huge lump.

I hadn't realized he was thinking about Rory as anything other than an opponent. He'd been so intent on his campaign to knock her down that it'd never occurred to me he might want her by his side after he'd brought her to her knees.

While my best friend had been looking out for me tonight, I'd been betraying him without even knowing it.

There must have been signs; I just hadn't picked up on them. I'd been too caught up in getting to play good cop —and thinking with my dick rather than my head. Fuck.

What the hell did I do now?

CHAPTER TWENTY-FIVE

Rory

I f I had to pick a favorite class at Villain Academy—
because while I was stuck here, I might as well—it
should have been my Seminar in Physicality. My instincts
seemed to be strongest in that area, probably because I'd
spent so much time bringing my imagination into reality
in my former life, and it was my only class that didn't
force me to deal with any of the scions or Victory and her
main gang.

Basically, everything was perfect except for the fact
that I was starting to think that Professor Viceport
hated me.

I couldn't have pointed to one obvious piece of proof.
It was just a whole bunch of little things. Whenever she
called on me or answered a question I asked, her tone
sounded several degrees chillier than with the other
students. Her nose appeared to wrinkle in mild distaste

when she examined anything I'd conjured or transformed. And even though I'd managed to work more magic in this class than any other, she hadn't offered a single encouraging word.

I'd have thought she simply wasn't the encouraging type, except right now she was gushing over a spoon the girl next to me had transformed out of a stick. It didn't look like an especially amazing spoon to me. Maybe there was some special hurdle in spoon creation that I wasn't aware of.

In any case, after three classes of that treatment, I figured it couldn't hurt to bring up the subject. If I was screwing up in some way I hadn't realized, I'd like to know before my impending assessment.

When Professor Viceport dismissed the class, I waited until the other students had filed out of the smaller gymnasium in the Stormhurst Building where we'd gathered today. The professor crouched down to gather the supplies she'd brought along. As I approached her, she peered at me over the top of her rectangular glasses. She was skinny in a way she managed to make look elegant rather than awkward, her ash-blond pixie cut wisping along my forehead. It didn't soften the ice in her eyes.

She straightened up. "Can I help you, Miss Bloodstone?" she asked in a tone that said she really didn't want to.

I clamped down on my nerves. I was a freaking scion. It was her job to teach me. I shouldn't be anxious.

"Yes. I just—I've gotten the impression that you're not totally happy with the work I've been doing," I said. "I'm trying my best, but obviously it'll take some time for me to get the hang of things after being out of the loop for so long. If there are any factors you think I should focus on more, or any other corrections I should make…" I trailed off at the pursing of her lips.

"If you're 'trying your best,' I'm sure that's all I can expect," she said crisply. "You are a Bloodstone, after all."

What was that supposed to mean? It wasn't as if I'd gained any benefit from a family I'd never known.

"I only meant, if I'm missing something—" I started.

"Don't worry yourself about it. You've got all the advantages you need." She spun on her heel and strode out of the room, cutting off any further conversation.

Okay, then. That hadn't been the most productive conversation of my university days. She *definitely* had a problem with me, but she also definitely didn't want to talk about it, so I guessed I was shit out of luck if I wanted any advice from that corner.

I shouldered my purse and slipped out after her. April showers had rolled in again late last night, and the sky was still clotted with clouds. I tugged my jacket closer against the damp wind.

Two clusters of guys had gathered on the field near Ashgrave Hall. The farther bunch I didn't recognize at a distance, but the one closer to me was made up of the four scions. Wonderful.

As I eyed them, a dark shape swooped down out of the sky. A hawk. And then another, diving from a different angle toward the same spot. Both groups of guys let out a cheer, urging them on.

The first hawk jerked up at the last second, its feet skimming the ground. It rose again with a chipmunk clutched in its talons. The scions let out another whoop. The other group muttered with frowns all around. The first hawk soared over to Declan, dropping the limp chipmunk at his feet and coming to land on his shoulder. The other bird perched on the wrist of the boy at the head of the opposing group.

"Best two out of three!" that guy hollered.

"If you want to get beaten that badly, how can we turn down the invitation?" Jude called back.

Just another one of their cruel little games.

My gaze lingered for a moment on Connar at the back of the pack, but he didn't glance my way. All of them were so focused on the competition that they hadn't noticed me heading toward them.

I wasn't sure I'd have wanted them to. Remembering the way Declan had told me to stay away from him yesterday after he'd kissed me made me queasy. Veering to the left, I gave them and their playing field a wide berth.

I kept my eyes fixed on the stone side of Ashgrave Hall looming ahead of me, as if I hadn't noticed them either. The guys were having a hushed discussion about the "bait." Ugh. I picked up my pace even faster.

Then a harsh voice carried across the space between us. "Yeah, just keep running, Princess."

My head snapped around with a lurch of my heart. That had sounded almost like—

Not almost like. Exactly like. Because it was. Connar had turned, his arms crossed tight over the expanse of his chest, his gaze burning into me so fiercely my pulse stuttered a second time. He was the one who'd made that snarky remark, calling me "Princess" like he had last night.

My mind refused to compute. If it'd been any of the other scions, I'd have given him the middle finger and walked on. But—Connar— This had to be a mistake. He'd never torn into me before, no matter where we'd been. He'd said—

The other guys had turned to watch. Malcolm clapped his hand to Connar's shoulder. "You tell her, Conn," he said with an amused grin.

"What are you staring at?" Connar said, so sharp the words stung my skin. "Do you need another reminder of who you're messing with?"

A lump rose in my throat. "Connar—"

He cut me off before I could get out more than his name. "How about it, Princess? We're still going to need to see you on your knees. You don't mind getting down in the dirt, do you? You can start begging any time now."

I backpedaled and swung around on abruptly shaky legs. The other guys' laughter pealed after me. "Nice," Jude said to Connar.

That wasn't the guy I'd talked to last night. But it was. It was exactly who I should have known he was.

My earlier nausea surged up from my gut. I clenched my teeth and all but ran the last several feet to the building. Heat prickled behind my eyes.

No. I was not going to cry over that bastard. That fucking bastard who'd been so tender with me before and then—

Why had I let myself trust him? I *did* know what everyone in this place was like, the scions especially. How had I been so stupid to think the affection he'd shown me was genuine?

Just like the guy before him, he'd gotten what he wanted and kicked me to the curb. Only the fearmancer version of the kicking was a lot closer to literal—and much more painful.

A few of my dormmates were hanging out in the common room when I burst in. Imogen was carrying a cup of tea from the kitchen to her bedroom. Her steps faltered when she saw me, and a flicker of emotion I couldn't decipher crossed her face.

"Hey," she said. "I was about to head down to the library to grab a few books. You want to come with?"

She hadn't looked like she was heading to the library, and her voice was weirdly bright. Or maybe I was doing a better job of hiding my inner turmoil than it felt like.

"No," I said. "That, um, that's okay."

"Come find me if you change your mind," she said, raising her cup of tea, and breezed past me out the door.

The girls who were sitting in a cluster in the lounge area leaned closer to each other with emphatic murmurs that might or might not have been about me. I glanced toward Shelby's door, but a hoarse coughing filtered through it at the same moment. My stomach twisted even harder at the thought of turning to her. She'd looked pretty out of it when I'd seen her this morning. She needed *my* help more than I should need hers.

I couldn't tell her even a tenth of the things that were bothering me anyway.

I hustled into my own bedroom. My magical security system was still in place, at least. I ducked inside, recast the spell with a few muttered words, and collapsed onto the bed.

The tears I'd been fighting started to leak out despite my best efforts. I squeezed my eyes shut as if that would keep them in.

A faint rustling sounded from the wardrobe. A moment later, Deborah burrowed between my arms and my chest. Her whiskers tickled my palm.

What happened, sweetheart?

"Nothing important," I whispered. Was it stupid even to feel this hurt when I hadn't expected last night to mean all that much anyway? How had I gotten my head turned around so badly?

I stroked my thumb over Deborah's fur. "I hate it here. I hate all these people. I don't—"

I didn't know what I was doing. I didn't know if I could keep doing it, keep going, until I figured out some kind of plan to turn the tables on everyone here. But where could I go that would be any better?

They're awful, Deborah agreed without hesitation. *You've learned some tricks. We could make a run for it now. If we plan it right, we could probably get to California before they catch up.*

And then what? The joymancers would throw me in whatever jail they had, and the fearmancers would slaughter them like they had my parents to drag me back out.

Until I brought down this center of fearmancer society and as much of the rest as I could, there was nowhere I could run that would do me or anyone else any good.

"No," I said softly, petting Deborah again. "It's okay. I'll be okay." But for the first time since I'd decided to destroy Villain Academy, I couldn't shake the cold wash of fear that had come over me.

CHAPTER TWENTY-SIX

Rory

There was something deeply unnerving about meeting a figure in the flesh whom you'd only before seen in a sort-of dream. As I headed out of Ashgrave Hall, a man fell into step beside me. I glanced up at him, and my pulse hiccupped. I stopped in my tracks.

I'd seen that golden-brown hair flecked with gray and those familiar features grown tighter with age in my brief venture into Malcolm's mind. His father, because that had to be who this man was, looked even more like the Nightwood scion now that he stood before me in reality.

The apple didn't fall far from the tree. My stance tensed.

The man gave me a smile that was about as warm as his son's usually was—so, not particularly. "Miss Bloodstone. I take it you know who I am."

"Mr. Nightwood," I said automatically.

"*Baron* Nightwood," he corrected in a firm tone that suggested I'd better remember that title next time. "I was hoping we might speak for a bit."

A chat with one of the four current rulers of the fearmancer world. With the most powerful current ruler, if the dynamics between the scions were anything to go by. I swallowed against the sudden dryness of my mouth. Why was Malcolm's dad coming to me here and now?

What were the chances he was any less of an asshole than his son? I'd have to assume pretty much nil. He'd had at least a couple more decades to perfect his cruelty.

I'd never thought I'd wish to have Malcolm Nightwood in front of me, but I'd have been overjoyed if he'd swept in to replace Baron Nightwood in this moment.

"What did you want to talk about?" I said, relieved just to hear my voice stay steady. Was he going to remove me from the university before I even had the chance to complete my assessment? Malcolm had said the barons were the only ones who could reverse a dismissal, so no doubt they could also impose one.

Baron Nightwood ushered me away from the entrance to stand near a windowless portion of the building. I'd have taken more comfort from the fact that we were in view of the green if I hadn't seen how enthusiastically a Nightwood could make use of an audience for amplified torture.

"I apologize for not introducing myself and welcoming you home sooner," he said. "I thought it best to give you time to settle in before making more impositions on your attention than you must already be facing."

I blinked at him. Baron Nightwood was... apologizing... to me? Was this part of some weird reverse psychology voodoo?

"Um," I said, "that's totally okay. I've kind of had my hands full."

The corners of his mouth twitched so slightly I couldn't tell whether he'd mastered a smile or a frown. Maybe he was amused thinking of all the ways his son had contributed to my preoccupation.

"Well, now that you've had the chance to adjust, we of the barony wanted to invite you to begin stepping into your ultimate role as baron yourself."

For the second time in as many minutes, I found myself lost for words. "I thought—I was told that I couldn't become baron until I graduated."

This time Baron Nightwood definitely smiled, as coolly as before. "Not officially. But we've been without a true fifth in our pentacle for nearly two decades now. It has made effective governing somewhat difficult. We'd like to see you transition in as quickly as you're able to. The rights and the authority are unquestionably yours. Why should you be denied them even longer?"

This didn't make any sense. I'd been defying his son at every turn. Why would he want to give me *more* authority? I had to be missing something here.

"I'm not sure I'm ready for that," I said cautiously.

Baron Nightwood waved off my hesitation. "We wouldn't expect a lot from you to begin with. And this situation isn't without precedent, you know. Declan Ashgrave has been acting in nearly all respects as baron for a few years now even though his position isn't entirely official yet."

Something Declan had said before clicked into place in my head. His mother had died in the same altercation that my birth parents had. She must have been the previous Ashgrave baron. He'd been thrust into this role way earlier than I had.

Not that the fact gave him an excuse for being a jerk.

"What exactly are you looking for me to do at this point?" I asked. This guy did know that I wasn't even officially enrolled as a student here yet, didn't he?

"We have a meeting of the pentacle in two days," Baron Nightwood said. "We'd like you to attend so that you can... get up to speed on our current concerns. I can arrange your transport from and back to the university. Ms. Grimsworth has already approved your absence from the one class you'd miss."

He'd thought of everything, hadn't he? Why was it so very important to him—and maybe the other barons— that I get involved now?

Uneasiness prickled down my back. I didn't want to go anywhere in a vehicle owned by the Nightwoods, and definitely not into a meeting with the four most powerful fearmancers in the country. And it was conveniently right before my assessment. Could they do something to make sure I failed, something I wouldn't even be able to identify?

Malcolm had grinned when he'd talked about the pentacle families having me in their power.

On the other hand, it was possible the barons just

wanted to get on with their politics, and I might find out something useful there.

As I wavered, Shelby came out the doors of the hall, her ponytail swishing and her stride light with more energy than I'd seen from her in about a week. Whatever she'd been sick from, it must have passed. I caught her eye and raised my hand in a wave with a relieved smile. She bobbed her head with a shy smile in return.

Baron Nightwood followed the exchange with narrowed eyes. His lip curled with distaste when his gaze came back to me. "What was that about?"

"She's a friend," I said. Had he never seen someone wave hello before?

"A friend," he repeated in the same tone. "I realize your upbringing was rather unusual, but one of the first things you need to learn is that a mage of your standing does *not* associate with the feebs any more than you have to. You certainly shouldn't be considering them friends. It appears our guidance would be of a lot of use to you."

My hackles came up in an instant. There was the familiar Nightwood attitude. The words came out before I had a chance to think them through.

"I'm about as interested in the kind of guidance you're talking about as I am in your son's, which is not at all. The only person who'll decide who I'm friends with is me."

Baron Nightwood sighed. "Miss Bloodstone, I meant no offense, only counsel. Once you get to know the wider forces of our society—"

"And I will," I said. "Get to know them. This just isn't a good time. I've got too many other things to concentrate on." *Like making it through the next few days without getting crushed by your son and* his *asshole friends.* "Get back to me after I've passed my assessment and know what I have to offer, and then I'll see about attending one of those meetings."

A flicker of anger passed through the baron's eyes, but I wasn't inclined to stick around to find out how much I might regret the decision I'd just made.

"Now hold on a moment," he said, his voice going from cool to chilling, and I took a few steps back.

"Sorry, I've got to run. My mentor's expecting me for our morning session."

And then I took off toward Killbrook Hall as quickly as I could walk without literally running.

The barons wanted something, and whatever it was, I had trouble believing it meant anything good for me. Maybe I'd be better equipped to tangle with them later, but right now I was having a hard enough time just defending myself against their heirs.

I hadn't quite escaped yet. Baron Nightwood rolled a sharp syllable off his tongue, and my feet jolted to a halt beneath me. The soles wouldn't lift from the ground. I twisted around to see him striding over to me. The haughty expression on his face and the brutal gleam in his eyes brought out the same divine devil I'd seen in his son.

He stopped in front of me and peered down at me for just long enough that I wanted to squirm.

"I'll give you a reprieve in light of your current circumstances and your history," he said, low and cutting. "But the next time I call on your attendance, it'll be an order, not a request. You're not baron yet, and you don't defy the barons you have. Are we clear, Miss Bloodstone?"

Provoking him further didn't seem like the wisest idea, at least not if I ever wanted to use my feet again.

"I understand," I said. And I did. I understood that he was the biggest asshole of them all.

"Good." He snapped his fingers, and the magic holding me released. "Run along then."

The breeze chilled the sweat that had formed on the back of my neck as I hurried the rest of the way to Killbrook Hall. Professor Banefield was waiting for me on the landing outside the staff residences.

"Sorry I'm late," I said quickly, my heart still thumping double-time. "I—I got a little delayed."

"It's all right," he said, motioning me back down the stairs. "It just means I'll explain what I have planned for today on the way over. I've arranged a private session for you with Professor Razeden."

My feet nearly tripped over each other. "For Desensitization?"

Banefield nodded. "I understand your first session was rather traumatic, and I know you've been under a lot of stress with your approaching assessment. It hardly seemed out of line to allow you a chance to navigate your fears without an audience. Professor Razeden will be able to give his full attention to guiding you through."

I should have been grateful. It would be a real help to get a handle on the whole desensitization process without Jude and whoever else looking over my shoulder. But the thought of facing that murder scene all over again, especially right after my clash with Baron Nightwood, made me want to vomit.

I just had to get through it. That was the whole point —learning how to make it through. With every fear I found the tools to withstand, there'd be one fewer way for the scions to hurt me.

Baron Nightwood had already departed from the green. I breathed slow and steady as we came up to the tower that bore the same name, working to calm my nerves.

No one was going to see this except my mentor and the professor who must have seen all kinds of fears over the years. There was nothing to be self-conscious about. And at least this time I knew what to expect. It wouldn't be real. Nothing could hurt my parents ever again.

Not even me.

Professor Razeden met us in the room with the benches outside the main chamber. He dipped his head to me in greeting. "Miss Bloodstone. I'm glad we'll have the opportunity to develop your baseline coping skills in a more intensive fashion."

He didn't look all that glad, but I wasn't sure that gaunt face was capable of looking really happy. "Okay," I said. "I'd like to cope better next time too."

"I want you to listen to my voice now," he said as he led us into the chamber. His dry, even tone echoed through the room. "Focus on it, and keep listening for it after the session begins. I'll walk you through the steps to shutting down your fear. If you start to get overwhelmed, go still and avoid interacting with your surroundings until you have a plan of action. Shall we begin?"

I nodded, swallowing the lump in my throat. If we were doing this, better to get it over with ASAP.

My shoes rapped against the glossy tiles as I walked into the center of the chamber. Razeden took his spot near the door, Banefield standing a little awkwardly on the other side of it. Maybe it'd help him understand where I was coming from better when he got a glimpse of how horrible my "rescue" had really been.

"Begin," Professor Razeden said, and the light went out.

A glow spread out around me. I braced myself, but... it wasn't the shiny white of my parents' kitchen. The room seemed to have expanded into a vast space lit by yellowish panels overhead. Four figures stepped into the light in a ring around me, and my stomach flipped over.

I was in the large gym in the Stormhurst Building where I'd had my first assessment. But it wasn't the professors who'd conducted the test before who surrounded me. It was the scions.

"*Dance*," Malcolm said with a vicious smile, and snapped his fingers the way his father had. My legs leapt up beneath me, springing this way and that in a ridiculous cavorting. They spun me toward Jude.

The other guy's smirk looked even sharper than usual under his dark copper hair. He raised his hands, and a searing heat shot up over me, an illusion that set my nerves screaming as if they'd actually been set on fire. A cry broke from my mouth.

Declan's voice rang out behind me. "You know you're not good enough. Stop kidding yourself, Rory. I can see every thought in your head. You're hanging on by a thread. Any second it's going to snap, and we'll see exactly how weak you really are."

My dance was more like a flailing now. Tears welled in my eyes at the burn still racing under my skin. I stumbled around toward Connar, whose face was as hard as stone. He stomped on the ground, and a metal disc as high as his waist rose up, gouging the floor with its razor edges as it screeched toward me.

Through the blur of pain and panic, I managed to make out Professor Razeden's voice. "You can do this, Miss Bloodstone. It's their power that frightens you, but you have power too. Summon your own magic to push theirs back."

Right. They weren't real. I just had to prove to myself that I was strong enough to withstand them. I pressed my hand to my chest, trying to feel the hum of magic there amid the burning.

My legs ached as they jittered on beneath me. "Don't make me laugh," Declan went on with a sneer. "Everything you've done since you got here has been a mistake. You keep shooting your mouth off without a clue how to back it up."

I dodged the razor disc, and Connar swung his arm. The air shoved me into the spinning edge as if he'd pushed me from across all that space. The blades sliced through my side all the way down to my ribs. I cried out again at the spear of pain that shot through my chest.

"Fight back!" Razeden hollered from beyond my view. "Shield yourself and hit them hard."

"Stop," I mumbled, but the word didn't catch any magic inside me. I tried to concentrate on the steel wall I'd snapped into place around my mind the other day, but at the same moment Jude switched up his illusion. The heat fell away just in time for a cloud of shrieking wasps to descend on me. Fresh pain pinched all over my body where their stingers jabbed me.

Where was my magic? I did have it. I should be able to do *something*.

"Away," I murmured, with a surge of energy from behind my sternum. The wasps shuddered, several of them disintegrating into the air like the nothing they were.

Then Malcolm's voice rang out again. "*Hand to your throat.*"

My arm jerked up before I could stop it. My fingers clamped around my throat. I tensed my muscles to wrench them away, but they didn't budge.

"*Squeeze*," Malcolm said.

My hand clenched. My breath cut off with a ragged gasp. A deeper ache shot through my throat and the sides of my neck as I fought for air. I had to stop him. I had to shut them all out.

"You think you're so perfect, but you know we have the real power here," Declan said. "You're on your own. Why would anyone want to help you when you can't even hold yourself together?"

I strained, but I couldn't reach my magic past the choking pressure on my throat and the panicking through my chest. I couldn't grasp hold of one more shred of the energy inside me.

My head started to spin. I dropped to my knees.

The Desensitization session faded away around me, leaving only the bare floor, the black walls, and the two professors watching my hand fall limply from my throat.

I'd failed an imaginary assessment. If I didn't perform better at the real one, I'd end up in an even worse position than the torment I'd just survived.

CHAPTER TWENTY-SEVEN

Declan

E very time I stepped into the room where the meetings of the pentacle were held, a little vise closed around my gut and didn't let go until I was in my car driving away again. The other barons dipped their heads with due respect and smiled their thin smiles, but I could hardly call any of them friendly colleagues.

And then there was Aunt Ambrosia, both my closest living blood relative and the person who'd most like to see my blood spilling all over this fine hardwood floor, always hovering at my side watching for the slightest slip.

She still had the right to sit next to me at the large rowan-wood table with its pentacle etching, the two of us on either side of the Ashgrave point. Until I finished my last year at Blood U, her word would hold some weight here.

"You look a little tired, Declan," she said in her syrupy

voice as we took our seats. "I hope the additional workload isn't wearing you out too much."

Today, her black hair coiled in loops over her ears before cascading down her back. It was a style my mother —her sister—had often worn when she'd been baron. I'd seen it in many of the old pictures. Aunt Ambrosia's dress, heavy velvet that didn't fit the season, recalled my mother's fashion sense too. It made me feel ill watching her trying to transform herself into the long-gone woman whom I'd barely known, as if the imitation would make it easier to take my mother's place.

I'd taken on the teacher's aide position specifically to show how much work I could handle, and I didn't imagine I looked any more tired than usual. If I did, it had nothing to do with schoolwork. More likely the memory of a hot mouth against mine in the dark.

"Everything is going well, but thank you for your concern, Aunt Ambrosia," I said.

"Have you heard from your brother lately? It is such a shame having him so far away when we have an excellent school right here."

I resisted the urge to clench my hands. Needling me about how I'd influenced my younger brother's life since I'd taken over guardianship of him from her three years ago had been one of her favorite bones of contention.

Marguerite Stormhurst, Connar's mother, jerked open the curtains to let what light and warmth the windows allowed to enter the gloomy space. She moved with the same athletic power he had, but her body was wiry rather than bulky with muscle.

"Do you still have Noah in that school in France?" she asked me in her blunt way. "Do you really think they'll teach him anything over there he won't learn just as well here?"

"I figure it broadens his horizons to spend some time studying with fearmancers he'd never have met otherwise," I said. "And now that I'm an aide at the university, it wouldn't be right to risk inadvertent favoritism. When I graduate, I'll have him transfer over here the following semester."

All of that was true, but the larger reason that I'd never have said to anyone in this room was I'd wanted to keep Noah away from the politics at home and the potential threats that circulated alongside them. The kid was only seventeen. He'd been just an infant when our mother had died, but he was nearly as much a target for Aunt Ambrosia as I was. The longer I could ensure he stayed far from this vicious circle, the better.

Baron Stormhurst wouldn't have understood my concern at all. She was only baron because she and her husband had destroyed her older brother's family thirteen years ago. No one had any proof that the series of accidents and illnesses had been their fault, of course, because that would have been sloppy, but everyone *knew*.

Just like everyone knew what had happened between Connar and his brother right before they turned fifteen.

Edmund Killbrook, Jude's father, rested his elbows on the tabletop where he'd already taken his seat. He was even more sharp angles than his son, his hair a sandy blond. Jude's deep red came from his mother.

"I hope he doesn't come back with the airs the European mages like to put on," he said flatly.

Julian Nightwood, Malcolm's father, strode to his seat with a click of his dress shoes against the floor. Looking at him was like looking thirty-two years into the future to the middle-aged man Malcolm would become.

Baron Killbrook's gaze slid to the empty point of the pentacle where a chair sat waiting for the next Bloodstone baron. He turned to Nightwood as the other man sat down. "I thought you were going to bring the Bloodstone girl."

Nightwood frowned. "The Bloodstone girl is in need of several good slaps before she sets foot in this room. The joymancers clearly addled her head. The sooner we can wring that influence out of her, the better." He glanced at me. "You've had plenty of chances to observe her and intervene, Ashgrave. It appears she's proved beyond the abilities of both you and our sons."

"She lived with the joymancers for seventeen years," I said, as impassively as I could. "She's only been at the university for four weeks. Retraining instincts and inclinations takes time."

Stormhurst let out a huff as she dropped into her chair. "We've given it enough time. We've been *waiting* seventeen years. To be on the verge, and then—" She sucked a breath through her teeth. "There has to be a way to speed the process along."

"From what Malcolm's said, he's come up with an idea he expects to throw her off before her assessment," Nightwood said. "If her magic fails to activate fully, it's likely she'll be dismissed, and then we'll be in a much better position to direct her."

"Are we going to leave it to the scions again, then?" Killbrook said.

Nightwood leaned back in his chair, his gaze going distant for a moment. "Malcolm has made some progress. He's intimidated her enough that she was frightened just seeing me. I think we should be above meddling with the university procedures." He raised his eyes. "But if his next gambit fails, we'll want to turn to other tactics. I agree that we've waited long enough already."

Other tactics. I didn't know exactly what the rest of the pentacle had been waiting for or how Rory would fit in, but it must have been big. It was only the core laws of our society that couldn't be overturned without the agreement of five rightful barons—which meant when you only had three or four, there wasn't even any point in talking about it. The best I'd gathered was that the pentacle had been preparing to make some major move before the confrontation that had left them missing one and with only a regent for another.

Whatever their intention was, I didn't think my mother had agreed with it. I had vague memories of her venting to my father about "the four of them" and how they meant to "destroy everything" in the weeks before she'd vanished from my life.

Sometimes I wondered if her death had really been entirely at the hands of the joymancers, or if someone else in the vicinity might have shoved her into the line of fire with the thought that a child would be easier to mold to the attitudes they wanted.

Stormhurst grimaced. "All right. I trust you're prepared to carry out the necessary measures as needed, Ashgrave?" Her cold eyes met mine.

Whatever the other barons were after, they wanted it badly. I could taste the current of impatience that ran through the room. The vise around my gut tightened.

Challenges between students was one thing. All of us mages on campus stood on at least somewhat equal footing. If the *barons* started sabotaging Rory's progress, that wasn't just natural squabbling or familial in-fighting. That was plotting treason against the sole remaining member of one of the pentacle families. We were supposed to each govern our own.

My frustrations with Rory were far more my fault than hers. That moment in the library—so close to her with so many emotions stirred up, her scent everywhere and her hand brushing over me like a caress—I'd lost control for one reckless, blissful, stupid moment. *So* fucking stupid.

It wasn't just my brother I was shielding as I staked a claim at this table but the other scions too. They deserved to be able to complete their time at Blood U unencumbered by the weight I'd had to shoulder so much earlier than most barons did. Rory deserved better than a double-edged welcome home. She'd barely had a chance to find her feet. Given a little more time, I had the feeling she'd become something magnificent, just perhaps not in the way these people wanted.

But if I said anything against the suggestion that we

undercut her position, I'd be putting my neck—and my brother's—on the line. No one here liked Aunt Ambrosia. I'd seen that quickly enough, and it'd worked in my favor more than once. But if I actively protested the other barons' plans, I expected I'd find those treasonous intentions turned against me in two seconds flat. They'd hand her the knife and point out exactly where to stab it.

So when Nightwood's gaze came to rest on me too, I smiled the same thin smile back at them and said, "I'll do whatever I can in support of our interests on campus."

CHAPTER TWENTY-EIGHT

Rory

The morning of my second assessment, I stood under the shower for several minutes with the hot water cranked. Steam hazed the air and filled my lungs, but the heat didn't melt the nervous tension in my chest.

It had to be okay. I'd felt tons of magic since that last assessment. I'd cast all kinds of spells. Maybe I was still getting the hang of it, but there was no denying I was a mage.

But what if I wasn't enough of one? What if whatever had gone wrong last time went wrong again?

I dashed across the common room to my bedroom and slipped into the outfit I'd already laid out on my bed. My dragon charm settled against my collarbone. Then I turned to study myself in the wardrobe's mirror.

Still damp despite my efforts with the towel, my hair looked almost black as I combed my fingers through the tight waves. My dark blue eyes stood out starkly against my pale face. The black pantsuit I'd picked out had struck me as powerful on the hanger, but seeing it on my body only emphasized my overall impression.

That was a fearmancer staring back at me. Powerful or pathetic, every inch of me fit the role now.

No matter how hard I fought, Villain Academy was absorbing me.

The uncomfortable thought made the tension in my chest twist sharply. I shook it away and knelt down to get a little last-minute encouragement from my familiar.

"Deborah?" I murmured, waiting for her to poke her little white head from between the socks.

She didn't emerge. Maybe she'd gone for a walk around the room to stretch her legs? "Deborah?" I said again, as loud as I dared while a few of my dormmates lingered in the common room.

No streak of white fur darting toward me. No patter of mousey feet. No reassuring voice popping into my head. The twisting sensation turned into a knot of fear.

She'd never left the bedroom before. She'd have told me if she'd decided to, wouldn't she, so that I wouldn't freak out?

I inhaled deeply and tried to exhale my nerves along with my breath. Jumping to conclusions wouldn't do me any good. She'd probably just fallen asleep somewhere and hadn't woken at my voice.

I pawed through the socks gently, my spirits ready to leap at the sight of her curled body. It never appeared. I checked the other drawers and then all around the bed and the baseboard, my heart thumping harder with each spot I found vacant.

Either she'd suddenly gone off exploring without giving me any warning, even though she knew this morning was the key to my future, or... someone had taken her.

I'd replaced the security spell on the door before I'd gone to the shower, hadn't I? It'd become so automatic, I couldn't remember whether I'd needed to take it down when I'd come back in afterward.

Of course, even if I had, there were at least a few mages around here strong enough to break through my work.

My stomach listed as I came out into the common room. One of the girls sitting at the kitchen table looked up. She took me in, and her mouth flattened.

"Victory and Malcolm Nightwood were doing something by your room while you were washing up," she said quickly, as if she'd been waiting to spit out that line.

My stomach, my heart, and the knot in my chest—they all plummeted to my feet. "Do you know where they went?" I asked, my voice sounding weirdly distant to my own ears.

"They mentioned hanging out in the basement," the girl said with that same reciting sort of tone. Had she volunteered to tell me, or had Malcolm persuaded her into it?

It didn't really matter. I ran for the door.

The basement. What basement? The question chased after me as I raced down the stairs, wishing I had a few fewer flights to descend instead of my lovely bedroom view. Was there even a basement in this building? Had she been talking about the Desensitization chamber in Nightwood Tower? I couldn't imagine anyone hanging out there, and the girl hadn't said it that way.

At the bottom of the stairs, I circumnavigated the library, following the curve of the lower hall. I'd never gone that way before, assuming it was for maintenance. At the far end, I found a narrow door. The sign hanging on it held a pentacle symbol and the words, *By Invitation Only.*

Fuck if I was going to wait for an invitation to crash the scions' party.

The door swung open easily. Maybe they expected the sign to be deterrent enough, or maybe they wanted me down there. Even if it was the latter, I didn't have a whole lot of choice.

I barreled down the steps and swung around the corner to find a tableau of my least favorite people in the world poised for my arrival.

The space was set up as a games room, a pool table at one end, a cluster of sofas and loveseats around a widescreen TV at the other, a substantial mahogany bar cabinet standing against the opposite wall. A vent over my head gushed warmth and a faint piney scent. The ceiling was high enough and the artificial lights strong enough to make the space feel much airier than your standard basement. But looking back at the assembled figures, I had trouble drawing in any air at all.

Victory and her two most devoted friends were sitting on one of the loveseats facing me, the lackeys on the seat cushions and Victory perched on the arm with her shapely legs crossed and her mouth already curved into an amused smile.

Declan and Connar had propped themselves at opposite ends of the sofa kitty-corner to the girls. Declan's posture was stiff, and his gaze didn't quite meet mine. Connar looked tensed to spring, his jaw tight.

Malcolm stood behind the sofa, leaning his arms casually against its back. A spark of triumph lit in his eyes at the sight of me, and his grin stretched wider. He nodded to Jude, who'd been lounging against the wall next to the TV with his hands slung in his pockets.

As the Killbrook scion pushed himself upright, my attention snagged on the one other person in the room—the last person I'd have expected to see in this company. Imogen shifted on her feet where she stood near the bar cabinet, her lips slanted at a pained angle. Understanding clicked in my head.

"You told them," I said with a flare of anger and betrayal.

"Rory," Imogen started, her voice wavering.

Victory sliced her hand through the air. "Shut it."

I couldn't tell whether she'd cast a spell or whether Imogen was just scared that she would, but my supposed friend's mouth snapped shut.

"Told us about what?" Jude said languidly. "Oh, you mean this little treasure?" He drew his hand out of his pocket with his fingers curled around a trembling white mouse, his little finger resting against the black splotch on her left flank.

My heart just about leapt up my throat. "Give her back to me," I said, marching over.

"*Stop*," Malcolm said in his casting voice, straightening up behind the sofa. My feet halted. The same fucking trick his dad had used on me. I turned toward him as well as I could, seething and trying not to shake, and he just grinned back at me. "Hid a whole familiar from us. Very sneaky. Well, maybe not so very sneaky when it is so very small."

My gaze jerked back to Jude. "If you hurt her—"

"Then what?" he asked, cocking his head. "What do you think you can do to any of us, Snowflake? You don't really deserve a familiar when you haven't even got the power to take care of it. Better to put the poor thing out of its misery in a constructive way."

He clucked his tongue, and the hairs on the back of my neck stood on end. His ferret familiar wriggled out from under the sofa and bounded across the thick rug to Jude's feet. It peered up at the mouse with an eager guttural sound.

"You'd like this tasty treat, wouldn't you, Mischief?" Jude crooned. As he adjusted his grip to dangle Deborah by her tail, the ferret's head bobbed.

"Leave her alone!" I said, the words catching in my throat before I could force them out. "You don't know—" I couldn't tell them how much more she was than just a mouse. They'd definitely kill her then. I turned to Declan frantically. "Isn't this against the rules you like to uphold so much? You can't let them do this."

I was sure when Professor Banefield had gone over the

school policies with me, he'd mentioned that students were forbidden from purposefully harming another student's familiar. Officially, at least. Apparently that didn't mean much. Declan looked down at his hands, saying nothing.

Malcolm chuckled. "He's just as sick of you thumbing your nose at us as the rest of us are. The only *real* rule at Blood U is not to get caught if you break the other ones. No one here is going to go running to the administration on your behalf. You can't even prove you had a familiar, can you?"

I couldn't. A shiver ran through me. Jude swung Deborah gently through the air, and the ferret stood up on its hind legs, its upper body swaying to follow the movement.

"You'd better listen to him," Connar said, his voice low and rough.

The question dropped ragged from my mouth. "What do you want?" Because there had to be something. This wasn't purely torture. This was a negotiation—one where they held all the cards.

"That's more like it." Malcolm crossed his arms over his chest. "If you want your squeak toy back, first you're going to grovel on your knees right here, telling us all about how you now recognize that we're the real powers in the school and begging us to help you find your way. Then we'll take it out to the green, and you can do another demonstration while everyone's on their way to class. And *then* we'll head over to your assessment, and you can prostrate yourself while the professors and the headmistress watch. Do that, and we'll make sure you pass too. We're generous when people deserve it."

I hugged myself to hold in a shudder. Throw myself at their feet not just in private but in front of the entire campus… I'd never recover the higher ground after that. I'd have proven to students and teachers alike that Malcolm and the other scions owned me.

"What's more important to you?" Jude said, waggling his eyebrows. "Your pride or your familiar's life?"

"Just—just give me a second," I said, as if I was going to see some way out of this if I just stood here a little longer.

"Nah, I think you've had long enough. You obviously need a bit more motivation."

He flicked his wrist, and the mouse sailed through the air to land at the edge of the rug. I cried out, lunging after her, but Malcolm's magic held me firm. The ferret pounced. "Slowly, Mischief," Jude said softly. "Take your time."

It sank its teeth into Deborah's delicate shoulder, and she squeaked in pain.

"You can feel it, can't you?" Malcolm said, his voice rolling over me as an echo of pain did bite into my muscles. "Through the familiar connection. Everything it feels, you feel too."

"Stop it," I said. "Stop it!"

"On. Your. Knees. And let's hear that groveling loud and clear."

Victory and her friends snickered. "Watch the mighty fall," she said.

Deborah squealed again. My legs wobbled, my knees starting to give. My gaze darted across the room in one last-ditch attempt to find something, anything, that could fix this. It settled on Imogen's face.

Her lips were still pressed tight, but her eyes were wild. The weird thing, though, was that I didn't see the same hopelessness I felt reflected there. Her expression was more frustrated, as if she already knew the answer and it was killing her not to be able to say it.

My lips moved instinctively, forming a word under my breath as I focused on her forehead. "Inside."

If I'd tried an insight spell on anyone else in the room with my mind in its current turmoil, I'd probably have smacked into a shield I had no hope of breaking. But Imogen wasn't guarded against me. I tumbled right into the whirl of her memories and emotions, flashes of hand gestures and laughter, and one thought so clear I heard it like her voice ringing in my ears.

...all a fucking trick.

I jerked my awareness out of her mind and caught my balance before I reeled backward. A trick. A trick?

"You feel how much Jude's familiar is hurting that little thing," Malcolm went on, and this time I recognized the faint casting lilt beneath the words. "Are you going to just stand there and ride out its last breaths?"

A fresh knife of pain ran through my chest, but it wasn't coming from the mouse on the floor, was it? He was persuading me to feel the pain I'd have expected to.

He'd only need to do that if... if the mouse on the floor wasn't really my familiar.

It might not even be a mouse at all. Jude specialized in illusion.

Something Professor Banefield had told me during our preliminary lessons came back to me. *The four magical foci exist on a sort of axis of opposing pairs: the inward Insight against the outward Persuasion, the concrete Physicality against the ephemeral Illusion.*

I'd seen through Malcolm's persuasion by leaning on insight. Now I needed something concrete to challenge Jude's illusion.

I *should* have a connection to Deborah, wherever she was. We were tied together with a magical bond. That was why she could talk to me inside my head. If I just reached out to her the way I'd drawn ice from the air and metal from the ground...

My hand came up in front of me. "Where," I murmured, and closed my fingers to my palm.

A tremor of sensation tingled over my skin from somewhere beyond the walls. She was down here. Down here, but not in this room.

I dropped my hand back to my side and aimed a glare at Jude. "That's not my familiar. You can stop now."

Malcolm muttered a curse. Victory let out a disgruntled sigh.

Jude gave me a sickly smile and flicked his fingers. The mouse his familiar had been toying with blinked out of existence, leaving the ferret jerking its head back and forth trying to figure out what the hell had just happened.

"It doesn't really matter whether we feed it to the ferret

or not," Malcolm said. "You're not getting it back until you get your act together."

"Then I'll just find her myself," I said. I shifted my attention to the floor, wondering if I could apply the same principles to freeing myself—how could insight unlock my legs? To my surprise, Malcolm released the spell with a wave.

I didn't get a chance to feel relieved. "You won't be finding anything right now," he said, his smile returning harder than before. "If you don't hurry, you're going to be late for your assessment, and *that* definitely won't be good for your chances of sticking around here, now will it?"

Fuck. I wavered on my feet. For whatever reason, Malcolm had decided he couldn't get away with actually hurting Deborah. That meant he wasn't going to feed her to the ferret now, right?

But who knew what else he might do with her once I was gone?

What would happen to both of us if I got myself kicked out of the university?

Malcolm glanced at the time on his phone. "Tick tick tick."

With a wrench of my heart, I made my decision. I spun and dashed for the stairs. Guilt squeezed around my chest as I bolted up them and ran for the main doors.

I needed to stay if I was going to get justice for Mom and Dad. I needed to stay if I was going to end all the horrors that happened here. Deborah would understand the risk I'd taken with her safety.

I had to believe that.

Passing students stared as I sprinted across the green. I slowed to a jog as I crossed the field and came up on the Stormhurst Building, my breath raw in my throat. Showing up hyperventilating wasn't going to be a mark in my favor either.

I strode into the gym just as the clock mounted on the wall clicked over to nine o'clock. Ms. Grimsworth looked up from where she'd been talking with Professor Banefield near the door. The four professors from before were already standing in their positions around the central circle.

"There you are, Miss Bloodstone," the headmistress said. "Ready?"

My legs felt like jelly and my breakfast was threatening to erupt from my stomach, but there wasn't much I could say other than, "Yes."

I walked to the testing circle, trying to shut out the clamor in my head. Fear for Deborah. Embarrassment that the scions had managed to trick me again so thoroughly. And doubt. So much doubt, worming through every other thought in my head.

The professors raised their hands. My body tensed automatically. "Just relax and accept," Banefield called to me.

Ha ha. Right.

I exhaled shakily and willed my body to loosen up as much as it could. The effort seemed to satisfy the assessors. They murmured together, and those simultaneous waves of energy blazed into me.

Their magic whipped through me like it had the first

time, but this time I felt the responding thrum behind my ribs more clearly. It pushed and pulled in the same moment, a straining of power against itself. *An axis of opposing pairs.*

A giddy rush of possibility shot through my mind with my sort-of victory against the scions fresh in my memory. What if *that* was what had gone wrong last time? Physicality vs. illusion, insight vs. persuasion—my abilities so closely matched at either end that they'd cancelled out each other's effects?

I didn't have time to interrogate that theory. I needed to let the professors' spells register every bit of my strengths. If my magic still wasn't enough, well, at least I knew I'd been assessed fairly.

I closed my eyes and trained my attention on the whirlwind inside me. The threads of energy that brought the solid sensation of conjuring a physical thing or the opening up of another person's mind—I tamped down on those as hard as I could, holding them back.

Two bolts of magical energy sang through me at a higher pitch and flung themselves back toward their casters. I released the impressions I'd suppressed and instead reached toward the quivers that spoke of shifting of a person's senses or the warping of their will. I yanked those down in turn.

The rest of the assessment energy crackled out of me rather than bursting inside me like it had a month ago.

When I opened my eyes, the woman across from me looked a bit startled. My stomach sank. Had my attempt to show my abilities failed after all, and she couldn't figure out how I'd given the same result again? I swallowed hard as the four professors moved across the room to consult with Ms. Grimsworth.

The follow-up conversation went on for longer than before, with a protesting "But—" here and an emphatic "Hold on!" there. My earlier nausea curdled in my stomach. Finally, the professors stepped back, and Ms. Grimsworth beckoned me over.

Professor Banefield was beaming. Seeing that lightened my spirits a little as I approached the headmistress.

"Did I do okay this time?" I said.

She laughed, but with an edge to it that set my nerves off all over again.

"Miss Bloodstone, your performance was far more than 'okay'," she said. "Even with much debate, no one can deny the results. You show great and equal strength in all four domains. This is the first time any of us has encountered a power that balanced or that potent in our time."

For a second, I could only stare at her. A smile crept across my face, and then a laugh of my own spilled out of me. "So, I'm staying?"

"I think you'd better," she said, with just a hint of a smile of her own. "Come along. I think there may be quite a few people interested to hear your results."

She was right. When we emerged from the Stormhurst Building, a few dozen students had gathered on the field. They all perked up at the sight of me, their expressions avid. The scions, who maybe had encouraged the audience in the hopes it'd be for my downfall, stood at the edge of the crowd, watching just as intently.

It really hit me then. I'd won. They weren't getting rid of me. And I now had official confirmation that I was not just a powerful mage, but that once I got a grip on my abilities, I'd have more strengths than any of them.

Ms. Grimsworth set her hand on my shoulder and pitched her voice to carry. "I'm pleased to announce that Miss Bloodstone will officially be joining us here at Bloodstone University as the only student currently or recently in residence with a strong talent in all four domains of magic."

A shocked but excited murmur spread through the gathered students. I caught a flash of fury in Malcolm's face, and then the headmistress was calling my attention back to her.

"You have your pick of the lot, Miss Bloodstone," she said. "At this point a student would generally pick a specialty and league to associate themselves with. What is your choice?"

I hadn't even considered that in depth before, I'd been so focused on just making it through the assessment. My thoughts immediately leapt to Physicality.

I'd always found so much joy in the act of creation. But the feelings around that type of magic were tainted now, too tangled up in everything I'd shared with Connar that he'd thrown in my face.

It was Insight that I'd learned from my parents before I'd known it was a skill I'd ever use through magic. It was Insight that had allowed me to stop Malcolm before I'd smashed the dragon bead on my necklace and saved me from giving in to the scions' demands this morning. Insight would have protected me from Connar's betrayal too if I'd pushed harder. I could take it so much farther with the training I'd get here.

I brought the word to my tongue, and everything in me hummed with the rightness of it.

"I'm going with Insight," I said.

Several voices in the crowd whooped in approval. "I'll have a new schedule for you tomorrow," Ms. Grimsworth said. "I think you've earned a day off."

I stepped forward, still a little uncertain that this could all be real, and the other students moved to meet me. At first they all just peered at me as if trying to glean how I'd done it. Then one girl said, "That's amazing!" and the floodgates burst. I was passed from one person congratulating me to another in a dizzying whirl of grins and awed voices.

Some of these people had probably helped trip me up over the last few weeks. I couldn't assume they were my friends now. I'd just been named the most powerful mage to attend the school in decades, and they were seeing how much that shine might rub off on them.

I'd be damned if the approval didn't feel good after all the tripping, though.

Somewhere in the middle of the impromptu celebration, a soft warmth pressed into my hand from behind. My fingers closed instinctively around a small furry body that sent a pang of recognition straight to my heart. Deborah.

I tucked her close to my chest and spun around, but whoever had passed her to me had vanished amid the other students. Had one of the scions decided they'd tortured me enough using her? Or had it been—well, I couldn't imagine it'd been Victory, but one of her minions?

I couldn't tell. Maybe it didn't matter. I held onto my familiar tightly with a sob of relief, and her tiny nose nuzzled my thumb as if to say what she didn't dare speak into my head with so many mages around us. She was back. She was home.

In that moment, I could almost believe that I was too.

CHAPTER TWENTY-NINE

Rory

My new cachet stuck with me throughout the day. Everywhere I went on campus, even in my dorm's common room, people watched me as if fascinated to see what I might do next.

It was a little exhausting. I holed up in my room for a while, and when I got bored with that, I looked out the window and saw that the field to the east of the main triangle was vacant. Next to a low, broad wooden building that I assumed was some kind of maintenance shed, I thought I saw the beginning of a path I'd never tried before at the edge of the woods.

I slipped out of Ashgrave Hall as surreptitiously as I could and hurried across the field. I'd just passed the maintenance building when its door clicked open and a voice I recognized reached my ears.

"Here you go," Malcolm was saying, his tone unusually warm. "About time for a run, don't you think?"

I eased back a step to peer around the side of the building. The Nightwood scion stood with his back to me, giving his wolf familiar a pat on the side as he motioned it off toward the forest. As the dark creature loped off, Malcolm reached to scratch the side of his neck.

The sun shone off his golden-brown hair. The collar of his shirt shifted to the side, revealing an angry mottled pink line across his shoulder that looked like a recent burn mark, large enough that I could see it even from several feet away. His fingernail brushed the edge, and he winced.

I never did have the best control over my tongue. "Are you all right?" I blurted out.

Malcolm snapped around to face me, his hand jerking to his side. "Why wouldn't I be, Glinda?" he asked with a haughty lift of his chin.

"You just looked like you had a burn or something on your shoulder." I sighed. "Never mind. I was about to leave anyway." I wasn't risking a walk in the forest with his wolf on the prowl.

Malcolm chuckled, but it was a dark sound. "So you're picking up the fearmancer mindset after all. Discover every weakness you can possibly exploit. Sorry, but you're never going to find me an easy target."

I stopped in the middle of turning away and met his eyes again. Anger flickered in my chest, but it was restrained by a quaver of a totally different emotion.

It was awfully sad that he couldn't even accept an honest question of concern without searching for an ulterior motive, wasn't it? How did anyone live their whole life like that?

For a second, I thought I saw something vulnerable behind the divine devil demeanor.

"I'm not planning to make you a target," I said quietly. "You know, even though I didn't want to be your friend and I'd rather you stayed as far away from me as possible, I'd care if I saw you get hurt. I'd try to help. Because that's what people with properly functioning hearts do for other people. That's who my parents—my *real* parents—raised me to be. And no matter how much of an asshole you are to me, you're never going to break that part of me."

We stared each other down for the space of several heartbeats. Malcolm folded his arms over his chest. His dark brown eyes bored into mine. "You should remember that no matter how many strengths you have, the guys and I have a much better idea how to use ours. We were holding back before because you couldn't do much to defend yourself. But believe me, we're just getting started."

That might be true. And I still might not know exactly how I was going to make it through the days ahead, but I had a much better idea than I'd had before. I was a fearmancer raised among joymancers, and I was going to hold onto all the joy I could gather until I was ready to burn all the fear away and make things right.

I held Malcolm's gaze and let a smile cross my lips. "So am I."

ABOUT THE AUTHOR

Eva Chase lives in Canada with her family. She loves stories both swoony and supernatural, and strong women and the men who appreciate them. Along with the Royals of Villain Academy series, she is the author of the Moriarty's Men series, the Looking Glass Curse trilogy, the Their Dark Valkyrie series, the Witch's Consorts series, the Dragon Shifter's Mates series, the Demons of Fame Romance series, the Legends Reborn trilogy, and the Alpha Project Psychic Romance series.

Connect with Eva online:
www.evachase.com
eva@evachase.com